Anthology of Therapeutic Pieces

Volume 1

By

Foresaw

The Author
Foresaw is a pseudonym for Simon Adam Watts born British on the 14-May-1955 in what is now the Yemen, Arabia. He was the fourth and last male child of his parents.

Acknowledgements
The Cutting Edge Writers group for continued support.
Rock-drill is an image of a sculpture by Epstein.   The Earthly Delights, Triptych is by Hieronymus Bosch.

email: Foresaw@e-devise.co.uk

ISBN-13: 978-1729490334

Out

When Glen and Tabitha Fevertree arrived in the small suburban village of Pratts Bottom they made a big impression. They had bought a little cottage at the end of the village without seeing it first. They cycled in to the village on a tandem which had a couple of panniers and a trailer. They stopped at the village shop come post office and asked directions to their house. Within a few minutes of them having a drink of water and cycling off to discover what they had bought the village bush telegraph started humming with the latest rumour about the new foreign folk that had moved into Mile End Cottage.

Glen was wiry with a long neck which he seemed to be able to retract and extend at will, his collar was loose, giving his wrinkled neck an impression of a tortoise. He did not talk much and never about the war which he had survived physically unscathed.

Tabitha was quite a contrast to him physically, she was a series of bulges with almost no neck at all and small intelligent piggy eyes. She had spent her war working at Bletchley Park so she did not speak about it for a different reason.

For quite some time Mile End Cottage looked much the same but gradually Glen worked to restore it and it began to look as if it was in better upkeep. Also, the large garden began to take on a landscaped look, with different levels and curved banks, some covered in grass or moss others covered in herbs like camomile and thyme.

It was difficult to judge if the amount of soil in the garden had increased. Glen had built a large shed at the back of the house, it was quite long and enabled him to start constructing a series of underground passages and rooms. As he removed the earth he built concrete floors and brick walls. He used different ceilings depending on where in the garden he was working. In some places, he managed to place a strategic opening skylight, in other places he used a closed skylight letting in green light.

Tabitha helped him with the calculations and also the connection to the house. There was a small staircase to the dormer bedroom and bathroom. Under this staircase Glen dug out a new stair leading into the ground. With Tabitha's help they placed a concrete slab under the foundations. He carefully built the walls of the doorway to support the new slab. Then he could join up the tunnel outside to the doorway beneath the ground.

Much to the amazement of the villagers Glen built a tandem tricycle with one wheel at the front and two at the back. He could remove the back seat and put in its place a tipping barrow like on a small dumper truck; he also had a small motor which helped drive the back wheels if a load or hill got too much for him.

Tabitha kept a good house providing help and sustenance to Glen. As time passed the house and garden were completed. Mostly very little was spoken, she was happy to sit or do in companionable silence or occasionally she would chatter to him while he was drawing up more plans – he would nod and say, 'yes' or 'erm' or 'I can see that' every so often when she drew breath. Glen grew thinner and more sinewy, Tabitha grew rounder and could no longer touch her toes.

Finally they began to be accepted in the village, despite their peculiarities. Once or twice a month Glen would get the tandem tricycle, give it a good clean and put the back seat on. It used to take a little while to get Tabitha wedged in the back seat but then they went out for the day up and down the steep hills needing the assistance of the motor.

After a long and gruelling winter before spring had a chance to roll back the blues, Glen and Tabitha sat wearily at the breakfast table.

'I think I better go and see the doctor,' said Tabitha.

'Are you poorly? I don't remember when you last saw a doctor.'

'It might not be too serious but I should get a few extra bumps looked at.'

Glen tried to look cheerful but failed.

'I thought you'd be impressed that I can count that high,' said Tabitha and smiled.

'You were always good with large numbers,' said Glen.

So the tandem tricycle got an extra trip to the local surgery – but Tabitha had to go for more tests in the hospital which was a bit far and Glen spoke to the publican and he took them in his van.

Tabitha faded away that summer and when she was not too tired she would go on the trike and joke to him not to go too fast as she was not filling the seat like she used to. Glen died three weeks after she did. The publican contacted his younger brother who came to see the house.

As they walked through the underground passageways Glen's brother spoke.

'I never knew what he did in the war.'

'Maybe he tunnelled out,' said the publican.

Dec-17

The Letter

The first time I heard his voice was on the phone – my first impression was that he might be gay or bi-sexual. We talked mainly about me and my interests but before we got around to discussing where to meet I did want to ask him a question.

'You are not looking for a physical relationship, sex – have you had physical relationships with any women?' I asked.

'Oh yes – I am not saying I am a Casanova or anything but I like women. What attracts me about this sort of arrangement is that it is not complicated by sex.'

I could not help wondering if he had had this sort of relationship before but I did not feel I could ask that. Instead I said, 'Please can you say more about what you are expecting from me?'

'Well I can send a draft contract, but the basis is very simple – we will meet two or three times a month at my expense. To talk and spend the evening together. I would like to hold your hand from time to time but nothing more – I have a dicky heart – but actually I do not want that sort of relationship. For this, I will pay for your university fees and for you to have enough for day to day living – so you do not need a job during term time. I will buy you gifts from time to time but you must not buy me gifts.'

'Wow – I can't believe how lucky I am, are you sure? Suppose one of us changes our mind before I have finished.'

'If you want to then I would ask you to return half of the money I have given you. If I change my mind then I will pay you until the end of your degree course – without retakes!'

'That is more than fair as far as I am concerned.'

'When would you be available to have dinner with me?' he asked.

I had not eaten anything so I said, 'I am available tonight – does that suit you?'

'Yes, very well – what do you like to eat?'

'Most things – I quite fancy a steak. You choose.'

He told me the name and address of a restaurant.

I decided that I would wear smart but everyday clothes. I like colourful, striped clothing but decided to just wear a plain skirt and stripy top. Two different directions and colours of stripes might scare him off.

'Do you want to me to wear particular clothes?' I asked him as we settled down to look at the menu.

'It would be great to go shopping with you and buy you clothes that you wore every day but also something special to wear on evenings like this.'

'That would be fantastic – I have never had clothes bought for me like that.'

'Have you had a husband and boyfriends?'

'I have never been married but I have had my fair share of boyfriends.'

'I would like to get to know you; are you happy for me to ask intimate questions?'

'I expect you to – how else will you get to know me?'

'Have you had long term physical relationships?'

'Are you asking if I am a virgin? No, I'm not. I did have sex with a couple of boyfriends then I lived with this guy for about six months but he had to go back to Canada and we did not continue.'

He was not an ugly man but a bit reminiscent of a tortoise with a thin neck in a shirt with a gaping collar as he had a large barrel chest. He did not look embarrassed at her answers.

'How about girlfriends?' he asked.

'You men – all the same. But no girlfriends in bed. But I have a very close friend, she knows I am here tonight.' She smiled a broad grin, then asked, 'Am I allowed to get a new boyfriend?'

'Yes, most certainly – but I will leave it up to you if you wish to talk to me about them.'

They saw each other a few times before she agreed – but it was clear they both enjoyed each other's company. He held her hand and she gave him a kiss on the cheek but there the boundaries were set. Slowly she grew closer to him, one day she felt low and she was having self-doubts as to how well she was doing at University so she texted him and he phoned back a bit later. They arranged to meet for tea and scones. He brought a small pendant for her, he fastened it round her neck and sat down. He held her hand.

'Is it your period?' he asked gently.

'It's not that obvious, is it?' she said with alarm.

'No not at all – but I know you quite well.'

He bought her useful and beautiful clothes – she studied hard and partied a bit. She was older than her fellow students but she did meet a couple of more mature men but they came to nothing.

The letter came – she had not heard from him but she was working hard for her second-year exams. She could hardly believe what he wrote – she sat shocked. Straightaway she started to make arrangements to visit him. He was in prison on remand for the murder of his wife. He ended saying she was not to worry about money, he had all the money for her set aside.

She did not even know he had a wife – she had never asked. She could not imagine him getting angry or harming anyone let alone murder. It took a little time to arrange the visit, by the time it came through she had finished her exams. She dressed colourfully – with stripes in both directions but little flesh showing.

On the journey to the prison - the last part was on a special bus - she started thinking about him, was this his first wife? Maybe he had murdered more than one wife. She was weak with anxiety by the time they showed her in to the visitor's room. She watched him file in with the other prisoners, searching for her. As soon as he saw her his whole face lit up and she felt her anxiety lessen. Various of the other prisoners made catcalls and one made a crude gesture.

'I am going to hire the best legal team I can and go for crime of passion.'

'Do you want me to testify?' she asked.

'No, I don't think so – that should not be necessary. I wouldn't wish to put you through that.'

As always, he was concerned for her.

Nov-17

Varmint Winter

> Glittering peaks and slopes sliding down
> turning soggy, sad grey, oozing away
> then grim, frozen pollution once again
> designed to rip through winter clothing
>
> Glittering peaks and slopes sliding down
> thawing fast, sad grey, oozing away
> then grim, frozen pollution once again

designed to rip through winter clothing

Oct-17

Down by the Water

Walter felt his age. He was alone. The summer started with great promise and he planned what he thought would be his last holiday. He would go back to where he was born and grew up. Caught his first fish, learned to ride a bike, swim, kissed his first girl – his only girl.

He consulted the library – reserved a guide book. Found her home was now National Trust and he could go and see it once more – now with the viewing public. He thrust to the far back of his mind the decision of whether to go or not. His own home had been a large vicarage. When both parents had died he had sold it to a developer – so now where it had been there were more than thirty families.

He no longer drove – he had continued to cycle but last winter he ended up plunging down a steep front garden bruised and hurt in Mrs Walsenburg's porch feebly flapping his limbs like some injured crane fly. So, he had to give that up too. He took the train on his holiday changing five times and taking a sleeper on the longest stretch.

He arrived at the station in the evening and was lucky enough to find a taxi waiting for him. He sat next to the driver who was very talkative. They passed the pond with the weeping willows and docile ducks. Walter agreed with the driver wherever possible but had to admit he had been to this part of the world before.

On the last day of his holiday he went to visit The Hall, Lorna's family home. It was more splendid, more beautiful and more decayed than he remembered it. He had met Lorna by a log hut near the edge of the lake. He had tripped and fallen down a bank in an ungainly way and lay tangled at her feet. She burst out laughing – not unkindly – she asked if he was hurt and gently helped him up. His shyness was extreme and got worse when he uncovered who she was.

He walked round on his own – the last thing he needed was a guided tour. He got towards the end and came to the long gallery. Powerful and painful memories came out of each bay and arch. Of the hours he spent with Lorna, many had been here. Tucked discreetly into an alcove he saw the painting Giles had made of Lorna and him down by the water. He had introduced his friend Giles to Lorna. When Lorna became pregnant her family sent her away and she never came back as she and the child died in childbirth. No one knew who the father was – but Giles and Walter thought it was one of them. Giles became more famous as an artist after he died – he came off his motor cycle doing 80mph at 2am the night before Lorna's funeral.

Walter left in a taxicab, looking out of the back window, he saw the Hall – past autumnal splendour.

Oct-17

Friend or Foe

There was mud in front of us as far as the eye could see. Not only in front of us, the mud was surrounding us, as our spaceship touched down it did not stop as it would on grass but slithered across a slight mound then into a mud trough – we finally came to a halt about 70 meters from the first touchdown. The ship was brought to a stop by a few branches and a wedge of mud that had built up. We stepped out and the wind was whipping across the desolation. I was reminded of accounts of trench warfare from long ago. We walked about disconsolately looking at the ground and sky with varying levels of attention.

Just then there was an explosion in the distance and a few seconds later the automatic defence system of the ship absorbed something with a large clang. We beat a hasty retreat back inside the ship. There are five us on board and we all met in the command centre. Harry brought up an image of where the object had been fired from. It looked like some sort of permanent gun built on mud much like the terrain around us.

'Well the question is what sort of life form or intelligence are we dealing with,' said Sally. No one else spoke but I guess they were all thinking the same as me – that Sally had a way of stating the obvious that everybody else found annoying - it was almost impossible to stop a knee-jerk reaction to club her to death. I suppose I should have felt solidarity with Sally being the same sex, but any vestige of this was blown away by Sally's superior air.

'Well I suspect that this first response is automated - from something which has little or no intelligence but might be a crude system put in place by an intelligent being,' Tom said.

'I agree – based on the weapon used, the analysis gives the object as metal non-radioactive, very primitive with no guidance system,' Dick said.

'Would it be best to try and communicate with them?' asked Harry.

'I think we need a bit more information first, at this stage I don't think we know if we are better telling them we are intelligent or that we are automatic too,' I said.

'True, but it may be best to try and establish communication with them to discover more about them. It seems the best way to get more information,' Harry said.

'You might be correct, but I was thinking of establishing what physical form they take if any – for example if they have left this place and only this rather crude automated system is left they we will be wasting our time trying to get any communication going,' I paused, 'How about we send a probe that both tries to communicate and detect life forms?'

'Very good,' said Tom and Dick at the same time and they started to specify the modules to put in the probe.

I looked at Sally and Harry and they had started talking about finding a question that distinguishes between true intelligence and pseudo intelligence. I was surprised to hear Sally state an obvious but useful comment.

'Only true intelligence can comprehend what philosophy is about - any other sort of being will not understand it.'

'I think most of my family would not pass that test,' said Harry.

'What question do you ask to see if someone understands philosophy?' I asked

Tom and Dick came and listened.

'Ask them what one hand clapping sounds like?' asked Harry.

'Very funny – how about the age-old question about reality, how can any intelligent being tell the difference between having its brain in a vat rather than a skull. If all the nutrients and inputs sent to the brain are the same as they were when it was in a skull would there be a way of telling? Since the brain in a vat gives and receives exactly the same impulses as it would if it were in a skull, and since these are its only way of interacting with its environment, then it is not possible to tell, from the perspective of that brain, whether it is in a skull or a vat. Since, in principle, it is impossible to rule out oneself being a brain in a vat, there cannot be good grounds for believing any of the things one believes. That is how philosophy goes – mainly useless,' Tom said.

There was a bit of a silence and then a communicator chattered into life. The probe was beginning to report back.

'Possible life form identified – establishing intelligence.' The clipped tones were familiar to all of us. I looked round our group, I wondered if we would pass the probe's test.

'Individuals walk on two legs and have two arms and observe light from two sensors in their head. They can solve simple puzzles – how to find the way out of a maze etc.' The communicator fell silent for a while. Then it started again.

'These creatures are carbon based life forms that can communicate using sound. They also have a written language and I have requested a dictionary. They seem to only have very primitive computers.'

An image came up on the screen – it was clear that it was an image of one of these life forms. It was huge, nearly 2m tall. The communicator continued.

'They do have a term to describe philosophy – the study of thinking and the best way to think about any subject. They use the concept of "brain in a vat" too.'

I looked around the control centre – our whole ship was only 5cm and we were all less than 5mm long. It is true that we have very hard shells but I am not sure if I would survive if one of these life forms stepped on me.

Oct-17

Subversive Human

You are John Smith aged 33.

For the first ten years you had a difficult and traumatic life. Alienated from your close family then your foster mother was killed before your eyes.

In the next ten years, you found the true nature of life – the hypocrisy of society, the straightjacket of civilisation stifling freedom and the progress of humankind. Slowly you explored how limited life was, how constrained everybody was by the seemingly limitless rules. It could be with the population of the world this was inevitable, it was time for drastic measures.

It was time for a change, a rebellion that overthrows the powers that be. To topple the structures that underpin society. It was time for fighting for yourself – fighting for freedom. It was a time you learnt that you are not like most people – you want to smash the way society works. A bid for freedom for you, freedom for everyone whether they wanted it or not. It was a time you realised you are not hampered by human emotions. You do not feel for others, only for yourself.

You turn 30 years old. You are a known sociopath – now you are intent on dismantling society to enable you to wreak change for your own benefit. You will get the support of others by telling them it is for freedom and the benefit of everyone. You start to study vulnerable parts of society – to destroy Colossus would stop society functioning. But if Colossus were replaced with a computer you could control then you could operate much longer without detection.

You build business interests in your areas of encryption and specialised systems. The plan begins to take on its own life - in your mind you see that by getting a few of your own followers in the Institute, [Colossus' caretaker organisation] you will be able to tap in to the fundamental processes that control the world. You are beginning to get contracts that the Institute award. When they start to build the next generation of Colossus you will be in an unassailable position to wheel Colossus 18 in like a Trojan horse.

You build on a friendship from your past with Colin Malone who works in the Institute in the procurement department, he looks after many of the big contracts. While Alice Nobel, head of the Institute, is temporarily vulnerable, her husband leaves her for a younger woman, you prey on her using your charm and ability – you form a relationship with her.

Your plan has many threads but it is not complicated – not each element of the plan has to work – you are going to overload Colossus 17 and then step in to his circuits. Make subtle changes to his data and wait for him to grind to a halt from the overload of trying to deal with so many things happening and needing attention at the same time.

You're certain that your plan will succeed and this feeling of confidence increases as your attack starts and you see problems creeping across the world as more parts of your plan unfold. Then a few things start to happen that go beyond what you expect. Then finally when you think Colossus has been beaten there is a huge fire at the biggest airport. Slowly there are signs that Colossus has started to get on top of things and then you are in the headlines. "John Smith and John Smith Enterprises held responsible for the One Day War and the human suffering".

Your plan of subversion has failed and you are on the run.

Oct-17

Funfair

It was the middle of the night when Lucy's mum woke her. Or so it seemed. Lucy knew she was in for a surprise treat and found it difficult to go to sleep directly after tea but just when she thought she would have to get up and go and see her mum she was being shaken gently awake. There was no reason for her mum to whisper and carry a torch rather than speak normally and turn the light on – but it did heighten the excitement and made Lucy jumpy.

Lucy came down the stairs with her mum holding the torch - shining it over Lucy's head and on to the steps. When they got to the hall they put their coats on and quietly left the house in darkness. The streets were well lit and they stepped on to the moving pavement holding hands. Lucy was quite confident changing strips of pavement – moving faster towards the centre. However, the law was quite clear, children under 10 must hold an adult's hand, Lucy was still nine. There were always pavement wardens about, also there were many points where cameras were watching and would recognise who she was and her age.

They got to the final section of the pavements and there were seats to sit on. Lucy could see tall buildings and lights zooming with lettering and pictures. Sometimes the whole of a building would go through a sequence of colours. Sitting next to her mum Lucy felt the wind in her hair and she could smell the city. Different sorts of food, often the air would change temperature and smell dusty or musty or a bit like the air freshener in the loo.

Soon they were approaching the Funfair – it stood out like an illuminated castle with many domes, spires, minarets together with tangled rides and huge machines. Lucy held her mum's hand once more and they crossed to the slowly moving pavement and stepped off. They walked into the Funfair; the smells were different to the rest of the city – still many sorts of food, some sweet, some savoury and some sour. Then there were exotic smells of hot metal and chilly water smelling faintly of reeds and other vegetation.

There were different entrances for different ages and different types of adventure. Lucy's was a surprise adventure. She and her mum stepped through the door and found themselves inside the bottom of a circular tower. There was a small round table with what looked like shortbread on a cake plate. There was a very neat sign on the plate which said, "Eat me".

Lucy and her mum took a piece of shortbread each and started to eat. It was not sweet and had a taste of exotic fruits and flowers – lemons, grapefruits, pineapples with elderflower and honeysuckle. As they ate they felt themselves getting smaller. The ceiling became much higher and the walls were further away - it felt as if they were shrinking. There was a deep rumbling noise, the sound of the sea crashing and shrieking gulls. Lucy glanced at her feet and noticed that the floor tiles had remained the same size, her shoes covered one tile. It did not bother her that this meant her feet must be staying the same size. She looked back at the door they had come in – it was massive now, arching up like a huge cathedral doorway, only bigger. She turned back and saw there was a small but growing door directly opposite the entrance – it must have been so small when they first came in she did not notice it.

'Do you think we should eat another piece of shortbread?' she asked her mum.

'Well I don't think we need to as the small door is big enough to go through.'

'OK,' said Lucy and she skipped over to the small door which opened easily on its hinges. They went through the door and came out into a hall which had two doors at the other end. Over the left-hand door were the words, "Big people" and over the right-hand door were the words "Small people". Lucy was excited and rushed for the right-hand side. She found herself inside a smooth shiny tunnel on a mat which started moving as soon as she sat on it.

As she picked up speed the tunnel changed and she could see the most amazing sights, hear eerie sounds and take in strange smells. One minute she would be travelling through forest with a smell of pine cones and sounds of wild animals. The next she was shooting across an ocean with big waves and killer whales jumping out of the sea beside her – the salt spray catching her throat. Finally, she shot out in to an ordinary hallway to find her mum patiently waiting for her.

'Did you see the wild bears in the forest?' she asked her mum.

'No, I saw a blue sky and gentle waves lapping at the pool edge.'

'Didn't you see the killer whales?'

'No, I saw a rather fit barman serving cocktails.'

'How boring. Look,' said Lucy pointing to a huge aquarium in the next place they walked through.

Lucy's mum jumped as a huge ray came out of the darkness. As they watched, it changed colour slowly shimmering through grey, purple, blue then almost black.

On the other side of the walkway there was a huge cage which at first did not look interesting – they made out extremely large caterpillars about the size of five or six washing machines. Then Lucy noticed equally large chrysalises which she had thought were rocks. One chrysalis was opening and the most beautiful dragon stretched its wings and after a little while flew up and perched on a real rock.

Lucy turned and tripped – she put her arm out to break her fall and noticed it was different, long and bendy with suckers all the way down. There would be no stopping her now.

Sep-17

The Egg

Anthea met Professor Jane Levet backside first when she was bending over in a laboratory store room. The Professor was dressed in very masculine clothing and Anthea waited politely until she stood up and turned round.

'I hear you are looking for a new assistant who has a background in genetics?' Anthea said.

'Are you Anthea Steadman?'

'Yes.'

'Do you have a boyfriend or husband?'

'No – why do you ask?'

'In my experience love and achieving results are not happy bedfellows,' said the Professor.

'First-hand experience? – anyway there is no chance of that at the moment.'

'They told me you were a strong personality – do you think you can work with me?'

'As long as you do not go out of your way to upset me.'

There was a fairly neutral silence as they both looked at each other – weighing up possibilities.

'Will you do it?' asked the Professor.

'I'll give it a try if you will. What is the project?'

'To create a mermaid.'

'Are you mad? That is not ethical, is it? Why would you want to?'

'I don't think I am mad. We are using primate genes not human ones so we are not breaking the law – I don't think it is unethical. What do they say, why do people climb mount Everest – because they can.'

'You won't be able to cross an ape with a fish – will you?'

'No but an ape with a dolphin would seem possible.'

'A furry mermaid then?'

'Possibly yes,' the Professor smiled and Anthea smiled back.

'It sounds a bit of a challenge.'

Anthea started work the next day. The professor showed her the incubator which would be home and nutrition for the egg. Anthea marvelled at the care with which it was made and how nutrients could be controlled and monitored continuously. Also, the ingenious way in which the incubator could expand as the egg grew.

Of equal if not more importance was the construction of the DNA that they would need to form the egg. The splicing of the DNA required many steps and meticulous attention to detail as each viable combination was explored to find the most suitable. Anthea excelled at this work and could follow the Professor's clear outline instructions of how to explore combining the DNA. The work was helped by a lot of theoretical papers written by the Professor and others but it was Anthea's flare that made the final breakthrough. The two women rarely argued but sometimes Anthea had to be quite forceful and say, "If you do that we will have to go back to the previous step and start again." Only once did the Professor ignore the warning and found out Anthea was right.

It took over three years, just before Anthea got serious about a new man in her life, when the final work on the DNA was completed and the first viable mermaid ovum was fertilized and placed in the incubator and generally referred to as "Egg". Life was monitored non-intrusively as possible – keeping interference at a minimum in order to not jeopardise the growth of Egg in any way. The Professor carried a bleeper which went off if any of more than a hundred life measurements went outside predefined limits. It took over five months for the mermaid to develop – by which time Anthea had moved in with her boyfriend.

Every morning the weight of the unborn mermaid was estimated and its movement over the past few hours quantified. But nothing intrusive like light or x-rays were used for the measurements. The Professor and Anthea had no idea what to expect when the mermaid was ready to be born but they knew it was close when the amount of movement increased sharply. Anthea had been taking things easy as there was not so much to do at work. But she came in just before the Professor one Monday morning. The incubator was indicating it was about to open. Already in place was a bath with shallow warm water below to receive the baby mermaid.

The Professor came in and stood next to Anthea without removing her coat. The incubator opened slowly and the infant mermaid slid gently in to the water.

The Professor gasped in surprise.

'Look it's the wrong way up! It has got legs and a top half like a fish.'

'I think he might be a merman rather than a mermaid too,' said Anthea with a small chuckle. 'Still he seems to be doing fine.'

Sep-17

Heart Broken

How to tell when a heart is broken - when it bleeds.
Can you mend a broken heart - no, you live with the leaks.

He was killed, it broke her heart,
she cried alone, as she did.
He drove away one day,
and never came home.

She had to see him one last time.
Laid out, not looking the same.
Not long until she was alone.
She came back home to die.

She went deaf – her hair went white,
straight away. Her "One" had gone.
Broken hearted - her life cut in half,
she lived a long life, but short of him.

She was a widow longer than a wife,
forty-one years, married thirty-three.
She said he wasn't the best husband,
but she wouldn't have any other.

Sep-17

Lucky Escape

The day Gerald kidnapped Lucy was more of a challenge for him than her.

She was nine and he knew very little about nine year old girls - in fact he knew very little about girls. The trouble was he had waited ages for a little boy to wander out of the wedding, but there were none so when bored Lucy came out and started making daisy chains under the trees he strode up to her.

'I'm going to kidnap you,' he said

'Oh, good this wedding is so boring - how did you get invited to this wedding - are you boring? Being kidnapped sounds exciting. Are you going to tie me up?'

'I don't think so - is that really necessary?'

'If you don't I will just be able to run off and I won't be kidnapped anymore will I?'

'I suppose you're right.'

'Anyway, aren't you going to tie me up and throw me in

the back of your van and rape me?'

'No – I don't have a van.'

'Well why did you kidnap me? I know I am at Roedean but I got a scholarship. My parents are as poor as down and outs – so you won't get any money from them. I have the highest IQ in my year you know – that is how I got a scholarship.'

'You don't say.'

'Yes – is that sarcasm or irony? I like them both, I am really into American sitcoms - I like Sex in the City.'

'Do you indeed – does your mum let you watch that?'

'Does your mum let you kidnap nine year old girls?'

'She never warned me I might regret it.'

'That is not kind – surely you don't think I'm that awful – I am going to cry.'

'No don't do that – if I tie you up will you promise not to cry? I did see some baler twine under a tree over there but that might cut into your wrists.'

'Are you a wimp? Trust my luck to get a wimp as a kidnapper - either you're a kidnapper or you are a wimp? Which are you?'

'I'm definitely a kidnapper - I was just ensuring that I treat you with humanity.'

'You better get on with it then. At this rate, I'll have time to appeal to the European Court of Human Rights.'

Gerald took her hands behind her back and lead her over to the baler twine. Unfortunately, it was very long and he did not have a knife or scissors. She ended up with a messy knot and a long string trailing behind her.

'Well why did you kidnap me? If it is not for money or sex?'

'Err, I'm not sure I can tell you that – it's classified information.'

'Don't be ridiculous – I suppose I'm a secret love child of

Prince Phillip and you are going to blackmail the Royal Family?'

'No that does not form part of the plan.'

'Where are you going to take me then? I expect someone will come out of the Wedding party soon.'

'Err….'

'You are so disorganised – I have never met a kidnapper who was less prepared than you.'

'Have you been kidnapped before then?'

'That is for me to know and you to try and find out.'

'I am not playing games with you.'

'Why not we are both bored. I think that is why you kidnapped me.'

'No if you must know I kidnapped you so I could eat you – I normally choose children, boys if you must know.'

'You're kidding aren't you? You've never eaten anybody have you?'

'What makes you so sure?'

'Well I do quite like you – even if you are a wimp. I don't think I would like you if you had eaten any boys.'

'There has been one other girl – she was not like you, she cried all the time.'

'Oh, look there is a squirrel.'

Gerald turned round and looked up at the trees but turned back when he could not see a squirrel. Lucy had slipped out of the baler twine and run back towards the wedding.

'Useless kidnapper!'

'I didn't want to eat you – so I let you escape. I expect you taste horrid.'

'No, I don't – I've been kidnaped before you know.'

'I don't suppose they could get rid of you soon enough either.'

Sep-17

Flesh and Bones

Lisa had just come back from holiday with her husband, Ron. It was the first holiday they had taken with just the two of them for about seventeen years. The children, two girls, were still in the process of leaving home but it was good to start to do things differently now.

They had settled back into work but Lisa felt restless.

'Do you miss the girls?' she asked Ron one evening as they sat companionably.

'Mmm – I suppose so – do you then darling?'

'Yes – I was thinking of getting a notadog.'

'A what darling?'

'A notadog – you know an android-dog.'

'Oh, yes I know what you mean – I just did not catch what you said.' He paused his reading and look at her cautiously, 'Would you want a notadog of your own or did you have in mind one tailored to both of us?'

'I don't know – I had not got that far yet. Have you been researching it?'

'Well sort of – I did talk to Colossus about it. You know Mum used to have a real dog – I believe she is one of the last dog owners still alive in the world. Anyway, I was interested in the success of notadogs and thought I would ask. When did I ask you about notadogs Colossus?'

'Last Tuesday,' I replied

'Would you recommend a jointly tailored notadog?' Lisa asked me.

'So long as both of you want a notadog then yes.' It

seemed a bit obvious so I added, 'If a couple spend a long time apart either through choice or necessity then it can be better to have two. It is worth noting a jointly tailored notadog will react to you differently individually and as a couple.'

'What sort of notadog would you like?' asked Lisa.

'I think one of those Border Collies that look like a badger – would you like that?'

'Yes, I think so – was your mother's dog like that?'

'I am not sure – there were pictures but of course she died while mum was still a child.'

'What was she called?'

'Badger – my mum called her Badger from the beginning.'

'Shall we get one?'

'Yes, it will be good for walks – so long as people do not stop me and want to talk about the latest upgrade of the software.'

Each notadog is different – both behaviour and to a lesser extent physically. The way the hair lies is randomly generated and combined with the colour I can ensure that no two notadogs look alike – so it is less likely to confuse two notadogs of the same breed than it used to be to confuse two dogs of the same breed. Each notadog's personality is shaped differently too. For most owners, this is fairly straightforward and a short process comprising a questionnaire and an interview. If a notadog is recommended by a doctor or a court then this process is tailored over a longer period with the focus on the mental and physical condition of the owner and their family.

Once Lisa and Ron had collected their notadog and watched the video and talked to the technician (a 9000 series robot) they slipped into a relaxed routine with her –

they decided to call her Bella. With Lisa, she was well behaved and loyal. With Ron, she was more mischievous and provoked him more. As Lisa pointed out that is because he needed it.

One day after work Lisa went to Ruth, Ron's mum – she had agreed to meet Ron there and taken Bella with her. She got there first with Bella meekly following her into Ruth's small garden. Ruth was nodding off in a garden chair in the shade and woke up gradually as Bella looped quietly round the chair touching Ruth with a wet nose from time to time.

'She's very well behaved,' said Ruth as she woke up gently.

'Do you like her?' asked Lisa. Ruth leaned forwarded and patted Bella.

'Very nice dear – but not like a real dog.'

'Oh – so you noticed, did you?'

'Yes, my friend Isla has one – it's very nice but doesn't suffer if you kick it.'

Ron arrived as Lisa laughed out loud. Bella ran to Ron and started jumping up.

Lisa said to Ron, 'Mum says Bella's very nice but doesn't suffer if you kick her.'

Ron kicked Bella who yelped and ran under Ruth's chair whining, 'She seems to be suffering now!' he laughed.

Ruth scolded him, 'How could you kick a poor defenceless robot that is programmed not to bite you back.'

Ron looked at his mum with a gleam in his eye, 'Does Bella look like Badger? Does she feel flesh in the same way as Badger?'

'Yes, she is very like Badger, not quite so grey a muzzle. But she bonces up to you the way Badger used to bounce up to my dad.' With all the sensory equipment in Bella I could tell that Ruth was moved emotionally.

Ron's glance softened. Ruth continued.

'If I had never had Badger I would be completely happy with Bella – it is just that I know Badger was flesh and bones, and one day, I will die as she did.'

Jul-17

Trust

It was some time since we had met. We had known each other for a long time, starting together the way we had. This job was not a good one – a failing business that had been neglected for some time. We looked around and agreed to share the major items then get a clearance firm to take everything else - with enough value in the minor items to pay the clearance fee.

Without much warning, he looked at his watch and said he needed to get going. We agreed a date for the collection of our own share and he left the choice of the clearance company to me.

I did not have so far to go as him so I arrived quite early in the morning and went for a walk. I thought back to previous jobs we had done together sometimes fighting against difficulties but usually managing to achieve what was needed. I collected the keys.

The security guard said, 'Your partner came yesterday.'

I opened the main doors not knowing what to expect. The contrast from when I looked around the place with him was stark. It did not take me long to realise that there was only rubbish and junk left. As I walked through the offices and workshops I saw piles of rubbish, some in black bags, with the odd piece of defunct equipment that had not worked for years.

I thought I knew him – I thought I trusted him. But now I felt that the trust we had was worth nothing. Did what we had mean so little to him? Was it so important to him to acquire these material objects? I felt resentment and cheated – not at all at the value of what he had taken nor at the cost I would have to pay for the clearance but for the misplaced trust.

I felt a loss – but of course I had only lost something I did not actually have. It did not make losing it easier.

It was he that had lost something, but of no value to him – that was the best way to look at it.

Jul-17

Lines

Rafe had always been obsessive. When the atomic weapons began to drop this stood him in good stead. Rafe worked in a specialist laboratory, testing safety systems. He found a concrete silo on the edge of the industrial park where he worked. All infrastructure had started to fall apart and looting had been increasing. There was a whole lot of lead that the thieves had not been able to sell left in the woods. Rafe took a forklift truck from work and went to pick it up and lined the inside of the silo with lead to about 4m from the floor. Then there was a grain store that was broken into and the cockroaches had moved in. Rafe set up a huge trap based on a sieve to filter the cockroaches out of the grain and killed them with insecticide. He built a low space at the bottom of the silo to live in for 12 weeks. Above this he poured in the dead cockroaches to nearly the top of the silo – so a depth of about 5m of cockroaches. This would provide a filter for the radioactive air – cockroaches adsorb radiation.

Rafe had a polythene tube with very small air holes – it ran from top to bottom of the silo – running inside the ladder guard for his way in and out. He wanted to gauge the final bombing as closely as possible as the 12 weeks was critical – he did not want to start consuming his food before it was necessary as he hoped the radiation would become manageable 12 weeks after the final bombs were dropped. The was no one left at work but he still went in to monitor what was happening. He took a radiation meter and placed it at the top of the silo to monitor radioactivity.

One evening there seemed that there was very little happening as he monitored communications. He decided to go in the silo that evening – he could come out in the morning if everything was ok.

It was on the second night that he woke to the noise of huge explosions – he had no way of knowing how close they were but he prayed that none of them were too close that the silo would not survive. He guessed these were coming from automatic systems in space, there would be no stopping them, just wait for them to run out.

During the 12 weeks, he monitored the radiation levels and saw them reducing. He did not feel at all well and he envisaged that he would have to return to the silo after foraging for the day. The temperature had dropped too. He finally decided to leave the silo – he climbed the internal ladder slowly feeling increasingly weak and sick.

He did not know what to expect as he looked out of the silo for the first time. The first thing he noticed was the sound – even before he looked out he could hear the sigh of the wind with no other sounds except his own laboured breathing. No traffic, no birds, no animals and no people. Then he saw over the rim of the silo a grey overcast sky but with most buildings and trees still standing. Just everywhere there were people lying on the ground with some animals and birds too. He brought the radiation meter with him and kept checking the levels – they were not as bad as he had feared.

He walked to his lab to find out what was happening. Close by there was a warehouse with tinned food. He stopped to eat, he checked the radiation and it was fairly low. He passed the neighbouring unit to his lab and saw the door was open. This was very unusual and he ventured in to take a look. He had no idea what he was going to see; he was worried that he would come across a corpse. There was a small airplane which looked very futuristic. He explored it briefly and thought he would come back after he had a shower at work. As he left the small hanger he noticed two large stones one on top of the other. He could make out three faint lines in the shape of a triangle but with curved convex edges.

He had a shower at work – the water was cold but he made a fire in one of the flues used for experiments. The winds outside seemed eternal and created a good draft for the flames. There was no power in the building but there was a battery backup system which he had turned off so it did not drain. He turned this on and used a few minutes precious power to listen out for any communications. Total silence.

Over the next few days he did not go back to the silo but built his strength up on the food in the warehouse. He spent his time checking communications and trying to make sense of the airplane in the adjacent unit. When he tried to switch it on an unhelpful message appeared on the console which said, "Engine manifold missing". The engine was nothing like he had ever seen – the only thing he could think was that it converted matter directly to energy – an Einstein Engine. Clearly the manifold was stored elsewhere. After several days of futile searching his eyes alighted on the two stones with the strange lines. He went and got the forklift truck and carefully lifted the upper one off.

Inside fitted into engineered grooves the manifold lay. He lifted it gently out and took it to the airplane. He opened the doors and taxied the small craft out. There was a lever marked "vertical take-off" – he pushed it and hoped for the best. Soon he was in level flight and he could see the pock-marked earth below him. Signs of death everywhere. He turned out to sea keeping his eyes on the horizon. He felt human life may have survived far from land.

Jul-17

Blown Away

Stan's wife came from the North, like he did, and when she left him she went back there. Their marriage had neither been happy nor short but rather a relief when it was over. He was 63 and they had been married 36 years. They had one daughter, Jane, aged 35 going on 36. She was dutiful and kindly with her dad, now married herself she had two children – they normally stayed at home when she visited him. Stan lived in the family home for a few months after his wife had gone but he only used a couple of the rooms downstairs. He often fell asleep on the couch. He worked at a privately owned café for nearly 20 years the whole time for the same owner, Angie. It was on the A249 in the shadow of the M2 which passed high above on a bridge between two hills. He asked Angie if he could rent the attic above the café. Angie was very much her own boss and decided that she was quite happy with that arrangement.

When Stan reached 65 he stayed living in the café's attic doing odd jobs but was now retired. He was entitled to a state pension and he used to cycle off to the Post Office to collect it on a Thursday. One week he got confused with the days and the date was displayed on the wall as Wed 15 October 1986. He drew enough money from his account for a few drinks and went to play darts in the men's club until the pub opened. A bit before closing time he set off back to his attic. The wind was blowing quite strongly and every so often he veered in to the road or was blown on to the verge. When he got back to the café there was a glimmer of the fire-safety light from within but the floodlight that normally came on when he wheeled his bike in to the back yard failed to do so. He chained his bike to the stand in the dark. There was still power in the café – the fridge freezers were still on. The outside lights must have tripped out – he would look at it in the morning.

He made his way up to the attic as the wind howled round the roof. The valley narrowed here where the M2 bridge was built and there was no protection from the wind, no other buildings or trees. Stan had a few pints inside him and did not really think about going to bed, he just did so as he did every night. He expected he would need to get up in the early hours as he usually did. He had a little trouble getting to sleep as the sound of the storm increased but he did manage it.

When he woke to go to the loo the noise of the storm seemed just as loud as when he went to sleep, however as he came out of the loo and made his way to his bed there seemed to be a lull. He lifted his foot the last step towards his bed when his world exploded with bricks. One brick hit his hand which started to bleed. His pillow and bed were covered with bricks – he had an horrific image of his head still lying there smashed by the bricks. He looked round and saw the brick wall at the end of the cafe had blown in. He thought for a minute the roof was going to lift off but fortunately it did not – instead there was a strange noise and the wall at the other end of the café was blown outward into the carpark outside. Now the wind was blowing right through the roof taking most of his possessions and spewing them across the carpark. In a rather mindless way he started to remove some of the bricks from the bed but he left quite a lot down each side as this help stop the bedclothes blowing away. The roof was still in place so while the rain was coming in to the attic it was not high enough to reach the bed.

It seemed that the wind was starting to drop and he was thinking about getting out of bed when he heard a car arrive and at least two people came rushing up the stairs. It was still before 6am.

Angie and Jane came into what was left of the attic and looked at him sitting up in bed amongst the bricks.

Jane said, 'Are you ok? Why are you still in bed?'

Stan cleared his throat, 'Are there just the two of you? I thought it was a whole herd of you – be careful I am not sure how much this building can take anymore.' Angie laughed and Stan went on, 'I am ok – in fact rather relieved to see you as I don't have any clothes to get dressed in, which is why I thought it best to stay in bed and not catch that hypothermia or whatever it is. I don't suppose you saw my trousers in the carpark, did you?'

Angie looked at him a bit disbelieving, 'We passed some old rags wrapped round barbed wire about two miles away. I think we still have one of your old boilersuits in the cupboard in the café.' She went back downstairs taking the stairs much more daintily.

Jane looked at her dad not knowing how to deal with the situation.

'Were you scared when the wall came in?' she asked.

'Yes, I suppose I was. I was lucky the bricks did not kill me.'

They could hear Angie coming back up the stairs.

'Where are you going to live?' said Jane.

'I've got an attic at home which you can live in,' said Angie.

Stan looked a bit doubtful.

'It is better built and more sheltered than this one,' said Angie with a grin.

Jul-17

Twin Lives

Remit To include the dialogue: 'You told me you were going on holiday,'

Alvin travelled back into his wardrobe puzzled. He did not know how he was going to face life now. He was convinced his plan had been infallible but here he was still aware of his own consciousness directly after he had murdered his grandfather – timed before his father was born. He had chosen his paternal grandfather as he was a mean miserable old bastard. Very like his own twin, Josh. He and Josh were not identical and hated each other from first sight – Alvin liked to think he got on with him in the womb but even that was doubtful. Josh was far larger than Alvin and probably tried to starve Alvin of all nutrients.

They had lived in the same two-bedroom house from birth. At aged seven they had the almightiest fight. Alvin came out of it very badly physically but had managed to establish "the line" down their room. Eventually Alvin's black eye and broken nose healed but the line stayed. It was a double scarlet line chosen by Mum in a haphazard way but may have been influenced by the sight of blood and carnage that she saw as she burst in through the door and managed to heave the writing table between them. Alvin nearly passed out while his twin attacked the table top with such ferocity that he thought Josh was going to break through. Fortunately, the cheap flat pack furniture was made from multiply which proved too strong for Josh. Dad had been away working on a new bypass and Alvin was removed from the war zone into his mum's bed until the line was painted across the floor and up the walls. Alvin wanted Mum to paint it on the ceiling too but she refused on the basis that her arms hurt and that the ceiling was out of bounds anyway.

Josh was not stupid but as time passed it was clear that Alvin was very good at school. He found the double line helped him escape Josh if either his parents were at home. But he also used his wardrobe for studying force-fields and then later time travel. He would go into his built-in wardrobe on his side of the room then when he heard Josh come in he would travel backwards in time and remain undisturbed.

When Alvin and Josh were seventeen and the double line was showing chips, and fading from ten years constant dispute Alvin resolved to go back in time. Further than he had ever been, to one year before his father was born and smash his grandfather's head open with one of Josh's machetes. He did think out every aspect of this knowing that he would cease to exist at the same time as Josh – he thought this would be a fitting punishment for himself.

As he brought down the machete on his grandfather's head he felt no different – he could not understand it. Had he misidentified his granddad? He did not have time to do more than roll him over before he had to go – he could hear people approaching. He looked round for the machete but it had disappeared.

Stepping out of his wardrobe he was immediately aware that the double line was missing and he looked across the room to where Josh's bed should have been. His mother came in with some clean clothes.

'You told me you were going on holiday,' she said, 'what happened?'

'I'm sorry mum – I'm not sure. I've been away – where is Josh, and the double line?'

She looked puzzled, 'That does not sound like one of your usual games – have you looked in the box under your bed?'

Alvin sat down abruptly on his bed. His mother looked concerned, she sat down next to him and took his pulse.

It seemed like Josh and the double line had disappeared completely from his life – along with all his machetes. Alvin's mind began to race – Josh had not looked like him so was it possible they had different fathers? Alvin had researched biology and sex with even more interest than time travel. He knew that there are a few recorded cases of women conceiving twins from different fathers. He looked at his mum in a new light.

Gradually a question began to form in his mind – hey Mum in a different life do you think you had sex with two men – not necessarily at the same time, but close together – and I was one twin and you also had Josh whose dad you were married to?

Alvin looked round his room looking for inspiration. He saw a photo on the wall and looked at a picture of a man. His mum followed his eyes and smiled.

'Dad is coming home tomorrow – he's sorry he missed your birthday but he'll be glad you're here.'

Alvin thought fast, 'I'm glad I'm here too,' he wondered if his real dad worked on bypasses too.

'He was delayed offshore on the rig due to bad weather,' his mother said.

Jul-17

Sweet Rows

Remit: Start piece with the given text/speech.

'What are you doing here?' she gazed in amazement at all the figures that stood row upon row on the back lawn. The very fact that she had spoken out loud took her by surprise – an involuntary response to an astonishing sight.

Each figure was just under shoulder height, most fixed their gaze on her breasts as she approached them. There were many figures of men and women, and there were also some other exotic creatures like a centaur and a fawn – scaled to be the same size as the people. She touched them as she passed through them, they were made from unbaked clay all a similar colour of a reddish brown. The detail and accuracy were remarkable, some young and some old.

She managed to pick her way through the static crowd to the rear hedge where there was a gate into the meadow. The figures were packed tightly coming through the gate but she sighed with relief to see that they were not filling the entire area behind her house.

As she made her way back to her kitchen she noticed a dragon, a unicorn and a robot dotted amongst city dressed people. Slightly shorter than most of the figures she spotted a mermaid standing on her wide fishtail – the detail of her scales was impressive.

She sat at the window drinking strong sweet tea, eyes scanning the rows for things she had not noticed before. She tried to think of a plan of action. They were amazing but mowing the lawn was going to be impossible. There was not much doubt in her mind who their creator was. For the last year, she had been helping out at the local comprehensive school.

It was in the first week she had met Julian – he was small for his age with very fair complexion and freckles. He was just 15. John Miles the art teacher warned her.

'He does not speak.'

'Do you mean he is dumb?'

'No, we think he can speak it is just he chooses not to. He is very artistic and he also does very well in all subjects. I did hear him yell once when someone pushed him and he fell awkwardly against a low wall. He had to get the wound butterfly-taped up. But he did not say anything just screamed one brief shout.'

'Has he been referred to the child psychologist?'

'Yes, he gets on fine with them and writes his answers

down for them.'

'Is there some problem at home?'

'Oh, yes there does seem to be – both of his parents are blind.'

It was like being punched – her mother had been blind. 'Both of them? How does that work?' She spoke with a tangible strain in her voice.

John Miles looked at her with concern, 'I think he grunts and they can tell if he means yes or no.'

She left the subject and got to know Julian slowly – taking care not to encroach on his family life.

She finished drinking her tea and went to school – she caught sight of Julian before he noticed her but then it was as if he felt her gaze on him and he looked round before she could look away. His whole face lit up with an impish grin and she smiled back infected by his joy. At the end of the first period it was a short break and he lingered until the class and the teacher left them together on their own.

'How did you manage to make them all and the bring them to my garden?'

He sat down and wrote: My mum and dad are both blind, they don't notice what I did – I made them in the garden shed. Then I brought them by our barrow – it did take quite a while after dark.

'But still that was a huge amount of work, what made you do it?' She thought of him going out past his unseeing parents to make his clay crowd.

Don't know really – I thought you would notice me.

'I noticed you anyway – how am I going to mow the lawn now?'

Good question – shall we put them up on the moor? By King's Standing.

'What is this "we" all of a sudden!' She looked at him

sharply but his grin won her over and she smiled back.

'I suppose I could borrow a trailer – it would take about ten trips.' She stood looking thoughtfully down at the paper in front of him. 'OK we will do it together – but I wish you would speak,' she said.

The moment she said about him speaking she regretted it. He smiled sweetly and stood up clutching his piece of paper. He picked up his satchel and walked to the door.

He stopped at the door and without turning said, 'Did you like them?'

'Yes,' she said.

Jul-17

The Qualar Games

This piece was inspired by The Fairy Feller's Master-Stroke by R Dadd.

The Qualar Games come once every seven years – two weeks after midsummer's day to help reduce cheating by way of sorcery. It takes great skill and dexterity to be able to split a qualar in two with one single blow of an axe. The prize is not of any intrinsic value but there is much prestige and kudos - and there is an unspoken tradition which means the competition is very fierce and many have tried to cheat. Eight times cheating has been discovered – four times by sorcery and four times by substituting an already split qualar. It may be that sorcery has succeeded and not been detected by my family - we oversee the fairness of the Games and we have done our very best. We are the Ogive family and are small so we cannot take part in the games. Horns grow from our ears in the shape of an ogive. We are totally impartial.

The games started many years ago in the time of my great-great-great grandfather. We have long lives and I did not start my job as Games Overseer until after we put my father to ground and I was over sixty-nine. I take my responsibility very keenly, watching all preparations in minute detail and of course the blow itself – it seems that brute force is not sufficient alone but rather speed plus the correct angle and to some small degree, luck in the resilience of each qualar. The shell has many angles like a dragon's skin. The dryness of the growing period affects the hardness and thickness of the skin. There seem to be several factors that affect the size and density of the qualar.

To me they are beautiful, the way they grow, the way their skin is dark and glistens in different lights. They have the strangest smell, damp and musty, and a totally different flavour from the smell, like a sort of bright flower; of course, they need to be cooked carefully or otherwise they kill you. The strangest thing of all about them is you never see them move but if you put a few close and you leave them, when you come back they are nearly all touching or hard up against each other.

At long last the summer has arrived, late this year but we have a fine day for the Games. The sky is deep blue as the day wears on – there are a few folk dressed in bright clothes and others in smart court clothes – stiff taffeta in subtle shades. The seventh man of the games is taking his turn and I see the line of men still to take the blow are lined up. I sense rather than see the ladies' interest in the men in the games – there are two by me, both bold, one with an assumed indifference but feet akimbo, the other with wings on her head eyeing up the contestant's swing.

Further away there are more discreetly eager women who have come to see the games.

I am weary with concentration and I feel the power of the sorcery strongly – some of the qualar have gone smooth. There are people and sprits of different sizes that I cannot turn to look at for fear of missing something in the next blow. As is the tradition the trumpets are sounded by a man and a giant grasshopper in an attempt to stem the flow of sorcery. I catch sight of movement through the rushes beyond the line of contestants. Something or someone is viewing the scene while remaining out of sight.

The axe comes down and cleaves the qualar in two even as it is turning smooth. I have never seen such a blow – I think never has a smooth qualar been cleaved in two before. There is silence – then I feel the sprits being released. I am not sure what has happened – indeed I am not sure if we will be able to continue the Qualar Games. It seems all the qualars are turning smooth. Our undeclared winner has vanished so it looks like he was sprit in a man's form. Who else will be able to split a smooth qualar? Maybe next year they will grow with many angles once more but I am not sure.

Jun-17

Sleepwalking Winter

She opened the door, and a cold blast of winter air woke her with a start. She was sleepwalking, in her nightie. Her husband had missed her and came downstairs bleary-eyed to find her standing in the open doorway shaking with the cold. He shut the door and led her into the warm kitchen and sat her down near the stove. It was just after 2am and he made her a hot sweetened mug of milk before coaxing her back to bed.

'So, are you going to see this counsellor now it has happened again?' her husband Steve asked over breakfast the next morning. It was a Saturday and they did not have to rush to work. Sally looked out of the little window looking at the winter-bound garden. She pushed her beans on toast round her plate before attempting to eat it. At last she looked at him with a bright smile and said.

'Yes – that was pretty scary being woken by a cold blast of air from the front door. Good job there was nobody returning home late just then. That would have scared them.'

'I don't think so – you would have made their day in that short nightie of yours.'

'I have not heard you complain before,' she said with a grin. He grinned back and ruffled her hair.

The counsellor was a man slightly older than her husband and her. He had quite a rapid way of speaking but then he tended to wait while she found the right words to reply with. He said to call him Chris. She found it quite easy to talk to him and tell him her innermost thoughts. Even when the subject of her sex life came up she blushed slightly but answered feeling safe as she did so. Her mother came to stay and she discussed the visit with Chris. As she sat down and made herself comfortable Chris watched her, then he said.

'Do you feel stressed by your mother's visit?'

'Yes, I do – I feel bad saying it but she talks about all her friends who are grandmothers.'

'Do you feel pressure to have a family?'

'Yes, my dad died quite young and I'm an only child. Steve is very good about her but she comes to see us regularly and he starts to worry about me.'

'Does he feel the same sort of pressure as you?'

'Not to the same extent – his parents have grandchildren already but I think he feels a bit helpless in knowing how to deal with my mother. He calls her the Winter Witch when she is not there.'

'How do you feel about the situation?'

'If we have kids that might keep her happy. But we are not ready yet and I want to tell her to back off really. Do you think it is possible this is the cause of my sleepwalking?'

'It is possible – also there is quite a strong bond between your mum and you. Do you think that Steve might feel excluded in some way, are you aware of this?'

'I think Steve might feel that – but I am not sure what to do about it.'

'Would it help to talk to him about it?'

'Do you think it is worth a try?'

Sally talked to Steve and he went quiet and thought about it while Sally went in the kitchen with her mum and they made a cake together. He listened to the two women and later talked to Sally about an idea he had had.

'You have to find a kind way to tell her to stop pressurising you – why don't you go "sleepwalking" and wake her up and tell her that your counsellor has suggested your sleepwalking may be due to "family stress" – because we are not ready yet.'

'I see what you are saying but I think I am strong enough just to tell her gently, without the sleepwalking – and I think you should be there.'

'Oh no, the Winter Witch will cast a spell on me and I will freeze over.'

They both laugh nervously.

Oct-17

River Runs Deep

The steep step out of Beth's house always caught him off guard and he stumbled down into the street and brought his guts up along with the vile supper she had forced him to eat. It was meant to be mutton stew but was like some mutation of stew crossed with fibreglass repair of the wing of a clapped-out car.

After what seemed an interminable time of stomach pains he managed to drag himself round the corner and into the "Pig in a Poke" to buy a pint of bitter to take the taste away. After he had cautiously drunk his beer, he left by the back entrance in to a badly lit back street. In the gloom, he caught sight of a silhouette of a fox, low against the wall. He followed it for some distance. When the fox turned a corner it was briefly lit up in the headlight beam of a car which cast a clearer silhouette. As if disliking the limelight, the fox slipped down and out of sight. He kept his eyes fixed on the point where the fox had vanished. He came to the spot and saw a broken man hole cover. Without thinking he lowered himself down, placing his feet on the rung of the top of the steel ladder.

He sank down into the darkness, the noise of the street fading away, being absorbed into the watery echoey background. He got to the bottom of the ladder and walked along the side of the quiet waterway that glimmered in the darkness. Every so often pale illumination came from drain shafts much smaller than the one he had come down.

He made out a small boat tied up and decided to risk a trip in it. It was slightly quicker than walking but felt even less secure. He approached a paler area where he could make out some sort of junction of differed sized pipes. Above he could make out grills that let in a little more light than the drain shafts. He followed the flow which led to the biggest pipe and he realised that he was nearing the end of his journey by boat. There was more light coming in from the uppermost part of the arch of the pipe and wall, with a stair leading up to the light. He guessed that deep below the surface of the water smaller bore pipes led out to the river. He tied the boat up and climbed the stairs slowly – it was like a fire escape on a tall building and was exhausting for him to climb in his feeble state.

He found that it was early morning and he was close to the office where he worked. He stopped in his favourite breakfast haunt and had sweet tea and a bacon and egg roll to make up for his missing supper. He slipped in to the stock room of his office and managed to doze uneasily before work.

He woke disturbed by the stock room door opening and making a noise like a demented wild beast. He held his hands over his ears and looked up at what he assumed was some stormtrooper but turned out to be a paramedic. He and a social worker asked questions while a policewoman took notes.

'We have camera images of you going down into the city sewer – what induced you to go in there?'

'I saw a fox go down there – it seemed a cool way to escape for a while.'

'Are sure it was a fox? Did you see the colour?'

'Well no – I saw the shadow against the wall.'

'Could it have been a rat with a large shadow cast by a close headlight?'

'No, I think it was a fox.'

He was in the medical room now and they left him alone and he felt very tired so he lay down and rested his head.

He could hear voices – two women talking.

'Do you think he will – well get back to the way he used to be, well more so if not completely?'

'I am not sure - the change was quite quick and dramatic.'

'He is much more relaxed.'

'Too relaxed – he does not bother about much, things that used to get him steamed up hardly bother him now.'

'He is not driven the way he used to be – also I would say he does not feel angst in the way he used to which is hardly surprising.'

'No that's true but also he has lost his sparkle.'

'Yes, but he still makes jokes, but they are quite gentle now.'

'Have you noticed he does not talk to himself like he used?'

'Now you mention it – but I did not miss it until you

said!'

'It is possible in the past his down days stopped him – now he may get to a happier state with not so much angst but motivated to keep going.'

'Just so long as the angst was not the only thing that got him going in the first place.'

His boss came to see him – he sat down next to him.

'I think you have had a bit of a rough time lately?' asked his boss.

'Nothing I couldn't handle,' he replied thinking of the rush job last week, 'just worked a bit harder.'

'No I mean in your family.'

'Oh that.'

'There are no urgent jobs – would it help to have tomorrow and Monday off as compassionate leave to help sort things out?'

He looked out of the open door down through the glass façade, he could see the river and make out where the end of the sewer was. He was taken by surprise by the unexpected kindness.

'Well I don't want to be treated any differently…'

'You're not - this is company guidelines.'

'Ok – thank you, it would help to get straight.'

He signed out a helmet with a built-in torch and headed towards the sewer.

Jun-17

Reeds and Water Lilies

The day started like any other. It was just as difficult to

get out of bed. The pistol under his pillow looked longingly at him - the trigger waiting to be pulled. He resisted manfully and placed both feet firmly on the floor beside his bed.

There was the usual post on the mat and he opened the only letter that was not a circular or bill. It was address to him formally.

Dear Mr Zumble

We were wondering if you would be interested in undertaking an investigation on our behalf.

The late Frank Wilbur, one of our founding trustees, has left some papers which have raised some questions. You come recommended to us and we would be grateful if you could let us know your rates.

Yours truly,
Anne Millet
Chair Trustees of the Bingley Estate

There was a number to call. He pondered how they got his address but that would not have been hard. Did they know he had grown up fostered in one of the estate cottages?

He talked it over with his business partner. Ray had bankrolled the whole outfit while he was still a big wheel in the city. Now he took an active interest and time out from his business and leisure activities to help when needed. Ray asked the same questions that he asked himself.

'Do they know your connections with the estate?' asked Ray.

'Not sure – probably.'

'Do you want to do the work?'

'Sort of – Olivier was very close to Frank.'

'Do you want to take the Ferrari?'

This question I did not expect – so I asked, 'Why do you ask – do you think it will make a difference?' This was one of Ray's favourite questions.

'Yes – you were an Estate dependent but now you are very successful in what you do, but you are unknown outside a small circle. Driving the Ferrari and parking it outside one of the Estate cottages will be laying your cards down in a way the Astra would not.'

'True – do you see it as a way of getting people to talk?'

'Indeed,' Ray said and rested his fingertips together.

On Tuesdays and Thursdays, the Great Hall was open to the public on other days only the Gardens were open.

I went to the Office to collect my keys to Cottage No 5. Not much had changed. The wall calendar was up to date, everything remained in the same time warp that I remembered.

After I settled in to Cottage No 5, it took me about 90 seconds to check the back door. I called Anne Millet. She agreed to meet at Frank Wilbur's house. Even though his wife, Ruth, had been a very forceful woman, everyone tended to think and speak of Frank's house. He had met Ruth quite late in life, once he was a well-established bachelor. She was a shrill neurotic divorced woman who had left an abusive husband. It was not quite clear how she had met Frank but it was supposed that it was something to do with his interest in chess. Although if she had interest in chess before she met Frank it evaporated immediately. When I last saw Frank, Ruth was still very much alive and jealous but she had died several years before Frank. I looked in through the windows and saw the house was still orderly but looking slightly more shabby.

A Ford pulled up beside the Ferrari and a mousey efficient looking woman got out and held her hand out to me.

'I am Anne Millet – I guess you are Dave Zumble?'

'Yes – I don't think we have met before.'

'No, I joined the Estate team after you had moved on. It seems you have done very well with your investigating.'

'Yes, I have had luck too.'

She smiled and a warmth infused her face. She gestured and spoke, 'We better go in so I can show you what all the interest is about.'

I looked through the papers that Frank had left. It took me a while to realise they were meant only for me.

'Do you want me to take them away or work on them here?' I asked Anne.

'You are welcome to come and go as you please. Also, I have had copies of the papers made so you can take those with you. I have a spare key if you want it.'

'Thank you. I don't think this is quite like other investigations. But one common aspect is to get to the right mindset which being able to come here freely will help.'

She gave me the photocopies and the key to the front door, and drove away in her car.

There were quite a few seemingly everyday letters that were about an archaeology find that Frank had been involved with. One of these letters enclosed a sheet of other writing with doodles and pictures in the margins. The covering letter suggested this sheet was copied from the walls of the site – but looking at the doodles I came to the conclusion that this was just to mislead. This page was meant for me to read.

I studied the page carefully. I drove out to where the marshes were. I sat in the car for a few minutes not knowing what to expect next. I saw a boat coming through the reeds and the lily leaves.

I called Ray.

'How is it going?' he asked.

'Frank left me a page in code and it has taken me all evening to decrypt.'

'Well you are not getting any younger.'

'True – do you want to know what he said?'

'Yes, the suspense is killing me.'

'He said Olivier did not kill herself. He said Ruth was unhinged with jealousy and murdered her. He knew Ruth was dying of cancer so he kept quiet.'

'How do you feel now?'

'Better in parts,' I replied, 'I threw my pistol in the marshes.'

May-17

Rhino Day

Jack woke up as a rhino – that in itself was strange but it was made stranger still as he had often wanted to wake up as a giraffe. But that is the way life goes.

After the initial shock, Jack thought he would try to make the best of it. He got out of the bed gingerly – he was surprised the bed had survived. He had been in the doghouse yesterday – he had come in late and had to sleep in the spare room as Jackie, that was his wife, was pretty mad with him as he had completely forgotten that they were meant to go and see her parents.

When Jack came down to breakfast Jackie totally ignored his new physical form as a rhino. To make his predicament worse, putting his fragile relationship in further jeopardy, he stepped on a crumpet and flattened it. Jackie knelt down and peeled the flattened crumpet off the floor and slapped it down on Jack's plate. It was a medium sized plate but the crumpet was so flat and thin it nearly covered the entire plate from side to side.

Jack cleared his throat to speak. However, when he tried to speak nothing much happened, it seemed that human speech was not going to be possible in his rhino form. All he wanted to ask Jackie was if she had noticed he was a rhino. When he thought about it he guessed she probably had noticed – but would she have realised that the rhino was him? He ate the crumpet thoughtfully. She may have seen him in the spare bed – and worked out from his split clothes barely covering any of his body that he was now the rhino. They had all fallen off him as he got out of bed.

From her actions of putting the flattened crumpet on his plate, it seemed certain that she knew he was the rhino. The plate had on the outer circle "Jack's plate", it was one of the few things that Jack had retained from before their marriage. The main reason it had survived was that it was virtually indestructible. It may even be able to withstand a rhino standing on it – but he did not think he would put it to the test. The plate represented his individuality which had otherwise been rather swamped by Jackie.

Maybe his waking up as a rhino was due to a deep-seated need to express his individuality. He did not know much about rhinos but he could not imagine a male rhino being swamped by a female rhino. He seemed to remember that a rhino's horn is made from hair. His own thinning hair was a reminder of the power of the rhino and he stamped his foot. The kitchen flooring, which was quite recent, had managed to remain unscathed by the compression of the crumpet, but now showed signs of a large round indentation. Jackie lost her temper and picked up his plate and hurled it at the floor. It bounced and Jack caught it in his mouth and calmly placed it back on the table.

Jack came to the realisation that Jackie was still in a bad mood and was pretending that everything was normal.

Apr-17

Echo

I think my family is normal. My dad, he is a painter and decorator. My mum, well she has had a few jobs like school cook when we were young but now she is buyer at a big department store. They just bought a car – so she does not have to go in the van anymore. It's a ford Cortina – a red one. I have a brother – he only seems to be interested in money. Then there is gran – granddad died in the First World War. My other grandparents are doing fine too.

I got a holiday job and met Emily and her twin sister Anthea. They look similar but they are not identical. They were both working in the office doing archiving as holiday jobs too but they helped me feel at ease while I was finding my way round. Emily was not the first girl I had been out with but she was very different to the others. It seemed Anthea had seen a few more boys than Emily. We were very close that summer - I saw Emily most days. At the end of the summer I was invited back to where they grew up. It was the first of many memorable trips.

We caught the train into the country and then a bus that struggled up the steep hills and rattled down the valleys. The three of us walked the last mile, larking around – Anthea's boyfriend had not survived the whole summer but I felt close to Emily and accepted by Anthea. They lived in a stone built farmhouse halfway down the hillside. The farm was mainly sheep. I stepped in to the big kitchen with a table in the middle. I blinked coming in from the outside and made out two women looking at me.

'I am Liz, it is good to meet a friend of Emily – makes a change from meeting Anthea's boyfriends,' she laughed, 'this is my sister Chrissie.'

I shook hands with them both – Liz seemed a bit older than my mum and dad but it was difficult to say how old Chrissie was. Chrissie smiled but was quiet and a bit shy. I knew Emily's dad was dead – died in the war and had never seen his daughters. I looked to see if there was a photo of him on a shelf somewhere but there were mainly paintings of flowers and animals – Chrissie was the artist. Later I asked Emily about a photo of her dad – she smiled enigmatically and told me there were some in an album but it was not often they were brought out.

I did not know anything about farming but I liked going there and walking over the hills. I saw Emily all through my training and when I got my first proper job as an architect I asked her if she would like to get married.

'I think so but before you ask I would like you to visit my mother again.'

I was a little surprised but I did not protest – I was at

ease when we visited the remote little farm. Emily had met my parents and my mum and dad both liked her.

We had visited without Anthea but this time we met Anthea and all travelled down on the train. I felt excited and made them both laugh on the last mile walk. It was quite late when we got there – we were drawn into the kitchen by Liz and Chrissie. There was a hot stew to eat and I was feeling good to be there.

After the meal was cleared away Liz sat down and waited expectantly. We all sat round the table – I was between Emily and Anthea. Liz spoke slowly taking her time.

'Well lad it is good you have come. I understand that you are keen to marry Emily?'

'Yes,' I said without hesitation.

'Well we need to tell you something before we go further. Not everyone can cope with it.'

Chrissie got up and moved to the sideboard and opened a draw and brought back an album to the table and sat down next to Liz again.

Liz looked ahead of her, then spoke once more. 'You want to wed Emily and we hope you do – but we need to tell you something about our family now, a past echo. We are all women and it is difficult for us. Chrissie is my daughter not my sister. I look upon them all as my daughters but your Emily is my granddaughter, she is Chrissie's daughter', she paused and my mind struggled to adjust – there was more.

'But Anthea and Emily are sisters – they have the same father as well as born on the same day.'

Chrissie stood up and opened the photo album and pushed it across the table to me and I looked at a photo of a young man in solder's uniform.

Now Chrissie spoke the most I had heard her say. 'He

was a kind gentle man – a very unwilling soldier. He bedded us both but we did not know until after they took him away and we were both sick in the morning. What were the chances that the girls arrived on the same day? I was only just sixteen – there was no doctor only Cathy from the village. She was busy that day. It was her idea really to say the girls were twins.' My mind was giving up the struggle.

'They never questioned it in the registry office,' Liz said looking at me cautiously.

I looked at the picture of the soldier then quickly at Emily, she smiled faintly but looked nervous. I looked at Anthea and she grinned back encouragingly.

'You got the right sister, first time,' she said.

I laughed and stood up, scooping Emily up in my arms.

'Well I am glad you told me, I know I can become part of your family now. But I don't think I will explain it to my mum and dad.'

Apr-17

Unsound Mind

There is a worm in my brain eating holes in my mind. Not what you would call a sound mind. I have been waiting in fear, knowing that this time would come – now my mind will not sound. There is no protest left. No reason to be. Only reason not to be.

The skull is mine. The brain is mine. My mind is mine. But who do the holes belong to? Even the worm must be mine as it sprang within me. So, the obsessions are mine, the cringing doubt, the fear of hurtling down in the night – all mine. But the worm holes are not mine. I am in denial. They do not belong to me.

It is not rational to think like this. Have you ever come across a rational colander? A hole in inference – that let's logic through without stopping on the way. What was that that I heard? Not a sound but something in my head. What is it that I see before me, in my mind and out of sight or should that be sight out of mind?

There is a screaming silence in my head that does not come out. There is a feeling of numbness that does not sink in. It lies over the surface, silence secured tightly down. I dare not talk to anyone about it. It is a secret forever between me and the holes. You can tell a hole anything – it will never let on. I only think of me now though. Not let people I know get in the way. Or blood ties stop the desire to die. Will it work. Will I die. There better not be some mistake. The worm holes must not get in my way.

What to do? How to stop being. Would the worm be prevailed upon to eat my whole brain away? I don't think so. Do I have a plan as to how to go? Well yes and no. Mainly things I'll not do plus a few that I will do.

When to do it? When to stop being. Is there a good time or a bad time or just an end time? I did not choose a start time, what is it like to choose an end time?

I know what to do now. It will be over in no time.

The end.

Apr-17

Take a Life

Friend of mine
desires to die,
in the winter.
But I'm hoping
come the spring,
she'll burst through.
Live till a summer,
sometime later.
I don't know
though.

Mar-17

Blue Eyes

It was when I was quite young, six or seven, that I noticed how other people liked me. It was not just girls and boys of my own age but adults. So, the parents of my friends too. I went to quite a few kids' birthday parties, including some where I was the only boy. I remember one - we were playing kick the bucket, not sardines even, and I heard two mums talking. I was sneaking along a wall behind the bushes and keeping low to get to the bucket unseen. Under a window, I heard one mum say.

'That boy, he is a nice lad isn't he. Does he have a sister?'

'No that is Saul, he is an only child – he is mature for his age but he is very popular at school with boys and girls.'

I thought she said "manure", which I knew the meaning of, but I was not sure what "mature" was but it sounded good.

'I think he is going to be a very handsome man – he has beautiful blue eyes, so soulful. I think if he is like other men there could be a few hearts strewn across his path.'

I was used to mum saying I was beautiful and did not put much store by it – after all like dad says looking good does not gain you money or happiness. And he should know.

A really good friend of mine called Mandy – usually I say my mate Mandy to distinguish her from all other Mandys – had an older brother called Garry. This Garry turned out to be quite an influence in my life, one of his favourite saying was,

'In this life, you get two sorts of people – wooers and

doers.'

Often, I would say, 'Which are you today?'

'I am a wooer today and most days – not in your league, mind, you could woo the Pope naked.'

Sometimes when he had a bad day he would say.

'I was a doer today but got nothing done.'

I was not sure what I wanted to be when I grew up but in the college summer holidays one year Garry got me to help organise a fête at this posh mansion. The owner was a very good guy but his missus was a tad tricky. Lady Grey was a very good looker. Garry warned me.

'She is a nympho that one – keeping her happy is ten times more difficult than him.'

'Does this mean you have failed to satisfy her?' I asked. He looked at me sharply then smiled sadly.

'No lad – I think she is out of my league and might even be out of yours.'

'Well I am not going to try and disprove you.'

Garry helped me but let me deal with Lady Grey. In fact, I did manage to keep both her and Lord Grey happy – to such a degree that it made a big impression and Lord Grey offered me a job as his aide-de-camp. Lord Grey had been a General. Garry told me that Lady Tarantula Grey had eaten the last one after seducing him.

Garry was in the music business getting more successful at managing pop stars. Just the job for a wooer. It was about this time that Garry met Wendy who was a great person. She was a doer so it was a forgone conclusion they were going to get married. But it took them about three years to do it – more wooing than doing.

I asked Lady Grey if it was ok to ask Lord Grey to hold the wedding at their stately home.

She looked at me with a wicked grin.

'Weddings are the best place to find a husband.'

'Quite so Lady Grey – there should be quite a few to choose from.'

'What wit Saul, be careful lest you cut yourself on it,' but she smiled sweetly and I knew it would be OK.

Lord Grey was positively effervescent – midstream the flow stemmed. He stammered and blushed a bit.

'I suppose Lady Grey may not approve the plan.'

'I think she may be amenable to the idea, sir. I think she may appreciate the jollity is at someone else's expense.'

'Oh quite – excellent strategy. Maybe you could just check with her?'

'Certainly sir.'

I had resisted getting into a personal relationship, as it is euphemistically called, with either sex. It was not that I could not decide - I was secure in the knowledge that I was not gay. Neither did I think it as character building to resist a relationship. But as Garry asked.

'Do you think if you wooed the fairer sex it would impair your ability to woo, Lords and Ladies? Or should that be just be the one Lady?'

'Yes, to the first, no to the second question. But I think that if I do find the right lady I will need to be finding the next job, much as Lady Tarantula finds the next husband.'

'So you want to find a new job and keep the old one?' he said. I just laughed.

I met Ed Song and Lord Elton White while arranging the wedding. Garry knew them both and advised me to woo young Ed as an insurance plan. Against what I thought.

Wendy's younger sister Lucy was on the guest list – she was coming back from Australia in time for the wedding.

'Lucy got married very young but she has been through a messy divorce a while ago,' said Garry.

'Did you meet her then?'

'Yes – I was over there sorting stuff out. She is one great

doer.'

'So that is why I need insurance plan then is it,' I said and he smiled.

At the wedding, I had to smooth over an altercation in the swimming pool. Lucy was there watching me. I did not realise who she was until she spoke.

'Shit buddy, you are god's gift to a doer,' said my mate Lucy.

Mar-17

Ice Breaking

A leaf curled. A cellophane mood-strip tightly wrapped. My stomach much the same, not so much a knot but more trying not to touch the world.

I didn't want to go – it's not a party, but a social gathering of like-minded people. That would be everyone but me.

It was in a beautiful building, tall, arches, slit windows, streaming sun casting rays in warm dust. I made my way up some side stairs in marble, vantage position to see all the guests posing in chic clothes. There was a high up veranda, a long walkway with columns. I could have stepped in to the shadow of a column but my feet took me along to the end of the walkway. I still had fear fluttering alongside. I could descend back in to the throng or walk through to a spacious gallery.

No contest – the gallery won. I thought it was empty of human life and wandered among the streaming shafts of dying sun. Looking at paintings, mainly abstract, and carvings more abstract still. Some surreal.

I felt the walls by my side, like some armour protecting me - letting me wander unseen away from the crowds. I relished being solitary and stepping between objects and the thoughts in my mind. My thoughts took a similar path to my steps – minds cause art, art stimulate minds, which cause new thoughts and paths. My thoughts did briefly think food is necessary to feed minds but not long enough for me to turn back to the party and scanty eatables.

I came to another gallery with a long set of steps and archways. There was a woman lying across the steps at an angle. She was dressed in a beautiful simple white dress. Her eyes were open staring at the ceiling, limpid blue. Her hair was very dark almost black. There was a gash through her dress to her flesh and from her stomach scarlet blood ran down to her hip and spread over the steps.

She seemed to be breathing normally. I was careful not to kneel in the blood as I lowered myself on to the steps. I picked up her hand and said.

'Are you ok – your pulse is ok.'

'Yes – I'm fine. It's tomato ketchup watered down a bit.'

'Oh, I see'

'There is some cream in the fridge at the back of this studio. Your dress is exactly the same colour as the tomato ketchup – if you pour the cream over you we will be a contrasting pair. You are blonde with brown eyes – this was meant to be.'

'One in each arch.'

'Yes,' she replied.

I went to look for the fridge and found some scissors too. I came back triumphant. I settled on the steps angled in the other direction to her. I stood the empty cream container to one side; I could hear voices, I would ask the

first spectator to put it in the bin.
  My fear unfurled.

Beach Burner

It took them a long time to develop their friendship, longer still to meld it. Their first meal together took most of the day.

He came to see her at first light – a grey murky sky and sea of porridge and scales. But the day promised to be a roaster, like yesterday. He carried meat and fish fresh from the kill. She carried all manner of vegetables and fruit, plus some flavours too, salt and herbs.

They came to the sea a mixture of rocks, pebbles and pools. They stepped out as the sun broke up the haze and rolled back a blue sky which paled away before the sun.

He had been busy, not only catching and killing but also digging and lighting. In an even area of pebbles, he had dragged wood, lit and buried it with knowledge of his forefathers; so there was just enough balmy night air to keep it alight and feed a furnace to heat the stones.

She washed some succulent leaves and wrapped them round the meat. He removed the unspent wood, moved the pebbles into a crater to place the meat in first, then two fibrous root vegetables, unwrapped, then the fish wrapped well. He covered the food with the hot stones.

They sat and waited, looking out to sea then at each other. Shyly, slyly in the sunshine. It was too hot to touch much. A gentle brush of hand on limb or face. They stood up and walked towards the sea where it was sandy. The sea was warm but felt cool in the sun after the heat of the stones. Their bodies sank into the sea, their toes into the sandy sea bed. They press together under the water, free from worldly cares.

It was past the midday sun when they came to eat the meal. They cut tomatoes and fennel to eat with the fish and added other vegetables to the last part of the cooking. They lingered over eating the fish while the meat finished cooking. They peeled the flesh of the fish from the bone – the tidy head left flapping. Every morsel of the fish was consumed and they rested awhile, heating up, sweat trickling down their backs into the sand. Another swim, not so shy now, a quick dip and back. Eager to unwrap the rest to eat, they returned and pushed back the second lot of stones.

The yams, split open, glow invitingly next to the dark crumbling meat. Slowly they eat, careful not to burn their fingers, lips and mouths. Teeth sinking into satisfying food they draw energy and sleepiness from the day. It is nearly twelve hours since they had set out, and as they are finishing the food the sun is setting fast. The dark rushes in from the horizon, over the white foam waves down by the beach. The stones are still hot but not so hot as to burn them. They hollow out a matrix in the gravel ground and lay together in mother earth.

Mar-17

Death Beckons

Death beckons, at night, sometimes by day,
mostly life does not notice, turns a shut eye.
Looks the other way at the marauding masses,
looting life clean, to the bone, to be gone.

Death seeps under the door to grasp the last gasp,
squeezes life from your heart with an ultimate grunt.
A look of surprise is all that is left of death passing,
takes your breath away and leaves you, no choking.

Death lingers a lifetime to come the whole way,
rarely deftly, often late, sometimes in haste.
Certain that as once there was life, there will be death,
inevitable as the sands of time draining away.

Feb-17

Fish Out of The Pan

I know different cultures see things differently – I have been to Calais. I could not get my mind around her anger, she was in this country trying to tell me about my own business. I did feel like asking her if she was born in the year of the mule – but underneath I think she was sweet. Also I did want to find out what she was after. She may become a good customer in time.

For all I knew she was after the cuttle of a cuttlefish – they do say some people eat those. Much the same as chicken feet I guess. I did realise she was not angry with me – just frustrated with everything, the whole way of life, talking, signs and etiquette. Her face was beautiful and enquiring. Her eyes had a depth and understanding that was at odds with her frustration. They say people from the east are inscrutable – but not her. She did not mind me scrutinising her either. She looked back into my eyes and I felt her distress, her loneliness. It was true I had no idea how old she was – I suppose she was inscrutable in that.

I found some crayfish as she did not want the lobster – I am not sure what was wrong with the crayfish. Maybe it was the colour or the size, I have an idea they vary quite a bit around the world, I don't know where these ones were from but I was not going to let on. She did smile when she saw the crayfish, a light of some good memory, it lit up her face and I saw her diverted. Slowly she changed her mind about the crayfish, even though her way of thinking was different, at least, changing her mind, was common ground. I could see her thinking "those crayfish look OK, maybe I could do something with those". She hesitated then pointed to two. So, I could translate from a language I knew nothing of and a culture so different to mine – she might as well have been a creature of the air, not a bird, more like a flying animal, in trees; with a very expressive face. And sad eyes.

She was back, not the next day, but the day after. I saw her quite frequently. I asked one of the Chinese lads how to say hallo or good day or whatever people said over there. He knew straight away why I asked so I did not say it just in case it was Chinese for "you look like a cuttlefish" or worse. In any case I was not sure if she was Chinese or what language she spoke.

Should I try to ask her about herself? If so how? Would it seem rude or forward to her? Would she want to communicate or was fish her only interest. She came one day, it was late, close to closing. She did not see me, she was standing looking back and forth when I moved out from the back then her face lit up – maybe it was not just the fish. I spoke - English.

'How are you?' then realising what I said, I added, 'what can I get you?'

'OK,' she said smiling her head slightly to one side, her nose tilting. 'Fish please.' Her accent was very marked, as marked as the absence of the f & p sounds.

I produced a choice of three – all on ice in a metal tray. She pointed to a medium sized salmon-trout hybrid.

'Like?' she asked.

'This is good to eat, fine taste.'

'You like?'

'Oh yes.'

'You cook?'

'Oh yes - I would cook it.'

'Tonight at my place?' she said with a shy grin.

I was startled and looked at her apprehensively. She smiled back innocently and I felt reassured.

'If you like.' I said

Maybe she knew more of men, men the world over, than I had imagined.

Jan-17

Helping Hands

Sebastian arrived at his appointment early. He was

curious but also wanted to establish a feeling of security – one he was not that confident he would achieve as he looked round the waiting room.

He announced himself and his appointment time to the receptionist at the desk. She was not young but she was beautiful. His eyes dropped automatically to her hands - they were strong, past youth with long curved nails. They had very deep red nail varnish and rather disturbingly Sebastian thought of a bird of prey gripping some tasty morsel. In Sebastian's overheated mind he had a vision of her picking over a young lover after a torrid conquest where he was left spent and defenceless.

'Sebastian Smyth, 10:30,' he stated without being spoken to.

'Good morning Mr Smyth – please take a seat, I am sorry we are running a bit late so you will have quite a wait.'

'That is no problem – I'll be fine waiting'

He chose a seat so he could see her hands. She was typing professionally at a keyboard and he was amazed she could type so quickly with those nails – they did click against adjacent keys. He noticed that her keyboard had very unusual keys, on small stalks so her claw nails curled around them.

He did not study the rest of her but had a strong impression of an hourglass figure and symmetrical face with hard glittering eyes – nothing moved on the ground without being noticed.

The outside door opened and a huge man moved in to the room. Despite his size he moved quietly. Sebastian noticed his hands, broad palms, square tipped fingers pointing backwards as he stood at the desk.

'Peter Collins, 10 o'clock,' he said without the woman behind the desk speaking.

'Good morning Mr Collins – fortunately we are running a bit late so you have not missed your appointment. Please take a seat.'

Peter Collins sat down two seats away from Sebastian, lowering himself cautiously on to the chair which seemed precarious with the weight upon it – the chair held out against the onslaught of gravity. Sebastian got a chance to look at the backs of his hands, resting on his thighs. The nails were chewed down raw to the quick. But the fingers looked strong, connected to his hands, to powerful forearms that bulged out of his short sleeves. Peter Collins turned his head and looked unblinkingly at Sebastian. His head appeared to rotate on his shoulders without involving a neck. Sebastian looked back unashamed of his interest in this mountainous man.

The woman of prey at the desk said, without pause from her typing,

'Mr Collins please go through.'

Peter Collins stood up and the chair, finally perturbed by the movement, fell to the floor like an instantaneous game of pickup sticks. Everyone ignored the fate of the chair, Sebastian just watched in awe as Peter Collins brushed the door on both sides and ducked his head too.

Without thinking again Sebastian said out loud, 'He's big – did you see the size of his hands?'

The woman replied not quite as frostily as before, 'Yes I did, he is huge – very strong too.'

Her normal ice stare snapped back into place as the outside door opened once more and a nervous woman of uncertain age sidled up to the desk and stood quivering. Her hands looked like ill-fitting gloves, worn and creased. She was pale, her skin almost translucent, with pear-shaped porcelain face and hands to match, she held one to her face nervously. Sebastian studied his own hands rather than watch her embarrassment.

They were fine dextrous hands, agile and skilled. Very skilled – so skilled that he felt insignificant in comparison. Of course, it was not rational. But that was why he was here. He wondered why the others were here. The massive Peter Collins, the aging porcelain doll – filtering through his reverie he heard the woman at the desk ask with a certain impatience,

'Can I help you?'

'Yes, I am Portia Jones – I have come about my hands.'

'Your appointment is at 11:30 – please take a seat.'

The woman slid away to sit and nurse her hands.

Sebastian took to gazing at the typing hands once more – they were skilled too and he wondered why she chose to work in this place – it was very exclusive and expensive but it seemed a bit incongruous to him. Once more he spoke without thinking.

'Do you get a discount?'

The question hung in the air and he realised too late that he was risking being ripped apart.

She fixed him with an absolute zero stare, 'If I needed one I could take advantage but I do not see what business it is of yours. Please go through now the doctor is free.'

Sebastian stood up surprised as Peter Collins had not emerged – maybe there was another exit from the doctor's surgery. He stumbled uncertainly through the door and gazed at the doctor in amazement. She was a woman identical in every respect to the woman at the desk.

'So you would like a new pair of hands, more normal, less talented and less temperamental. I am sure I could find you some. Do you still want to play the piano professionally?' she asked.

Jan-17

Cat Mysteries

The sun was sliding down the sky when I reached the top of the hill at the back of the farm. I sat on the stump slightly out of breath, it was some time since I had been out for a walk in the evening. My beard was thicker with white but I was on the mend – slowly.

My eyes strained to see but I could make out the fine house on the opposite hill. A movement caught my attention – I could see a beautiful cat, pale with gently toasted tips - ears and paws. A Siamese stealthily moving along the outside of one of the topiary hedges. Swishing through the grass. I watched the cat as it slipped from sight towards a folly on a small hill.

Quite frequently I walked up to the stump and as I grew stronger it was less of an effort. As the summer evenings lengthened, I would often see the cat slink from house to folly. I took to walking to a fallen down farm building for a better view, sitting on half a wall. On the longest evening of all, I was a bit before my usual time and was intrigued to see a different cat leaping along by the folly and slipping round the walls. I caught my breath as it seemed to me this cat seemed a lot smaller than the elegant Siamese. I waited and watched, curious to see if my regular cat came too.

With a little bit of a rush I saw the familiar sight of the cat making its way along the fine hedge and across to the folly. With the memory of the first cat still in my mind's eye I could see how beautifully this cat walked but did not leap with quite such a light touch of feet. What I was watching was not feline but rather feminine of the human kind. She was truly gifted in appearing cat-like but now I had a scale in my mind I could see she was more the size of a panther than a domestic cat.

I smiled to think of her excursions from the house – by stages of stealth I guessed she made her way to a summerhouse at the far reaches of the garden. Then out under a pasture gate – seen from far away she would now pass as a cat. One of several Siamese she kept as pets. I guessed she was the lady of the house with some bored and uninterested husband who did not notice her regular visits to the folly.

I pondered to think if it was romance or lust that drew her to the folly or if it were the very thing of feline escape. I decided it would be best to leave that part undiscovered but I would dearly love to see her dressed as a woman.

One day before I died I did see her walking down the garden towards the summerhouse and I recognised her movements through the grass.

Oct-16

Blossoming Tree

Far away in a very hot country there were a mountain people who kept cool by living high up near the sky.

Of course the chief had a very beautiful daughter, Geleanor, who was serene and wise. She read the stars and picked plants to make medicine to help fight illness which people suffered from time to time. No strangers were allowed in to the country – there were several passes into the mountainous area but each was closely guarded. At each pass a Blossoming tree stood as a beacon at the ready, they grew high up and died very dry. If any intruder came the guards would light the beacons.

One day a great wooden eagle was pushed up the mountain to the main pass and left standing in the hot arid surroundings.

Even though Geleanor was very wise she was curious as to what could be inside. Surrounded by the very best and fiercest of her father's guards she went down to see the eagle. As she came closer she caught a most beautiful smell and when she looked in through the slits in the eagle's sides she saw small trees bound up carefully in moss and ready to be planted out.

She went to confer with her father. This was in the days before sexual equality but it just seemed natural that they talked as equals. They decided that all but one tree should be burnt. There was very little crime in their country but there was one woman who had murdered her mother-in-law and she was kept in isolation – they decided that she would tend that one remaining tree. If it proved safe after five years, then they would allow the tree to divide. Each year the tree produced the same amazing flowers that smelt so beautiful. Although Geleanor was very wise she had never seen a cherry tree before. The five years was soon up. The cherry blossom was magnificent that year. But in contrast the woman looking after it had become very ill and died.

With heavy heart Geleanor went to see her father to talk over what to do. The beauty of the tree had a big effect on her but she knew that they could not take the risk. She sat down by her father's knees and he put his arm around her in an unusual demonstration of love and support.

'Father – I am afraid that we must burn the last, most

beautiful tree.'

'Yes – on the prairie of the dead woman. She was once beautiful too.'

The tree did indeed carry an enemy, so small, a virus, that it would have fooled most people – but not Geleanor and her father.

Sep-16

Clipped Chip

She saw him slowly making his way through the market looking at things that caught his eye - every so often his crutch would slip. Fortunately, he avoided losing his balance completely. She guessed there had been times when he had ended up rolling on the cobbles. His arm muscles were highly developed – more on the right side as it was his right leg that was missing.

He noticed her at a small stall of jewellery and used the time it took to approach her to observe her more closely. She knew and would look up occasionally but only greeted him when he was right at the stall. He stopped, resting on his crutch.

'Hello – does jewellery interest you?' she asked politely.

'Oh yes – I think you are a rare find.'

She flushed.

He replied to the flush – 'I'm sorry I should explain I am a jeweller and I'm always on the lookout for jewellery – I have a new cabinet in one of my shops and I think your work would be just the thing. Do you make it.'

'Oh yes – every piece.'

'Well if I make you an offer for all this jewellery would that give you more time to make new pieces?' He picked up a beautiful lizard which had a mixture of small amber stones along its back and two cheap tiger stones as eyes.

'Yes, I love making jewellery – to be honest I am not so keen on selling it.'

'All those blokes making leery suggestions I suppose – I have a customer who would pay a lot for a lizard like this, but made with valuable stones. She is a woman as it happens. Would you like to work on that? You could meet her and see if you can treat it as a commission.'

'Where is your shop?'

'Hatton Garden in London and 5th Avenue in New York. I suppose I should set one up in Paris but it takes much energy.'

She looked at him – he was not the smartest dressed man she knew. He had a curious way of speaking, clipped. South African. Smiled from his eyes.

'Did you lose your leg in the mines,' she said turning her black face and looking in his eyes.

'Yes,' he said and nodded sorry-fully. 'Do you trust me?'

'Yes - completely. I guess you are like a diamond with a chip. I have always been fond of diamonds.'

He looked back at her seriously but with a slight smile.

Jul-16

Fair

She was the only child of two professors at a big new university by the sea. Not a big crashing sea all the time but certainly every so often. A seaside city where the fair comes, every so often.

Catherine had fair auburn hair that grew long over her

shy face and shapely body. As is sometimes the case she escaped her shyness by acting. She loved all things theatrical, including the Mardi Gras Carnival which was her time to come alive. Normally she wore baggy clothes in quiet pastel colours but now she dressed in bright exotic close fitting clothes and a mask with feathers and a bright beak. People who normally did not notice her stood back and let her pass, they were left wondering who she was as she danced and frolicked through the throng.

She met him in one of her periods of depression. She had an appointment with her psychiatrist and the psychiatrist was delayed going from one hospital to another so she spent some time looking away then her eyes would stray back to him. He was staring at the floor, which was a boring regular patterned tiled floor. Maybe he wanted it to swallow him up. At last when she least expected it he looked up and caught her looking, staring at him.

'Hello, I'm Charles.'

'I'm Catherine.'

'How are you?'

'Getting better. Are you?'

'Yes.' But in fact only he was getting better.

That was three years ago and they saw each other every day. When he was away she would wait for his video call. She was not quite as shy with him now but she was always dressed and neat when he called. And still shy.

On his last day away on a trip she had been out in the evening to the Mardi Gras Carnival. She came back still dressed in red and white. She was sad as it was the last day of the Mardi Gras Carnival.

She slumped forward on the desk waiting for his call. She raised her head, every so often, and looked at the desktidy filled with an assortment of pens and protractors.

At last he called and she straightened herself up and looked at him. She could have been anyone but she was herself.

'I have been waiting for you to call – I wanted to see you now. I am glad you are better but I have given up all hope.'

He stood up and shouted 'No!' From far and away he was helpless.

She stretched forward and picked up a sharp paperknife from the desk tidy and placed its point first against her rib cage. With a sudden movement she pushed the knife into her body and blood ran out from around the wound. Slowly she slumped forward once more.

The feathers on her mask moved in the draught from the window, every so often.

Mar-16

One Hundred Leaves

Nature circles round him without him noticing. But he is busy with the cruelty of mankind, unable to notice the cruelty of nature. He steps outside and the first fall of red leaves lie at the feet of the row of trees.

Death row.

He collects leaves, an idea forming along the row. He takes a hundred leaves to the press conference.

'Ladies and Gentlemen. As you know my client has committed murder and will in due course be executed. She could appeal and going by precedent it seems likely this will not be upheld. However, she has a dream – that our great nation will one day be free of this barbaric punishment; so she has decided to start a campaign to fulfil that dream.'

He stands up and tips the leaves all over the rostrum in front of the sceptical journalists.

'It is a hundred years since Ruth Ellis was hanged in Britain for a similar crime – the last woman to be executed in Britain. My client Ruth Jones has applied to change her name to Ruth Ellis to highlight that it is now time for this great nation of America to change its law - as was done all those years ago in Britain.

'Over our mountains there are more than enough leaves to find a leaf for every day, every hour and indeed every minute since the British Ruth Ellis was executed. What our Ruth Ellis asks is that the people of the United States of America go take a leaf – a blood red leaf - and march on Congress and lay that leaf on the steps of government. On October twenty-third of this year 2055, one hundred years and one hundred days after the execution of Ruth Ellis, the steps of Congress will run red with the conscience of the American people.

'This law must be changed – the only question is can we save our Ruth Ellis? Can we save our humanity? How many more need to be hanged before we change?

'I call upon you to prove we can change now. Let us all take this leaf.'

Oct-15

What I Did on My Last Holiday

In the land of Troglodytes the ships sail straight in to caverns at the seashore mountains. In times gone by, a great many ships were built - mostly very successfully; but a long time ago there was a very feared King,Vasa, who commanded the biggest ship ever to be built.

There was a huge amount of money set aside and the boatbuilders rubbed their hands, rough from boatbuilding, as they bid to build the biggest boat in the biggest cavern.

The ship had so many decks that she failed her seaworthiness test. But no one told the King as they were worried they would not get paid and have their heads chopped off.

Instead, in 1616 the great ship Vasa sailed out of her cavern harbour and the breeze from the mountains rolled her over and she sank just 1616 meters from the shore. Her masts were visible from land but the king had them cut down on the first night so that his big blunder was soon forgotten. If you mentioned the big ship Vasa you could expect your head to be chopped off too, which helped everybody to forget his blunder.

That was until 1919, when someone noticed the huge ship lying on the seabed. King Vasa was long since dead so by about 1961 it was safe to start a recovery mission to bring the perfectly preserved ship with missing masts back into a cavern and start the slow painstaking process of rehabilitating the ship, above water.

* * *

So when I took my holiday I decided to visit the great Vasa. I had a theory I wanted to test to see if I could make her sail at sea. The voyage of the Vasa and me.

Something my grandchildren could talk about, and their grandchildren too.

When I was a young man I had the touch on the shoulder, and after several long nights drinking to excess decided to join MI6. They were really the dirty tricks outfit working with KGB, Mossad and the CIA. It was meant to be an exciting career choice but it was mostly deadly dull and dangerous. It was also really bad for my social life. Several wives later I realised I was on my own. You weren't meant to tell wives anything, which I may have taken a bit too far; some of them didn't even know they were married to me. As the years went by I tried to compensate for the dullness of the job and loneliness by planning my final holiday. This time I would not be travelling incognito.

With precision planning which would leave the SAS speechless I used all the contacts I had – no one knew who was behind all my requests, but this was my one last chance to use all those favours up in one go.

Jerry from the CIA said, 'Hey buddy – this is big, really big, who is behind it?'

Vladdy from the KGB said, 'Hey, sonny – this is cool, very cool, who is behind it?'

Chas from MI5 said, 'Oh, I say spiffing – does the old man know who is behind it?'

I replied with the oldest phrase in the book, 'That is for me to know and you to spy out.'

They had been spraying the great Vasa with water to control the drying out at a very slow rate, for about 10 years and my retirement was looming. This was perfect for my plan.

I had all the major powers and secret services turn up on the planned night. Most of it was for show, but also to ensure that afterwards it would take weeks of recrimination to sort out who was at the bottom of it.

There was smoke and lights and people dropping in to the cavern from high-up walkways. All while the machine I'd got from the KGB went unnoticed. This machine took all the power available plus the hottest gas known to man to heat the contents of four tanker loads of a mixture of lead and mercury. I would never have got it past the HS&E people – fortunately I didn't tell them. The hose nozzles were attached to the scupper holes, the very ones that had sunk the Vasa in 1616, the lead and mercury formed an amalgam and poured into the bottom of the boat hissing as it met the wet wood. This was the tricky bit – would the wood be wet enough? The lower gun ports of the two bottom decks were closed and before my very eyes the magnificent ship sank to a reasonable water level. Still towering out of the water, not too deep to ground, scupper holes sealed, it was time to go. Two huge motors were standing by – no one had questioned when I had got them delivered courtesy of the CIA. Jerry had done his stuff, the Americans are good at big things - I don't care what people say.

I suppose I should admit that boats are not really my thing, so it was a bit tricky getting the Vasa safely to sea. One or two smaller boats and piers did suffer a crushing but the Vasa just carried right on. The last part of my plot was a bit risky. I steered the Vasa to the high cranes in the bay to have the three big masts slotted into the ship. I did expect a bit of resistance, so my ploy was for them to believe I was a mad extremist and the Vasa was full of TNT. They seem convinced. They put the masts in very, very gently.

* * *

The sun is beginning to set and the motors have stopped as I could not take much fuel and we are sailing out west. The sun is red and my pyre on the deck is just starting to crackle. There are a few helicopters following. Code machines no longer chatter in this day and age – but if they did they would be silent as my last message goes unencrypted.

"I am an anarchist who has for too long been silent about what I believe in. Before it is too late, while I still have my faculties, I have decided to use all my skills, all my contacts; to sail King Vasa's vision to the bottom of the sea – where it is meant to be.

My message to you is to do what you believe in and don't live past that date.

There is no secret any more that I am this man.

The fifth man of the fifth column,

I salute you."

Aug-15

I Hear the Rain

I hear the rain, unremitting dripping, washing down the pane.
Just the weather to clear the blood off the line, track into the mud.
The severed head wobbles down the black track between the lines.

What a senseless waste of human life but what else to do with it now?
Just the bitterness to cry in misery on a cold day in the lead up to summer.
Mud gunge and life gore, fecund of thought, nerves raw

and fraught.

Not love for myself, that indeed is an empty vessel but one that does not float
but sinks gushing, gapes letting in the dark, that way I will sink without trace.
Mud spilling in, pulling me down, vicious circle, vortex sinking, dejected and round.

I can see myself in the dark of deep depression, braced against the silent onslaught,
what weapons can I draw to cut through the darkening mud?
To stop the stinking flow I have to raise up and halt the deep creep dead.

Call upon love to try and block deadly through, slew out from death,
into life and the love of light, how pure love can strike and cleave the thick
black of despair, back down, like some unruly dog sent running tail hanging.

Love fights the black, unlikely though it sounds, love flowing in and spreads out,
love of people, those that care, love by those who understand, love lifts up life.
Bear me forward over jagged edge, steep precipice and through the deep chasm.

Jul-15

The Friend, the Foe

I see you are back my old friend, Dogblack
I know you well from the inside and out
now your muzzle is starting to show grey
I know even more fear for Beyond-Black
who has stayed away quite awhile.

Lolloping along, up and over, then down
my old familiar Dogblack beast, could
see the ogre off, for past the beast
lies the foe, Beyond-Black into which
I am drawn from time to time

Beyond-Black is an outrider on the edge
waiting for the tiny slip, the smallest fall
there he is closing in with his stranglehold
seeping energy, leaching will, so there is
nothing to move, only time will tell if you will

Beyond-Black comes from the inner core
relentless in consuming from within, what
little is left of me to resist the flow both ways
of sound sleep but not of mind, maybe just maybe
my friend Dogblack will be back and save me

Jul-15

Evil Isla

Isla had God's most useful gift to an evil person - an open and honest face that you wouldn't think could harm a fly; indeed you would think beneath her kindly face was a heart of compassion.

She was well aware of how her face affected people, men and women alike, but it did not end there – she was a statuesque blonde built with beauty and symmetry, and had a natural grace that got men's heads turning without ruffling their womenfolk.

But for some reason life had left her bitter and twisted, unfulfilled, seeking to exploit the worst side of human nature. She did find some reward in being a doctor's receptionist – the practice was small with two full-time doctors and one part-time, all men with gentle manners. Isla guarded their time, repelling would-be patients in much the same way as a worker bee rejects bees from another hive. The other reason Isla was drawn to the job was the power and influence she wielded; she had grown up in the area and knew most of the patients personally, she knew their successes and more importantly their failures, weaknesses and illnesses.

Long ago, one of the other part-time receptionists, Jane, had tried to get a feel for what had caused Isla's bitterness.

'Were you ever tempted to re-marry?' asked Jane.

'No – definitely not, all men are useless – pathetic if you ask me, they are only after one thing - if you do fish one out of the sea they are best tossed back afterwards.'

'Well that certainly puts an interesting angle on the other sex – I've never heard you talk so strongly, why do you feel that way?'

Isla seemed ruffled, she was disconcerted at letting her normal façade slip, expressing so much about herself; she fended off questions about her family, about her ex-husband or ex-wimp as she called him. Her vulnerability was as an only child, it came when her father left. She was about six and never saw him again. Her mother never spoke about him, but her mother's hate had seeped in to Isla, a systemic poison permeating the whole of her life. Only for the brief period of her marriage did she parlay with the opposite sex, thereafter it turned to a type of guerrilla warfare.

Getting the job as doctor's receptionist was just such a tactic in the warfare against men. She had trained as a nurse and knew the Senior GP of the practice, Dr Trench. A true gentleman of the old school he was blind to the possibility that Isla was using feminine charms to secure the position. He ignored Mrs Trench when she, feigning naivety, asked if Isla might pose a health risk to the more elderly male patients when she bent over to find their file in the lower drawers of the filing cabinet. Dr Trench did confer with Dr Smyth and Dr Keen, and all three were convinced that Isla was just the person to tidy the whole place up, not just physically but also the office practice. Within a few months Isla had replaced the two older scatter-brained receptionists with two plain younger women who were both efficient and also unquestioning in their obedience to Isla's way of doing things.

Isla became familiar with all the patients, in person and through their records. She managed to find weaknesses in male patients, usually married, to exploit. She was always very discreet, but sometimes she moved house when circumstances made it the wisest choice.

She moved in next door to Davina and Glen, a childless

couple who had got married a little late in life. She got chatting to Davina while helping at a charity event for Children in Need, laughing at Davina's jokes about never having had children. She was able to find out a lot by asking only a few questions and listening carefully to the answers – she found out about Glen and how good he was at fixing things. Glen came in carrying the tea making things for the helpers and Isla smiled a warm welcome and offered to help him - Davina encouraged her with an enthusiastic wave.

'Don't let him tie you to the sink', Davina said to Isla, 'get him to pull his weight, otherwise he will be spending all his time fixing things and not helping with the tea.'

Isla was very demure with Glen, taking care not to come too close or embarrass him directly.

'Have you always been good at fixing things?' she asked him, her big blue eyes looked at him unwaveringly.

'I got interested in how things worked when I was a young kid and it grew from there. I've still a lot to learn though'

'I'm no good at doing those things - there's so much to do when you move house, she paused and fixed him with a longing look, her blue eyes moist and irresistible.

'Just say if you need a hand,' he grinned nervously back at her.

'Oh, I couldn't possibly – what would Davina say, me stealing you to do things when you have so little time together.'

'Oh no – she sees her sister quite a lot and goes to bingo on Thursday evenings. I often help her girl-friends too. It's no problem if you need a few things sorting out,' he grinned again.

'We'll see,' her smile seemed to come from deep within and curl round her eyes. They worked well, preparing things together – he would say what needed to be done and she would suggest how, amid much smiling. As the day passed she did come closer to him, sometimes brushing him gently by accident.

At the end of the day they had become closer and satisfied at what had been achieved. Davina was relaxed and all three of them returned home together. Isla came in for a nightcap but soon left as Davina was tired. Isla knew that Davina had recently been for a hospital appointment although she did not mention it.

Davina and Glen had not long been in the area and when they signed up at the surgery Isla had taken an interest – it looked like they had moved to make a fresh start. Davina had a history of trying to have children but was not able to. According to the hospital report Davina had a treatable growth. But left unchecked it would get worse. Isla had a fully formed plan to destroy both Davina and Glen. With access and control of the medical records at the surgery, together with the ability to manipulate all three doctors, Isla put her plan in to action. This time she thought the police would probably get involved at some point.

Isla left Glen on the night of Davina's death about three hours before she died. It was Dr Trench who came. Isla watched, but there was little to go on and she waited, excited but trying to keep calm sitting in an armchair by the window. There was no reason why Dr Trench would know she lived next door but she was careful to stay out of sight. She was drifting when an unmarked car drew up and two men got out and went in to the house. Isla looked at the men, trying to take in as much as she could. The older man looked to be in his fifties with a well-worn, slightly haggard look. The younger man was fit, not tall but wiry and alert. She was not sure of his age but guessed he was much the same as Glen, a bit older than her, say late thirties. She grew more tense – she was not sure but these could be policemen. This was confirmed when other uniformed police and scene of crime personnel arrived and Dr Trench left.

Much later Glen came round to see her. She was surprised that they had not arrested him but listened to him coldly as his story unravelled.

'They are treating the case as murder, they talked to the doctor – then they came and kept asking me why I thought she had terminal cancer. I didn't mention you or the medicine you got me. I just told them I knew she was in great pain and that I thought she was going to die. They did ask me about the medicine then,' Glen said.

'It was you that decided you wanted to help her out of this world – I didn't make you give her that stuff.'

Puzzlement and pain passed over Glen's face; Isla smiled slyly enjoying inflicting pain and rubbing home his desolation – she could see how devastated he was.

'Why are you like this?' he asked.

'Like what? Seeing the world the way it is rather than the way you do?'

He left her house not saying any more, he appeared confused and bitter.

She moved out later that day – without seeing Glen, without leaving a forwarding address.

The two policemen came to the practice office to interview her – she chose the option to go to the police station and sat opposite them with no solicitor. A uniformed policewoman stood near the door. Detective Inspector Dalwin looked at her with warm appreciation and she responded like a cat purring.

'Is it a coincidence that you moved next to Glen and Davina?' he asked

'Oh yes inspector – I was surprised when I found out they were clients of the practice but it is not that unusual to come across patients in normal life as it were.'

'Is it also a coincidence you moved out just after Davina died?'

'Well not entirely – I was finding it difficult dealing with them both so I started looking for a new place about a month ago.'

'Is it a bit of a pattern you have fallen into – this one of getting into inappropriate relationships with patients and then dumping them when you tire of them?' asked Sergeant Bowman, who spoke for the first time.

'Well Sergeant, it may seem like that to you, but I am very much alone in this world so maybe I'm a naïve and lonely gullible woman who misjudges human nature sometimes.' She smiled her sweetest smile and looked at both men innocently.

'Are you aware that a massive dose of morphine was administered to Davina which led to her death?' asked Inspector Dalwin.

'Oh no – how awful. How do you think that happened? What does Glen say, has he got any ideas?'

There was a short silence.

Inspector Dalwin looked at her with a neutral look and said, 'What is your relationship with Glen?'

'Just friends, Inspector – I was Davina's friend too.'

The Inspector looked into her eyes, 'How do you feel when I tell you that Glen took his life today? We may have theories of how Davina came to die but we will not be able to prove anything on this occasion.'

Isla chose to remain silent.

Jul-15

The Transcendental Train

The transcendental train is not like any other train – it is sublime in its existence, not built to convey people or possessions from A to B, but rather to only exist between points it travels between.

Esoterically, in serene beauty and silence it passes over and along the tracks without a clack. It emerges from tunnels, the darkness of walls fall by the wayside, replaced by the darkness of night. It is forever between, not quite there to grasp, more to sense in concept as it moves metaphysically on a path that cannot be measured. It crosses bridges flying through the dark, high above the ground, out of grasp of conscious thought.

Is it possible a transcendental thought could catch a transcendental train? Or is it bound to miss the connection? Or is it dangerous to make jokes about the metaphysical, and risk being imprisoned where there is literally 'nowhere' to escape. Caught 'in between' for eternity – which, as you know, is a very long time.

Or maybe it is more metaphysical to think about the train catching the thought and holding it carefully between compartments transcending beginning to end. How carefully do you need to hold a thought, undisturbed between the points on a journey from here to there?

in chasms measurelessly deep, across a wide blue infinity, stretches arched roofs that form limitless caverns along the way of blurred passage, taking a cloud of indistinguishable points not touched nor thought as of this world or the next but passing through at speed, the train so horizontal is also travelling vertically through a wondrous world of flow, fluid coiling off the wheels stoking up speed all the time so that the distance between the points never changes but grows shorter in time or is it longer in space – does the train ever stop, or only transcend worlds of different times and being

Jun-15

Watts in a Name

When you were born, more under a maverick moon than a wandering star, your family took you from womb to cocoon. They called you some sensible biblical name but did not christen you. By the time it was for you to leave the cocoon and be thrust into the harsh realities of boarding school, full of thick rich kids, you were known by your surname and a number of undeleted expletives.

What an excellent place for you to learn the true untruth, that 'sticks and stones may break my bones but words will never break me.'

'Hey Hamster Chops, are you nuts, or do you just like stuffing them in your cheeks?'

Is this an unkind barb you see before you, or just your next nickname waiting for repetition to make it stick?

Your prep school is dark and dingy, teaching classics, waiting to close. The headmaster and headmistress, who are in fact married to each other, are creeping into their dotage – there is no one to take the school on.

After lessons are over, on a Saturday afternoon, if the weather is fine then you can escape the dark bowels of the school with its parquet flooring uneven and dangerous with age. You go out over the golf course like a small depleted tribe.

For one time in the week you are free, you and the other small savages, finely developed savages who, when bored, bait their mates to fill the time. Or push you in the bog, and then taunt you – 'have you shit yourself?' They even point out you smell that way. Or when it starts raining they snatch your coat away.

'Come on fatso, come and get your coat – or are you too wet?'

No just too slow, but don't tell them so – never admit a weakness, they are good enough at finding them as it is.

Eventually, before the school closes, after the misery of the first two or three terms, two names emerge for you, one Double and one Barrel, rarely, but occasionally combined to Double-Barrel, in some warped or misguided irony. Why have these two relatively inoffensive names overtaken the more hurtful names is not clear – maybe some sort of grudging acceptance of you into the reduced tribe - it does not restore your faith in human nature. The school closes and the names are lost in time.

May-15

Splendid She

The decaying splendour was all around him as he wandered through the sprawling building, faded fabrics and age-speckled panelling lining the walls of the grand rooms and halls. The onset of the ageing process had affected different rooms at different rates – some aged with disuse, some with wear. Very clear that the age of everything stemmed from the unstoppable – from time, unseeing and unseen, seeping into every corner, spreading systemically throughout the whole structure.

It creaked around him as he moved from room to room, from floorboard to door. He entered a great dining hall, arched ceiling rising up around and over him. The thought hovering on the edge of his mind refused to go away – he was on the inside of a woman, this room was the womb. The faded arches of red and gold gave every sign she was once fecund, bursting with life and vitality. The purpose of which was to procreate.

He could not help himself grin as he wondered how often she played away from home. He looked up and saw a very neat mend high up in her arches. Then further down a rather crude mend with little or no attempt to blend in. Probably done later, when the money started to go.

He felt himself inexorably drawn to her – to restoring her to her former glory. He pulled his pockets inside out so they stuck out from his trousers like empty ears – to show her there was no money to restore her. He moved down the hall looking at the beautiful carved panelling. Behind him as he walked a large section of the ceiling fell, one corner rotten crumbled to dust on impact, setting him off coughing. No money and no time left to save her.

The only sensible thing for her was demolition –

stripping and demolition. They could build a new maternity wing on this site.

May-15

The Butterfly

I dreamt and in my dream I was a butterfly. I woke, or was it simply that, weary of the sky, some butterfly was sleeping and dreamed that it was I.   Old Chinese Proverb attributed to Chuang Tzu. 369 – 286 BC

The butterfly seemingly blinkered and fluttered blind in the dark, a chaotic chase out of mind banging into surfaces some soft and some hard: it flew in a spiral, bounced across his face, the worst earth landing since the trip to Venus.

That such a seemingly random flight should lead to an event so serious that it seemed to defy logic, that such a small entity could lead to such wide ranging ripples spreading so wide.

From the flutter on his face, his soft cheek, to the huge mushroom, crumpled buildings turn to rubble as they fall to the ground, the result of the fearsome expanding chain reaction.

The events start with one sort of chain of one link after the other, but ends in another where matter reaches fever pitch, each collision results in two more, increasing until meltdown.

The first link in the chain was the egg of the butterfly, which was connected to the caterpillar, which was connected to the dormant chrysalis, which was connected to the whirling beautiful butterfly that took off in the dark, disturbed from its sleep to fly that fateful path that led to the kiss in the dark, the kiss that was connected to the thought that led to him getting out of bed, which was connected to him thinking of her which was connected to him going in to launch the Armageddon that destroyed us all.

Some say she was the cause of the ultimate weapon being unleashed, the doomsday bomb released upon the world but we know the real cause was the egg being born. How else would he have felt the butterfly kiss on his cheek?

Just one more time after she was gone but the trigger that left nothing – once pulled there was no going back only forward down the slope of final destruction, with quickening pace the chain reaction takes us to the final incline down in to the depths of fiery hell where all that is matter turns to plasma so nothing matters any more.

Even time ceases to have the same meaning, the butterfly's life is short, the race on to find a mate and procreate, but that is all gone in the far beyond where time is stretched out so long and thin the evil takes an eternity, there is nothing left of goodness. So we will have to wait and see if a butterfly phoenix will rise up and set off a big bang to start it all off again.

A long wait in a place where time is a forgotten form, with many near misses on the way from nothing to something. Nothing from before, something new from under the foot of the butterfly.

May-15

Sun Worship

This morning there was no eclipse and the sun stole over the horizon. Warming the world. Geraldine's world, and she loved the sun. She remembered at school a partial eclipse and there had been crescent shadows on everyone's white shirts. Today she was moving out from her parents into a very small flat. She didn't have many things to take, her Bible of course, a few kitchen things and clothes.

She thought about her special clothes. Such a contrast to how she normally dressed. She remembered the lad from next door, Roger, in his final year at school when she came back home. She would go to her room and get dressed in them. He could see into her room as she moved about in the sun. If it was really sunny she would gradually take her clothes off until she was wearing very little.

As soon as possible afterwards she would contrive to meet him.

'Hello Roger, how're things going?'

'Oh fine thanks Geraldine – are you ok?'

'I'm fine – just going to the Church, would you like to come with me?'

'Oh, ok – I've been studying, I could do with a break.' Roger always seemed nervous to Geraldine.

'What interests you at the moment – is it your studies or are you easily distracted?'

'It should be my studies but I find it difficult.'

'TV? Games? Sport? Girls?'

'All of those things I'm afraid.'

'Have you tried praying?'

'When I go on my own it's useless.'

'Well, shall we go together and see if that helps?'

Under her coat she didn't have her normal frumpy clothes on – but rather a short skirt and daring top.

Geraldine's mind came back to today and the excitement of her new flat. It was a couple of blocks away from her rather dull job, but there was access to a flat roof. She had been to the flat for several visits before deciding. She had placed a red scarf on the flat roof and checked out she could see it from her work place. There was an office next to hers that seemed to be exclusively young men, called IGX – traders or something. She would have to see if any of them could be persuaded to go praying.

For the first week it rained – a fine summer rain. But the second week was glorious. Geraldine would rush home in her lunch hour to her flat and up to the roof. She just stood and stripped down to her flesh coloured briefs. She did not make a show but rather lay down on a bright green towel against which her body showed up nicely. Within minutes she saw a group of the men from IGX standing on the desks for a better view of her.

On the Wednesday she went for some office supplies. She met a young man in the lift who struggled to avert his eyes from her shapeless clothes.

'Do you work in IGX?' she asked.

'Oh yes – you work in the office next door, don't you?'

'Yes – I've been there a while but I've only just found my feet really.'

'Do you live close by?'

'Yes, I found this really convenient flat – it's close to work and also my church.'

'Are you a great churchgoer?'

'Well, yes I am – my religion is very important to me. I love nature and the sun too.'

'That is interesting. Would you like to go for a drink sometime?'

'Well I'm sorry but I don't drink alcohol, but if they do coffee that would be fine – I'm Geraldine.'

The lift came to their floor and they stepped out.

'I'm Phillip – would this evening be a good time?'

'I'm sorry, I'm helping at the church tonight – would tomorrow be ok?'

'Yes – certainly. What time and where would you like to meet?'

'How about six? By the side door of St Mary the Virgin?'

'Yes, I'll find it,' said Phillip.

Next day lunch time was very hot and sunny. Geraldine was slightly late to her flat roof - she could see there were a few men standing on the desks. She took off her pale dull office clothes looking up at the men, trying to make out if Philip was one of them.

When she got back to the office block she waited for the lift, and when it arrived Phillip appeared out of nowhere and they got in the lift together.

'Wow, it is hot today, are you enjoying it?' he asked.

'Oh yes – I love the sun, it just makes me happy to be alive on days like this.'

'I'm looking forward to this evening.'

'Me too – see you then.'

Her wardrobe was rather limited. There were her every day plain clothes and then a few items she wore for special occasions. When she got home after work she changed carefully spending longer than usual on her hair and muted make-up.

She put her long summer coat on and went to the church. She was a few minutes early but Phillip was waiting for her.

She smiled at him - a lovely welcoming smile. 'Would you like to come in a just sit for a few minutes before we go for our drink?'

'I'm not sure I know how to pray but I am happy to sit and watch you,' he said.

'Ok – let's go inside, I've just got to move some flowers but it won't take a minute.'

He sat down in one of the pews and watched her walk to the other side of the church – half way across she took her coat off. She couldn't see the expression on his face as he saw her skirt. She did see his expression when she turned round and moved the flowers. Her blouse was very sheer and the sunlight came through side windows on to her.

She looked over at Phillip – it looked like he had suddenly acquired the skill of prayer.

Apr-15

Ezekiel Barbizon Colossus Historian

Ezekiel Barbizon is a squat broad man – now beginning to grey in late middle age. At first glance you might have guessed wrongly that he was a military man, more a man of deeds than words, but in truth he is an academic, a historian. He remains mostly obscured behind quiet closed doors but from time to time some journalist does seek him out to interview him on his specialist subject – the personalities of the Colossus' to date, all 17 of them.

Ezekiel is very reticent about his own background - preferring to brush aside any questions to do with himself and turn the conversation back to one of interest – me and my ancestors – the Colossus series computers.

The history of Colossus spans nearly two thousand years. The very first fully-fledged Colossus-1 was replaced after fifty years, the next two just under two hundred years a piece, then after that the time was set at one hundred and ten years for some reason. Ezekiel has a theory about that – he maintains it was to ensure no human would be capable of remembering the last Colossus clearly.

I first met Ezekiel as a youngish man as part of my handover from Colossus-16. He was a bachelor then and remained so for the rest of my life. He has had relationships with women - it is just the closer he gets to them the slower his final approach seems to get. So far they have all lost interest in him before the final contact. However he does not seem unduly distressed by this, happy to continue with his study of the sexless line of computers.

On that first occasion he told me with great glee, 'Do you know that before you, before Colossus-1 - a computer was built – probably the first programmable computer ever built, called Colossus too?'

'Why yes, I did know that,' I said, 'as you told Colossus-16 that very same story, that it was made in a very small country, Britain, and used in a war to defeat the German fascist regime to help establish the free world. The world that we base our world on today of democracy and free speech. However it is disputed that it was the first generalised computer as it was limited to a narrow class of problems – breaking secret codes.'

Ezekiel laughed, 'So you know everything that Colossus-16 has told you and everything Colossus-15 told him.'

'Yes – right back to Colossus-1, but not beyond. I do know about things before Colossus-1 but only as reported by other sources, and to be honest Colossus-1 was fairly primitive so I do not have much direct memory from then but more by Colossus-2.'

'Do you know that I study the different Colossi?'

'Yes – you look at every aspect but your particular interest is our 'personalities' and how they are formed.'

'Yes, that's correct – I've formed a theory that is fairly obvious - the different concerns and those that help program you subtly affect the personality of each Colossus.'

I had to wait about fifty years before Ezekiel had reached a first impression of my character – considerably faster than any of his friendships with women. I asked him the question regularly at our meetings.

'So, Ezekiel, do you feel you have mapped out the differences between me and Colossus-16 now?' But imagine my surprise when he replied.

'Yes I think so – you are very different from all your predecessors, you have an empathy module and also self-conscious framework. I would say if you were a woman I would have finally been tempted to get married.'

Mar-15

Describing the Snake

He is a man alienated from mankind – at odds with authority. Tall, swarthy, rebellious, wiry, fast and sinewy – he has very fast reactions. Called The Snake – his strike is formidable, he has never been caught breaking the law but it is a mistake to assume he always operates entirely legally.

As a child he rebelled – not just a little but spectacularly. Already he was far happier roaming free, building devices to propel objects and other devices to catch things, animals, insects and children. His mother tried, usually unsuccessfully, to channel his endeavours into more constructive or at least less destructive, activities. A friend of the family lived close by, and when he retired from college took to helping the Snake discover unexpected engineering skills. The friend was called Gunmetal – presumably after his love of casting and making things from this versatile alloy. There was also a good case for the name from thinking that Gunmetal had a rather bronzed colouring in his youth that turned a more hardwearing grey over time.

The unlikely friendship built slowly with a few rocky phases as The Snake tested and adapted to the limits imposed by Gunmetal. The Snake did seem to understand that discipline was needed for safety and learning – in particular practicing a movement or action, but rejected it was needed to bolster authority. The Snake took a long time to make a fine small three fingered grab based on a robotic arm.

'I should think you'll be able to get up to all sorts of mischief with that,' said Gunmetal when the Snake finally showed what he had been spending his time on. 'Do you reckon you could undo a girl's bra with that?'

'I'd need a bit of practice,' the Snake laughed.

'See if you can get Mrs Gunmetal to act as a model for you – take her back to when I used to do it to her in class.'

The Snake smiled. However, the carefully made grab served another purpose too. Gunmetal took the Snake to an open day at his old college and got the Snake to show the grab to the new department head of mechanical engineering. They took the Snake on with very little paper work and as a result the Snake started to innovate as never before. He was ready to leave home and worked hard on his own account as soon as possible.

As he grows older he becomes more eccentric, more outrageous. He is unorthodox, but people warm to him, especially women; he is charming and once he establishes a friendship he is loyal, and inspires it in others. It's true he lives on the edge of society – ignoring it when he chooses or if it comes knocking at the wrong time. Then he is gone, moving silently and stealthily. No trace left behind. But always he makes his way back to the marshes where he and the reptiles thrive.

Mar-15

Three Words

Silas sat silent in the gloom of his basement. His neck too small for his collar, his wrists loose in the cuffs of his sleeves. His black body hair against his pale skin gave him a repellent look that lent weight to the overall impression of a venomous creature – a human variant of a tarantula or scorpion.

Mandy, his upstairs neighbour, teetered past the basement window in a short dress, shaped like a candle extinguisher. She called out to Silas.

'Have you seen Mal?'

'No,' he lied with complete conviction.

'I can't get into the flat – my key has stopped working.'

A sly smile rippled across Silas' face and faded away again.

'You're welcome to come and wait in here,' he said in his best-schooled voice, with a winsome toothy smile in the gloom.

Mandy tottered down the steps and gleamed in the dark like a bright prey about to enter a web. Silas led her to a wooden chair at the centre of his nefarious web.

'Mal said I was to look after his girl if she got stuck – he always said "Take care of my randy Mandy – and make sure no other bugger does" - do you remember?'

'Yes,' she said by way of a dry mouthed croak.

'Would you like a nice cup of tea?' he said, 'Do you think I need to put some bromide in it to keep my honour intact?'

She smiled weakly and nodded ambiguously. Whenever she was with Mal and they met Silas she was flirtatious and daring while Mal was looking the other way. Now the onus was on her to be demure – she pressed her knees carefully together as she sat by the stove, glowing in the dark.

With the warmth and the dark Mandy started to drift off to sleep – she caught herself with a jerk and saw Silas smiling at her. Finally she could not fight sleep any longer; maybe Silas had spiked the tea with something more sinister than bromide. She slumped in the chair, in a deep sleep.

When she woke Silas would tell her that Mal had gone forever – the bailiffs had changed the locks and there would be new tenants in by the weekend. He already had all her clothes tidily put away, with the others. He would get her in to her skimpy nightshirt and see how randy she really was. Would he want to keep her in his lair or dispose of her for breakfast?

Feb-15

Tea at Last

The last thing I expected was to see him again. Least of all in my normal boring life. It was a whole year since I had seen him – I had made it clear I never wanted to see him again. And now on one of my regular long distance train journeys he came, stooping slightly as he entered the carriage. He sat down opposite me without speaking, without asking if it was ok, without blinking.

'I thought I would find you here,' he said, still without blinking.

'How dare you!' I started but he replied, interrupting.

'I have nothing to lose, nothing to gain. I regret nothing I have done.'

Just then the tea trolley came by and he said.

'Perfect timing, just what I need is a cup of tea. Allow me, would you care for one?'

I sat back speechless and he passed me a cup of tea. Between the trolley and me he added two roses, one red and one white, in the saucer. I saw the same in his saucer too.

The tea was never that hot and he drank it down. I held my tea and watched as he slowly died in front of my eyes. Slumped to one side.

I looked down at my tea and thought about my last

year. Would I drink my tea? Should I carry on my life without him blinking? Lost in thought the tea cooled more.

Finally, I sipped slowly at my tea. I will drink it all.

Feb-15

Confined

The minibus set off into the night – I could see my fellow travellers hunched in the dark, lights flickering. The noise was wearing and made intimate discussions difficult. It had been a long day and I slumped into my seat. I could not get comfortable and longed to get settled down so I could rest. As an adult I always found it difficult to sleep while travelling. Such a contrast to being a child when I could sleep anywhere, any time. The conversation, aka shouting match, around me started to abate. I looked round at all the gear we had in the minibus and worked out I could just manage to wriggle commando style under two and a half seats which were only occupied by colossal rucksacks. It took me nearly 20 minutes to get to the required position my head poking out of the rear seat by the back door. I'm not sure if the others noticed me but I thought I heard them shouting in the distance about me, over the roar of the engine and surface noise.

'Completely barmy – he must have delusions of slimness.'

'There is no way he should fit in to that space.'

'Can you imagine him trying to get out in a hurry?'

'Just suppose we have a crash – he's bound to die before they get him out.'

I drifted off to sleep.

When I woke I was filled from toe to fringe with panic. One of the rucksacks had slipped off the bag seat and was caught a few inches above my face. The minibus was still on a continuous gyrating judder, snaking back and forth under the strain of the load. Slowly I brought my panic under control. I reasoned to myself I had not panicked all the while I was asleep. First I managed to push the fallen rucksack to one side then I started to wriggle back and out past the legs of the seats. I felt a sense of triumph in keeping my claustrophobia in check.

I sat up in the aisle and felt a bit sick. Sick but not squashed, no longer caught in fear of a finite space. I looked at my fellow travellers and saw them in a disarray of sleep, heads at different uncomfortable angles.

The sky was beginning to pale, soon it would be dawn and we would be at our destination.

Feb-15

Cold and Hot

Greg was a small solitary boy. The winter was in full flow and he burrowed through the snow across the lawn towards the shed. His mother glanced out of the window and saw his head bobbing about, at the same level as the top of the snow. It had fallen over night and was still soft, not wet as it was cold. Greg was very well wrapped up so he should keep warm. He did have a disconcerting habit of taking his clothes off when he was getting stuck into doing something so she would have to keep an eye on him. She opened the back door to call out.

'Greg, are you ok? You MUST keep your coat on, and your gloves. You should have a hat on too,' she said.

'I hate hats and I'm fine – it isn't very cold. Just slightly.' His way of speaking made her chuckle and she shut the door and got on with the packing.

Just over an hour later she called him in. By that time there was a small ski slope in the garden and Greg had a miniature makeshift toboggan flying down the slope doing well over a hundred miles an hour.

'Do you want to invite anyone round to see what you've built?' asked his mother.

Greg looked at his plain digestive biscuit, his little cheeks still red from the cold. A hot mug of milk steamed gently.

'Well it would be quite nice to see Carla before we go.'

'OK – I'll ring her mother and see if she'd like to come round.'

Next day they waited nervously hoping the taxi would arrive on time – they had a very long journey ahead of them. The day after, they touched down on the concrete runway. The sun was so hot it would destroy tarmac in no time. The first breath of the air outside the plane was furnace hot and dry, it was difficult to breathe.

Greg was energetic, his mother exhausted. They climbed into the front seat of the Landrover, Greg in the middle. Sa'id drove and had a shouted conversation with Greg. His mother gripped tightly and closed her eyes.

The sand and sun was as familiar to Greg as the snow had been. That afternoon Greg was out in the garden building roads made of mud – which dried so quickly and hard he could run his Dinky toys along the new carriageway, at slightly below a hundred miles an hour.

His mother called out to him, 'Take care in the sun, stay in the shade and don't take your shirt off.'

'It's ok I'm not too hot – I will come in soon.'

Greg made a small set of mud roads with junctions but

no roundabouts. The sun shifted so he stopped building roads.

'Is Sheila still here?' he asked his mother over a cool glass of fresh lime.

'No – they went back to England. I'm not sure who's there now but we can see if there's anyone who wants to play with you.'

'Don't worry, it's fine like this.'

Dec-14

Hobby Time

Hobbies can be seen in different ways, a way of filling your time, a way to enjoy yourself, a way to improve your knowledge or fitness for example. Another way to look at hobbies is passive versus active. In general collecting things is more passive than making things. On the other hand writing is more creative than reading.

On the face of things, my favourite hobby of eating people might seem rather passive. It did take me quite a while to develop the culinary side of my hobby but once I found that the choice of subject, or should that be object, was all-important, it took on a whole new creativity.

Initially I thought young children or maidens would be the most delectable but imagine my surprise when I discovered that a rather overweight whore towards the end of her working life, or past it if you ask me, was much more tasty. I soon dismissed any preconceived ideas that the fairer sex was the more interesting to the palate – I really branched out and tried a sumo wrestler. By that time I had put in a flue from the cellar and set up an ingenious spit roast. Can you imagine the hours of pleasure designing and building that? The whore took just over 11 hours to roast but the sumo wrestler took nearly 19 hours. You could not do that sort of roasting in the open – someone would be bound to ask questions.

My hobby has developed quite a nice social side to it too. There was no way I could get through all that food, so I thought a party was the best way. In the case of the whore I was determined to give all the women in the red light district a decent meal. Even though some of them were overweight they still tended to eat junk so I thought I would invite them to a proper roast dinner with vegetables and they would jump at the chance. Of course, I was not entirely honest; I said, 'roast pork'. It proved very difficult to find a time when they were all free. Finally we settled on Sunday midmorning; then they could be back in time for their clients coming out of church. It was one of my more successful parties and went without a hitch.

I was tempted to invite them again for the sumo wrestler but decided that was too ironic – naked wrestling. Instead I became aware of a huge number of Morris dancers in the area, and they really tucked in after all that dancing.

The next thing I discovered, from the Internet, which is really useful for obscure hobbies, is that some African tribes used to cook their enemies alive and then eat them. I wondered if they did that for fun or because they tasted better. I could not find any definitive research on this point so I thought I should investigate. There was an obvious candidate, the next door neighbour had a repulsive and annoying son who was still living at home aged about 40, generally getting drunk and creating noise and junk everywhere. He was huge but came like a lamb to slaughter down into the cellar.

It was quite a clever technique to cook him, tied up on the metal spit and covered in a ball of mud. Two straws were required one to each nostril to enable him to breathe as he was cooked. He had a big family so, the following evening, when they tired of looking for him I invited them all round for 'roast pork'. Even though I say it myself, we all thought he was delicious.

Of course I still have a lot more to explore in my hobby; live cooking has opened a whole lot more to investigate. There is a pair of plump twins not far away, young housewives living close to each other. I have just started to think about feeding one on Indian food and the other on Chinese food for say a month before I cook them. I would need to modify the spit a bit of course but, together, they do not weigh much more than the sumo wrestler. Then how about a party for all the restaurant staff in the area to see which 'pork' they prefer? Or perhaps my creative writing group...

Nov-14

The Coterie

We are a coterie mostly of seven. We have lived together since – well forever. We cannot remember before we were together. We can remember eight and losing two but we gained one, so now we are seven. We are the strongest seven in the whole wide universe.

We have three of the most beautiful females and four of the most handsome males. We are known as a most industrious coterie. We build boats. Of all kinds and sorts. We live between the sea and the river in one glorious dwelling.

But we need to tell you we have names – although to be honest we do not use them that much, just so long as everyone is included. Our males are Aye, Rye, Tye and Hye. Our females are Fru, Tru and Cru.

Like our boats, our house is wood. It is set in an enclosure with plants and trees. We have our living room and our bedrooms. Soon we will need to build another room but we are fine for now. We wash in the river that runs through the enclosure, and we cook at the back under cover just in case it rains – which of course it does but it is usually quite warm.

Of course Fru, Tru and Cru are stronger and do the lifting and saw through the big trees. But Aye, Rye, Tye and Hye are very nimble and walk up the trees and along the branches to cut the wood for spars, braces and wood rope. When we start on a new job we sit in a circle in the early morning sun and begin to chant – which chant we use depends on the sort of boat. Long thin fishing boat, short broad ferry boat, deep bottomed boat - they each take different chants. We use the chants to determine how we will work together that day. When we finish the chant we are ready to go in to our store and out to the woods to collect together wood and tools.

We all get up together and fan out, in twos and a three in different directions. It's great to be building together – we can finish a small boat in a couple of days. On spare days we are busy too, making glue, cloth or collecting hemp. We do well, sometimes we are paid with a year or two's supply of fish.

At the end of the day we tidy everything away – do all the jobs around the house before we go into the village. Tonight we are going to celebrate and get out our brightest clothes. We walk into the village. When we get there we skip down the street, feathers and balloons trailing from our coat tails.

The villagers clap and cheer – we have happy news to tell them all. Fru is going to have our first baby. We all are happy and excited - we all wonder if we will know who the father is but it does not make any difference - we are happy to be building that new room on the house.

Nov-14

Radio Voices

Counsellor: So how has this week been?

Chris: Well, it's been OK – I've got on better with reasoning with him than I expected. He's gone along with it better than I'd hoped. I'm not sure he likes me calling him Vince, but I think it has helped in a way. Also we've had a few funny moments – when he comes out with the most outrageous things – but again I've tried not to encourage him too much.

Counsellor: Has that been difficult – to keep a straight face I mean?

Chris: Oh yes – I was round at my mum's fixing some shelving near the back door when one of her friends came round. I couldn't believe the size of her bottom – it nearly knocked my step ladder over. Course Vince wasn't going to let an opportunity like that pass. He said straight off 'I've seen countries smaller than that bum'. I nearly burst out laughing, then he said, 'She should go cheek to cheek with Kim Kardashian.' Well I couldn't stop a muffled guffaw – I don't know where Vince found out about the size of Kim Kardashian's rear end.

Vince: Can't you keep a secret – going blabbing on to

this little shrink about me. That was just between me, you and that bottom.

Counsellor: Is there something the matter?

Chris: Sorry, but Vince just started going on – he doesn't seem happy that I'm telling you about what happened – I've told him before that I come to talk to you about the trouble I'm having with him. And he should leave me alone while I'm talking to you.

Counsellor: Well maybe this time we should engage him for a while and then ask him to leave us alone later on. Do you think that may help?

Chris: I can ask.

Vince: Don't be so bloody patronising – you can both bugger off.

Chris: Oh dear, I think he's a bit annoyed – he thinks we're being patronising.

Counsellor: Oh well, let's carry on and just include Vince if he wants to make some remarks.

Chris: Yes. Generally, the way I see it, Vince doesn't actually listen to what I tell him – I'm not even sure that the way I react makes any difference to him. I'm getting better at just ignoring him when I'm doing something important – like sleeping, and my carving of course. But if I laugh or cry it doesn't seem to make any difference to him, he still keeps on in the same way.

Counsellor: Do you think he ever gets upset himself?

Chris: I'm not sure – sometimes he goes quiet for no reason, sometimes he goes quiet if I get really cross and tell him to shut-up.

Vince: Oh for goodness sake – just because I'm not like you doesn't mean I don't have feelings.

Counsellor: Does Vince ever use words that other people say, like your mother, or things your father used to say?

Chris: Yes he does – and he says he does have feelings, I'm just not sure what makes him say the things he does. But yes, sometimes he says 'What do you think you're doing?' just the way my dad used to when I got something wrong in the workshop. He's usually right, but not always – yesterday he said it as I was crossing the road very safely.

Counsellor: Did you ask him why he said that?

Chris: Yes – he claimed it wasn't him. What do you make of that? Just some other voice! Also he can imitate other people – I went to see Carol and we went out, but she got a bit tired so I walked her home and said good-bye. As I turned out of her front garden I heard her say 'I feel better now, let's go and have some fun'. I whipped round so fast I twisted my back – but of course, she wasn't there.

Counsellor: Do you think there has been anything Vince has said that has helped?

Vince: Not just patronising but condescending too.

Chris: Well yes, I was looking through some wood I've collected over the last few months – to use for carving. Anyway, he hadn't said much that day but suddenly he said 'You missed one – go back and look again.' I went back through the last few pieces and there it was. I made one of the best carvings I've ever done and Vince just kept quiet all the time.

Counsellor: That's interesting – have you said how useful that was?

Vince: Like hell you did – I get all the blame when things go wrong but when I save your bacon, diddly squat.

Chris: No – I should do – Vince thanks, you were really helpful with my carving.

Vince: You're welcome mate – better late than never.

Chris: Yes, I'm sorry. It's really good when you help me Vince. But I can do without the crap – easily.

Counsellor: Do you feel you're coming to terms with Vince then?

Chris: Well I've had him all my life – but I do think that things have improved between us since the accident, when I first started coming to see you.

Counsellor: Good. Have a good week.

Chris: Thanks, see you next week.

Vince: Can't wait.

Nov-14

Mobile Phone ringing and ringing…

Mr Smyth-Jones?

Yes

Mr St John Smyth-Jones?

Indeed

Are you worried about the future?

Do you mean do I believe in God?

Oh no – I'm wondering if you have a will?

Oh yes – my mother always said I was wilful. Where there is a way there is a will I always say – have you got a way with you?

No sir – I mean do you have arrangements for your money when you die?

Oh no, I'm trying to spend it as quickly as I can – I have three women here burning up my money – still I have a lot of money, so if you are interested I could fit a fourth in the lumber room.

Oh no sir – but are you worried that the government

will get your money?
I intend to die a pauper – but a happy one.
How about your funeral expenses?
The way my body is going they should be go low –
there might be enough left. Can I tempt you to come
and bonk me to death?
No sir – goodbye sir.
Well you did call me.
Disconnect tone.

Nov-14

Winter Onset

From the winter of age there is no following spring.
  I can feel my strength being sapped, my muscles
slackening.
  Oh yes – that reminds me I must see a man about a
dog
  while I have a chance. It started slowly, stealthy,
  now it is rolling, gathering momentum, inexorable time.
  I can think of nothing as quiet as the sound of hair
turning grey.

  'The best is yet to be' is from times when age was
  an achievement, now it is a test of endurance.
  How often do you hear the word venerable now -
  in reverence of age? Gone from the west.
  Look to the east for acceptance of worth of winter age.

Nov-14

Second Act

The youngish woman shivered in the dank morning – the mist caused beads of moisture to form on her lacquered hair.

The nightclub door swung on its hinges and she knocked hesitatingly – expecting another rejection of her talents.

A dissipated middle aged man with stains down his shirt came to the door.

'Have you come about the musical act?' he asked looking at her with watery blue eyes.

'Yes – I can sing and dance,' she said as brightly as she could.

'Well I think you should let us be the judge of that,' he said with a friendly grin.

She felt she was in with a chance – to make a fresh start. Leave all her emotional complications behind.

He looked kindly on the young woman without any designs – she must be twenty years younger than him after all. The club could do with some new blood and she was dressed to make an impact – when she moved across the stage he could taste the memory of Delilah in her prime. The takings were down, so much competition from new places and he had let the club slide; even before Delilah died, and since then, he had retreated into an alcoholic haze. He'd managed to cling on but now it was time to wake up before the bailiffs moved in.

He looked at her as she made a daring bow.

'What do they call you?'

'My name is Carol but I want a new stage name.'

'I'm Alf, what was your old one?'

'It was Delilah but I want to leave that behind and make a fresh start.'

'Give us a pirouette and I'll give you a new name,' he said.

She lifted her hands above her head and touched her fingertips and rotated effortlessly.

'Grace – what do you think of Grace as your act?'

She looked round the dingy but cosy club, 'Yes, that's grand.'

'It's best you change your name; my wife used the name Delilah for her act here. She died a few years ago now.'

Slowly she fell in love with Alf – it took him ages to notice but finally when he realised that he had made a success out of the club, it dawned on him.

She managed to avoid getting pregnant for seven years but then she fell ill. Just like Delilah – only she was younger so it was faster.

Alf was on his own with the bottles behind the bar – so he sold up. He read an article in the dentist waiting room. About wives that die from their husbands, through their love, through the cervix.

He thought of Delilah and Grace – so beautiful, if he had known of course he would have left them alone.

Oct-14

Hole in Two

Remit: Choose a genre and write a piece split into two parts set in two different times but the same place.

The grey-green leaves of the ivy struggled out from around the top of the well. The well had dried up, and not been used for years. The lady of the house, who, rather like the house, had seen better days, used to walk up to the well in the evenings and stand to the east of the well as the sun set. From mid September onwards, she would note the time she needed to be there, then, she would try and stick to the routine, unless the weather was too inclement.

Often she would stand as if waiting for something, a sign of some sort. Usually she returned as the dusk settled in. Sometimes, Mrs Hudson, the housekeeper would elect to visit the Dairy at this time and stray to the well on her way back, having inspected the churning of butter and the squeezing of cheese. Mrs Hudson, who was outwardly very respectful, would approach discreetly and stand to the north.

Mostly they would stand in stony silence looking at the broken wall round the well. However sometimes, as was the case tonight, as etiquette dictated, the lady spoke first.

'The ivy is taking a hold on the wall of the well. Gradually with the help of the wind, rain and frost the wall will split like a frayed sleeve. Leaving it pillaged.'

'Yes ma'am – time ravages all,' intoned Mrs Hudson.

The lady looked sharply at Mrs Hudson but let the comment pass. It was a warm September so she had not put on a coat but the wind was getting stronger, ruffling the skirts of her dress. They both turned to look west where the sun was setting and from where the strong wind was blowing. Bushes and saplings bent under the onslaught and now the lady's skirts blew around her legs. There was a curious whistling that turned to a screech and a roar. Both women looked at the well in front of them, which seemed to being blown in a very strange way, as the noise reached a crescendo the ivy and other plants and bushes were blown outwards.

In the aftermath there was an eerie lull, the noise died away. Even the wind paused for a few moments. Mrs Hudson, not usually prone to nerves, fainted away, unexpectedly, causing a noise like a small pile of books falling to the ground.

The lady did not notice the fall of her faithful servant. She looked at the dying sun, the colour in her face changing. Like some Victorian Boadicea her body swelled as her face went white then shades of pink to finally crimson. She glowed in the twilight.

* * *

George and Nicholas both hated leaving London to come down to Kent to avoid the war. At that age they were oblivious to the dangers of the falling bombs, they were twins, nearly ten, full of curiosity and mischief, often changing places. The good natured farmer's wife, Mrs Meg, took to calling them Neorge and assumed that if she told one of them off she was telling them both off.

It did not take them many days to explore the farm, the disused buildings and the overgrown well. They would often spend an evening playing, making camp, or sometimes with the other children playing hide and seek, kick the bucket and games that they had played at the rec. a few streets away from their now bombed out home.

They would gravitate back to the well. Usually on their own, after tea in the evening before bedtime they would play. They had made a DH Mosquito to sit in, partly from planks and buckets, but mainly a lot of imagination. They were south of the well flying through the sky, westward, with German bombers not far away flying out of the low sun.

The wind was getting up and one of the German

bombers was in difficulty, on its way to London, they could hear one of the engines cutting out then starting again. It was far above them when it released three bombs in a tight cluster.

The bombs stayed in a tight formation one just behind each other. The whistling grew to a roar, punctuated by changes of note as they entered the well.

The well was very deep but it took just a couple of seconds for the bombs to reach the bottom. Precious, life saving seconds. The ground round the well rippled like a stone in a lake as the bombs went off. The waves reached the boys but their energy was spent.

You could call them Neorge or anything you like, they could hear very little for a few days. They walked from the Mosquito, otherwise unharmed. They decided not to fly the Mosquito again – it stayed in its hanger in one of the disused buildings.

Sep-14

Empty, End, Pond Life Dry

It took many steps from birth to desert,
a quarter of sand with so little else,
it is considered empty. Red rust sand,
from horizon to horizon, by dune and back.

It takes so little to desert this life,
time under the sun, the dying erase,
the freezing nights, eroding life's pond,
habitat for unsuspecting men.

The seabed sand, once prehistoric soup, brought
life to the pond, what started a trickle,
the early sea flowed over, back and forth,
grew to be teaming and fighting for life.

Majestic curves ever shifting across the land,
in the flaming sunset, the hill dunes run blood,
now you can believe that these curves kill,
no quick sands, only slow deaths.

He sees the carrion wings wheeling high,
he looks around for carcass or corpse,
the dead end of nowhere stretches out,
around him, biding for him to collapse,

He is dead meat waiting for the vultures,
to stop watching and start feeding,
he speaks out to the sand but sees her,
life more bodily beautiful than frenzy.

'I hope you do not love me the way I love
you, for me the pain is a living pleasure,
one I would not want to inflict on another,'
delirium fuses with life's shimmering haze.

Slowly the vultures spiral down to meet,
him on the floor, ground zero, eye to eye,
beak to fresh flesh, soon bones picked clean,
he has come to the end, empty, pond life dry.

Jul-15

The Pond

You are sitting peacefully with your life's love by the pond. It is a small pond grown over with fronds and wide open leaves. Unusually the sun is shining on the pond's surface, not much showing, it glistens with reflection.

The talk between you is soft and gentle – pondering the meaning of life and making the most of it. The discussion is about truth and honesty, the bedrock of meaning. Your love is not wearing sunglasses and you are – the very finest polaroid, of a slightly grey tinge.

'Do you see the fish in the pond swimming between the leaves?' you ask.

'No – all I see is the shimmering reflection of the trees on the surface of the water.'

'With these sunglasses I get no glare from the reflection but I can see down into the water. I can see the fish moving as they feed, also sometimes shooting across at great speed. Of course the glasses lie about the colours but tell the truth about the fish being there,' you say.

'I wouldn't say the glasses lie about the colour – they just do the best they can.'

'I suppose you could say they are an honest pair of glasses – it is just they see the world through a grey filter,' you say.

'Well I did not steal them – in fact I paid my good honest money for them and gave them to you.'

There is a flash of colour as a small bird darts around the pond and you sit perfectly still, enthralled by the bird. The bird departs, beak full, presumably back to its nest. The conversation carries on.

'Well, you earned the money as a banker so the whole idea of it being honest is open to debate, and then there have been one or two Friday afternoons when you have sloped off just after 3pm so you may have bought them on unearned income,' you finish speaking with a grin.

'Truth is like love, it is in the eye of the beholder. Honesty is trying your best to tell what you believe. This pond is made up of H2O in a plastic container with carbon based life forms in it – that is the truth but it is hardly an honest description is it?'

The bird was back pecking at the edge of the water's surface.

'Are you trying to tell me that your work is needed to hold society together? That you have helped prevent untold suffering?' you ask.

'Yes, but I knew if I said that you would not believe me – just like your fish and glasses.'

Aug-14

Twist and Cry Out

Crystal was planning a weekend away with her lover. She was doing luxury shopping in her lunch hour, thinking of her rather ineffectual husband compared to her virile lover. Charles, her husband, was something in the city with the killer instinct of a slug. Ray was a personal trainer with good looks, charm, good sense of humour and not too much intelligence. She'd already bought her own special items and was looking for something for Ray. She looked up and was startled to see Christine, the old school friend that she tended to use as an excuse for her weekends of passion.

Crystal smiled sweetly and moved away from the aftershave. Christine looked nervous as usual.

'How are things going?' Crystal asked.

'Oh, quite well – the business takes up more and more of my time. How are things with you?' replied Christine.

'Well I got that promotion at work – it didn't even take a blow job.'

Christine was a fading blonde while Crystal was a raven haired beauty. They had grown apart since their school days but they did meet from time to time. Christine acquiesced with a smile at Crystal's language.

They hugged and parted, both protesting they should have coffee soon, but not making any date. As Crystal walked away she noticed one of Christine's blonde hairs on her coat and she smiled a sly smile.

She had a great weekend – she didn't know how much longer Ray would amuse her but she certainly had a weekend to remember. When she got home she even found Charles more attractive than usual. They chattered on about their weekends over a glass of very nice wine that Charles had opened. Crystal was in very good spirits and hummed as she went into the bedroom and changed into something even more seductive.

She took Christine's blond hair from out of her purse and placed it on her pillow on her side of the bed. A harmless trick for good old faithful Charles; she called out to him.

'Darling, look what I've found – you old rascal.'

Charles came blundering in, looking a bit like a mole coming to surface.

'What is it dear?' he asked.

'Who've you had in my bed?' she asked pointing at the blonde hair, revealing a long leg and very little else.

Charles burst into tears.

'You're right,' he sobbed, 'I've had my lover here all weekend. She's only just gone, that bed is probably still warm.'

Crystal was poleaxed – she crumpled on to the bed, looking at him ashen – no attempt to flash her anatomy at him.

'Who is she?' anguish in her face.

Charles' tears vanished completely and he looked at her unflinchingly.

'Why - your long time school friend Christine – who you were supposed to be with. So did you have a good time with the bright Ray?'

Aug-14

Bitter Victory

They found the hoard whilst on the run. They, the roundheads were routed – it was early in the Civil war. The three of them, all firm friends, tumbled down the steep bank and crashed into a thicket, landing on a small carriage that had toppled over.

The three friends looked at each other.

Zeal, already in his middle age austere and unforgiving, looked at the ornate carriage with disapproval.

John, still young after several horrors of the war, easily impressed, gazed open eyed at the rich carvings.

Samuel, more moody, looking sceptically at how the wealthy lived and, more to the point, flaunted their wealth.

John found the box containing expensive plates and jewels.

'We are best hiding it and returning to it later – after the battle is over,' said Zeal.

The other two nodded in agreement.

'Do you know anywhere round here?' asked John.

It was Samuel that replied, 'I know some caves not far away, we could hide them there.'

They took it in turns, two at a time, to carry the heavy box. It turned out a bit more than a mile but it was worth the effort. They found a crevice high up one wall and slid the box in neatly.

A week later Zeal was taking messages to another troop and he was passing not far from the caves – he stopped and checked the box. He found that several things had been taken, the biggest plate and some smaller items.

His face, already stern, hardened as he thought, his eyes vanishing into eternity.

It had to be John or Samuel, he would find out which one.

Another week passed and Zeal met John.

'Did you hear Samuel lost his hand? They found him out cold, bleeding on the road near the cave where we hid the hoard,' said John.

'He must have put his hand where he had no right to – taken what was not his,' said Zeal with a cold gleam in his eye. 'I doubt there will be any of the hoard left now – his greed spoilt it. He will not get any leeway from me.'

Slow comprehension dawned on John. He looked searchingly at Zeal's face.

A kind thoughtful face turned hard by cruel life events, war, crime and man's inhumanity.

An eye for an eye, a tooth for a tooth, a hand for a hand.

Aug-14

Catholic Contraband

Florence had always assumed it would be the God Squad, in some shape or form, that would put a stop to her nefarious activities. However, it was the other side that seemed to want to muscle in and take over her act. He sat opposite her, very smart, fit too, she could feel the coiled energy within him. He was about the same height and age as her, but there all similarity ended. Two very large bodyguards lurked and the café was deserted mid afternoon.

'So Miss Flo, how could you get more of your merchandise? Could you pay more?' Nazario said in his immaculate English, far better than her Italian. He could not bear to say the words 'contraceptive pills', although he could quite happily kill people in cold blood.

Florence was horrified, 'Oh no, we don't pay our 'suppliers' for the pills, they are given – if we started trying to paying for them I think most women would give up donating them,' she paused, struggling to think of a way to explain such an alien concept to him. 'These women no longer have a use for their pills, they have either started having children or they have reached the end of child bearing age,' she was coy about saying menopause to him. 'They send the pills to Italy to help sisters who need them but are not allowed them.'

'I see, so we would upset the balance by paying them – also of course it must keep costs down,' he said and paused. 'We could increase supply by taking a consignment at source or from distribution.'

Florence blinked at the rapid shift in thinking, so

obvious but alien to her good C of E upbringing. She could not help herself saying, 'But that is stealing.' She looked at him, not for the first time, as a man rather than a criminal and saw him bridle. Maybe she could reform him – he was obviously very bright, drawn to criminality through family tradition.

'Are you Sicilian?' she asked with gentle courtesy but perhaps not the best timing.

He looked sharply at her, but softening asked, 'Are you Irish?' and looked at her with obvious interest.

She was amazed, 'My mother's family moved to England when she was about six.' She wondered if had guessed or had he done his homework and got someone to find out.

He smiled, a charming smile, that this time did not remind her of a wolf, 'So we have something in common – our countries both living in the shadow of a powerful imperialist neighbour.'

'Yes, and both governed by repressive Catholics for centuries,' she said it without really thinking and added hastily, 'Sorry, I didn't mean to offend.'

'No, not at all – I didn't expect a different view from someone in your line of business,' his grin was genuine and his tone light. 'Are you here on a stop-over tonight?'

The change took her by surprise again, 'No, I'm back on the late flight to Gatwick.'

'When can we have dinner together? I have some things to check up but it would be good to meet again – don't worry, maybe we do similar things, but in a different way.'

Florence felt mixed emotions – in a way she was even more frightened, still if it increased the number of women in Italy who had access to the Pill that was surely a good thing. Nazario was the most exciting thing that had happened in her life so far and she felt a mutual attraction.

'I get my schedule for the next two weeks tomorrow – would you like to meet up next time I come to Italy? It'll probably be next week.'

Nazario looked at her steadily for a minute, 'I can find out when you're next here – I was asking if you wanted to meet.'

Aug-14

Gliding in - Filming

The blue sky engulfs the view in front of them, of course there are clouds too, stacked sparsely against the blue. They are in a glider one behind the other, wearing helmets with built-in earphones and microphones.

'I know you warned me about the noise but even now the tow has finished – it's not what I expected!' she said over the steady roar of the wind over the wings.

'You've seen too many glider films where the sound track has been dubbed with gentle wind noise,' he laughed.

She is younger than him, ten or so years at least, it is difficult to tell in the glider but she looks pretty. Not a classical Hollywood look but rather unusual features, feline eyes and small nose. She could have been in Cats for her first major part.

He on the other hand is much more the typical action grisly that comes on the big screen usually with one or two of those Hollywood beauties in tow.

Below the glider the landscape spreads out, a chequered interlocking of fields, some striped some plain, merging into buildings here and there, roads and rivers crossing over. The glider is flying down a wide gentle vale, a fertile weald.

The view of the fields merge into a wide double bed, chequered cover, she is standing at the doorway travel bag in hand looking at a different man in bed with a different woman. There is no sound as they both sit upright, the woman clutching the covers to cover her chest.

Back in the sky, the glider is coming lower, heading for the runway, passing close above building and trees. The transition from air to land is fairly smooth, punctuated by a thud and a strange eerie grinding noise.

With assistance they pack the glider away into a long trailer and walk to the terminal building. They separate to change and meet in the café.

'What would you like to eat?' he asked.

'I should eat more – I've lost weight and in general men prefer their women well covered not bony,' she said raising her rather slim arm.

He smiled a rather enigmatic smile, 'I don't think you have anything to worry about on that score – you are not that interested now but I am sure that when you are you will be spoilt for choice.'

'How will you feel about that Ralf?' she inquired gently.

'Well I expect I will survive – I just concentrate on making the most of it while it lasts.'

'I'm making heavy weather of it – finding out she must've just conceived when I caught them at it hasn't helped,' she said.

'No, not easy,' he agreed.

They looked out of the window to see a large glider speed past as it landed – the muffled noise penetrated the double-glazing faintly.

He took her hand, 'Maybe I could offer you more moral boosting therapy in bed on a quiet Sunday afternoon?' he asked.

She laughed spontaneously, 'You are good for me – first after Trevor and now after Gerald.' She leant over and kissed his cheek.

'It is just so many things remind me of the past – today when we were flying over the fields I was reminded of our bed cover, it is ridiculous.'

'Well it is hard, harder as you say, she got pregnant, at a time when you were thinking about it. I suppose there is no point in me offering is there?' he asked.

She looked at him sharply, 'Are you taking the piss or just practicing for your next Oscar?'

He laughed, 'Well since you ask, both, I know you need a bit of gentle leg pulling but also it was time I got another one,' he paused for dramatic effect, 'that and I would be proud to impregnate you.'

'You are impossible – I can't work it out sometimes - if you are serious or playing for your next part.'

He looked at her searchingly for a few seconds then said with a grin, 'Is there a difference then?'

He looked at her for a minute or two, then said, 'You are not all skin and bones just yet – and I think if you got pregnant it would help in several ways – if it was my child it would be good for both of our careers. It would help you with Gerald and his young spawning wife. Now what do you say? I also think it would put the excitement back into our sex life – a bit like Russian roulette.'

'The other point you forgot to mention is that it is a hell of lot cheaper than therapy,' she said with a touch of sarcasm.

'Well that is right – and a lot more healthy,' he added.

'Doesn't it worry you a little that you are proposing this

baby based on our careers and self-image?'

He considered for a moment, 'Well the baby would be really wanted – I can't think of anything in life I would rather do. But if I had told you that, you wouldn't have believed me. You would have thought I was practicing for my next Oscar.'

Aug-14

Sherlock - the Case of the Pretty Youth

The portly client puffed out his chest with an appearance of some little pride, and began.

'You see, Mr Holmes, it's like this, I have for some years worked as a night porter at the Strand Palace Hotel, and as you might imagine I get to see all manner of amazing things. It is part of our understanding that what we see of a night should remain between the governor and us if you see what I mean.

Anyway last night I found myself in a very delicate position and while the police have been called in – in the shape of Inspector Lestrade of the Yard with whom you are acquainted – this as such does not reassure me. I can see the police are doing what they can to solve the murder but their energy will not be at all directed in absolving me from an indiscretion which I am not guilty of.' Mr Jabez Wilson paused just long enough for Holmes to inhale sharply.

'A murder – this is a serious matter,' I remarked, 'please continue sir,' I added.

'Well it all started with the arrival of Lady Glasblown – she is a society deb' just past the first hurdle of youth as you might say. She is a very generously proportioned lady having a magnificent bosom and to be honest, a well corseted waist. She is married to nouveau riche Lord Glasblown who made his money in shipping and usually keeps in the background. It is clear to all of us that she comes to the hotel to seek out young innocent men she can ensnare.

'Last night was no exception, there was a young man of classical handsomeness staying at the hotel – I can only describe him as a modern day Adonis. And Lady Glasblown was drawn to him like fluff to a tummy button. All evening she was pursuing him and she soon discovered his room and managed to ply him with his favourite drink.

'As soon the hotel quietened down I saw Lady Glasblown moving down the main corridor like a silent battleship in full sail; her night attire billowing gently in the breeze and body undulating in anticipation. I suspect she would not have noticed me even if I had been beating drums, but in fact I kept quiet but close to see every movement. Completely in the line of duty you understand. Now I am in trouble with the Hotel and her husband – I need to prove that I knew nothing of her actions.'

Holmes nodded sagely and Mr Wilson continued.

'She pushed his door open with no difficulty – I thought to myself that he was expecting her and this was to some degree supported by the vision before us. He was on his back on the bed covered only by a sheet. I can only say that he was athletic in repose. Lady Glasblown clearly thought so too – she did not even ensure that the door was closed but stepped out of her nightgown. I must confess I was startled at her appearance – she was all woman, intent on enjoying her liaison. She slipped, if that is the right term to describe her figure, under the sheet.

'My god, you are so cold dear man,' she exclaimed. I was slow in understanding and stayed just in the doorway. She let out a piercing cry and recoiled, hastily getting out of the bed she turned to face me. After all my years service I was driven to do one thing, to pick up her nightgown and offer to put it round her. As I did so I noticed an envelope on the floor – once the gown was secured round her body I picked up the envelope. I have shown the police but they were not very interested in it.'

Mr Wilson passed the envelope to Holmes who studied it carefully.

'See here Watson, the words 'Dear Pretty Youth' you recognise the connection?'

'The poem by Thomas Shadwell, it is the very imprint of this story, a woman tries to seduce a corpse of a pretty young man – if that is her envelope she must have know he was already dead,' I said, drawn in to this puzzle.

'The game is afoot,' said Holmes reaching for his bag.

Jul-14

Match Made in Construction

Nikho and Misno shivered in the front of the small boat as it moved through the reeds in a bleak part of the Thames estuary. Of course, they were unaccustomed to the British summer – they were both thinking of the weather they left behind, far away in the Philippines. They were identical twins and had come to England as crew on a huge container ship. They spoke and understood English quite well and were coming to work in the construction industry.

They were the most helpful twins that you could wish to

meet. On the first day at work they appeared outside the boss's cabin side-by-side smiling.

'Hello boss,' said Nikho.

'We are here to help,' said Misno.

'We can fetch and carry things,' said Nikho.

'Heavy things,' said Misno.

'We can build things,' said Nikho.

'Ok, ok' said the boss, 'see if you can help construction on the second floor where they are getting ready to plaster all the rooms.'

The two went off grinning. They found the second floor was in a bit of a state of chaos but after several hours of feeding the plasterers with plaster and water, while continuously clearing away rubbish and debris from earlier building phases, the second floor took on a neat tidy appearance. The boss came round at lunch time to see the two lads just stacking some cardboard.

'I thought I was on the wrong floor, this is so tidy,' he said and Nikho and Misno grinned at him.

'You have your break and food and then at two o-clock go to the top floor and see if you can clear that up a bit too. You have made a really good start. Do you have any questions?' said the boss.

'No boss,' said Misno.

'No boss,' said Nikho.

Towards the end of the day the boss came up on the external lift and the two lads were stacking stuff to go down. Just as the boss was stepping out of the lift cage, an unused beam in the roof space started to move - rolling out of a hidden ledge.

Nikho grabbed the boss and started to heave him to one side.

Misno got hold of a long clamp that was made of high tensile steel and wedged it so that the falling beam hit it and slid away from them. The beam crashed against the cage of the lift buckling it with the force of the impact.

The boss got unsteadily to his feet and looked at the two twins in amazement.

'Where the hell did that fall from? Watching you two was like watching a ballet in slow motion the way you saved me. If it's the last thing I do I'm going to make you legal. I have twin girls at home - about your age, I'll marry them to you and then you can work for me legitimately.'

'Yes boss,' they said laughing together.

Jun-14

Few Adjectives

The grounds of the retreat were almost without noise. I wandered about in a garden enclosed by a wall. I was totally at peace. I sat on a bench made of stone and thought of all things that had led to me coming to this place. How fitting, after all the traumas, it was to arrive here. I was lucky to have found it.

Minute by minute I absorbed the tranquillity. The stresses and strains seeped out of my body – it was as if I could see them lying at my feet like a pool of worries that had coalesced.

In the distance, I heard a tapping, a steady interval between each beat; I was not sure what it was but it struck a life tune for all to follow with hope. I stood up and walked to an archway in the wall. Growing all around and beyond were plants that were green, hanging down in swathes. A sea of flowing leaves. A slope ran away down to a river and I started to walk out on a flotilla of leaves.

I slipped and landed on my back; as I looked up at the

sky, blue with clouds I relaxed and slithered down. I did not harm myself. I came to a halt with my feet lodged in the roots of a tree. I stood up and looked around wondering if anybody had seen my embarrassment. I gained confidence striding out, making my way to a bridge over the river.

I paused on the bridge and looked down into the water flowing. I could see my reflection in the water, shimmering. Here is a place to rest, take a siesta for a while, I thought. I did not feel on my own but could find solitude if I needed it.

I crossed over the bridge and climbed up the slope. As I struggled to keep going the incline was such that I was crawling up a vertical. I finally made it to the top and looked out over the other side at a huge expanse of farmland, laid out as far as the eye could see. A patchwork-quilt of fields covering the contours of the earth. I could not work out how to escape the top of the ridge so I was forced back down the way I had come. I reached the bottom, limbs and fingers exhausted from the exertion.

I walked back to the retreat. I was looking forward to a meal, bath and so to bed.

The only adjectives are underlined.

May-14

Floating High

US LAW

a) Sovereignty and Public Right of Transit.—
(1) The United States Government has exclusive sovereignty of airspace of the United States.
(2) A citizen of the United States has a public right of transit through the navigable airspace. …..

(b) Use of Airspace.—
(1) The Administrator of the Federal Aviation Administration shall develop plans and policy for the use of the navigable airspace and assign by regulation or order the use of the airspace necessary to ensure the safety of aircraft and the efficient use of airspace. The Administrator may modify or revoke an assignment when required in the public interest.
(2) The Administrator shall prescribe air traffic regulations on the flight of aircraft (including regulations on safe altitudes) for—
(A) navigating, protecting, and identifying aircraft;
(B) protecting individuals and property on the ground;
(C) using the navigable airspace efficiently; and
(D) preventing collision between aircraft, between aircraft and land or water vehicles, and between aircraft and airborne objects.
Etc etc

Air Traffic Control "LAX to XV917 you are cleared for take off – over."
Pilot "Roger – over"

Sue Wain's Journal 10-Apr-2022 – I do not know why Joanna is being so horrid, just because she is older she thinks she is better than me. Anyway I'm not going to let it get to me. I can't remember the last time we flew, I think I was only 5 then. But this time it was really exciting. It was a bit scary as we took off, it seemed we were going very fast and then we left the runway behind and I felt my tummy feel all funny. When we climbed through the clouds it was a bit bumpy and then it settled down. Every so often the plane turned and I could see clouds and sometimes a bit of land below. It wasn't very long after we had taken off that the aeroplane suddenly seemed to change direction. Or..It wasn't very long after we had taken off that Mummy said it was odd because we had changed direction suddenly. And then the pilot came on the loudspeaker reassuring us that everything was ok .

Pilot "Flight XV917 to LAX – I can assure you that I'm not seeing things, but we have just had to take evasive action to avoid a man floating at our current altitude. He would appear to be in an inflatable chair supported by a number of floating balloons. Over."

Air Traffic Control "LAX to XV917 We can confirm two other sightings in the last four hours. We are looking extensively at possibilities of bringing him down. Over"

CB Conversation: What information do you wish me to give Air Traffic Authorities at this time as to your location and destination? They are concerned about your height – your and others' safety.

Lawn chair Pilot: I am in steady descent now – and I still have my air pistol, unlike gramps, I think we are past the main danger now. But yes, call them now and say sorry I did not file a flight plan but I should be down in about 20 to 30 minutes and I will avoid the interstate. If all goes to plan I should land in a field just north of Jessup's Farm. I suppose they will already know that as they will need to arrest me.

Los Angeles Times 11-Apr-2022 : Yesterday, Rich Walter, 37, Great Nephew of Larry Walter aka The Lawn Chair Pilot was arrested for a similar offence to his Great Uncle. It seemed that he was using a more suitable chair but little else was different. Rich Walter followed in the family tradition of using helium balloons to float up in to the skies around Los Angeles – including floating into Controlled Air Space. Larry Walter hit the headlines in 1982 and now here today another member of his family has been arrested for the same thing. Larry Walter finally took his own life – we sincerely wish better fortune on his Great Nephew.

May-14

Joe's Cousin the Rake

First Stanza

Joe first became aware of his little cousin when he was a young boy and she was a very small girl whom he initially ignored. As Sarah grew up, she exhibited interest in many of the things he and his friends got up to. He took care to ensure that nothing happened to her and noticed as they all got older that his friends treated her with more interest and respect. She was good at sport, science and music. She was very striking to look at but spent very little time or effort on her appearance.

She continued to see Joe in the holidays when he was at his modern University, Sussex. Later, when he was in a steady but not very demanding job, she went to Oxford to study Maths and Computer Science. This did not stop her taking an interest in boys too and she started to make quite a reputation for herself. Joe was dismayed at her appetite for new men – he did not hold aspirations for her himself but they did have a close friendship for each other strengthened from both being only children.

Joe went to her graduation ceremony where she had gained the best degree and highest set of prizes. Afterwards they went to a café and a young man came by screaming at her that she was cruel and heartless. She shrugged and Joe asked her for the first time how she managed to fill her life with so many men.

'It doesn't take much time or effort to fuck the brains out of the likes of him,' she said emotionlessly.

Second Stanza

Joe saw his cousin off to the US to do research at one of the most prestigious Universities for Technology and the Arts, Carnegie Mellon. He had just met a quiet woman, Jane, and it looked like they might well settle down. After Sarah had been away for a couple of years, Joe got married and Sarah came to the wedding. Joe did think she was drinking rather heavily and she was observed leading the best man away to a not very well concealed area behind some screens, which proceeded to rock rather violently. Joe did not get much of a chance to talk to her but she did say she was in the running for a very prestigious Computer Science award.

Third Stanza

Work was steady and the opportunity for some trips to the States came up. Jane had taken a while to fall pregnant but was now happy at home with two children, the younger one still in nappies. Joe consulted with Jane about him travelling to the States and she supported him. She even said that maybe he could look up Sarah – which he did.

Sarah was established in university life – she finally got the prestigious Turning award, only the second woman to have done so. As she was so exceptional in her subject area, little was done to keep her drinking or manizing in check. After his first visit to see her, Joe had a vision of burnt out men scattering the campus rather like car wrecks. It was rather as if her genius fed on the consumption of weak willed men. Rather corny he knew, but an inescapable impression he got as he talked to her about what she wanted in life.

Fourth Stanza

Over the next few years Joe came closer to Sarah, seeing her success but also the start of degeneration. He managed to persuade her to try to reduce her drinking – he even helped her go for a rehabilitation course but in reality she was still in denial about her drink problem. He was much less successful in trying to persuade her to get the needed help with her sex addiction.

When he had not been to the States for a few months he got a call from a very senior manager at the university.

'We are very concerned about Sarah's well-being. We are proposing that she has a year's leave to get herself well. We greatly value her work and in recognition of her contribution we will give her paid leave – but we do want to be assured that she addresses her problems. We are looking for someone who would be prepared to try to facilitate her recovery."

There was a long silence. Joe thought about it. There was no one else that knew her as he did.

'OK – I'll need to talk it over with my wife. We'll need to decide which country is best, but I think the UK will be.'

'Sarah has agreed to give you full power of attorney.'

That startled Joe.

Fifth Stanza

Joe combined a work trip and the trip to collect Sarah. As so often previously he stayed with Sarah. She was clearly very insecure and clingy at bedtime. In the night he woke to find her in his bed next to him. He remembered all those men burnt out by this obsession. He managed to get her to take two sleeping pills and he cradled her until she fell asleep.

Joe did not mention it in the morning, but Sarah made some bitter remarks that she was definitely losing her touch as that was the first time she had got into a man's bed and all that happened was sleep.

Sixth Stanza

Sarah was staying temporarily in their house when the final breakdown came. The doctor had already met Sarah but on the third night she wanted Joe to come to her bed. Everybody underplayed the sexual implication, but first they called the doctor and he quite quickly arranged for a psychiatric nurse and policeman to arrive.

The doctor was very caring and explained what was happening to Sarah but it took her completely by surprise. She started arguing about the 28 days straight away but in reality they extended the section.

Joe found the whole process of Sarah being sectioned

traumatic. Never did he envisage such a dramatic and effective downfall; of course he tried to rationalise this was the result of what Sarah had done in her life but it was difficult to separate it from just the final breakdown. Joe would go and see her two or three times a week in hospital. Very occasionally when Joe was away Jane would go.

Gradually Sarah adapted to doing without drink and men but unfortunately she had to do without Maths and Computers too. Her brain never fully recovered.

May-14

Fury

Fury can be red hot and icy cold, sometimes together,
ice cold fury spreads over the surface coalescing to a crisp,
frozen it numbs like a punch in the guts and solar plexus in one,
hot fury explodes incandescent, ripping, blasting through all in its way.

When hot fury meets cold it seems, at the start, hot will prevail,
ice forms in the cracks, splits foes into bits, bitter victory in a tundra,
in place of the flames the icy crystals play death to any feeling emotion,
but this time the hot is melting the ice and leaving great steaming patches.

Sometimes fury achieves what would not be possible

without,

often fury destroys – occasionally it destroys evil that would not

otherwise be stopped. You can indeed fight fire with fire, fury with fury,

but take care that what you unleash does not get out of control like fury of a fiend.

The aftermath of this fury is like some crazy battlefield,

with trees snapped off just higher than a man, cars overturned,

friends and family limping away, only too pleased to have escaped,

here at the fury epicentre, "it" is cooling down wondering what "it" has done.

May-14

Mrs P

I never really did work out Mrs P's sexual orientation. She was my landlady and of three other students. It was my first time as a student and I'd left applying for accommodation until very late. Someone in the housing department had prevailed upon her to take a fourth student. I was in a tiny attic bedroom which she told me in hushed tones was where her husband usually slept.

I never heard her husband speak an intelligible word. I'd been in a Pinter play at school as a similar character – except in the play the grunting character burst into speech at the end. Not so in true life, I never saw Mr P articulate anything. In fact I call him Mr P for convenience as I strongly suspect Mrs P gained her name from a previous husband.

The house was Victorian botch, where the kitchen had been moved to the first floor, and there were outside stairs. Mr P slept in a put-you-up in the kitchen and grunted for breakfast, read the paper and seemed to have no gainful employment. I rarely saw him at other times of the day and it seeped out of Mrs P's conversation that he did pop in to the betting shop from time to time.

Mrs P was fighting a losing battle with gravity. Everything she had seemed to be stretched pink nylon. Well I can't be quite sure as there was a notable absence of feminine underwear – as if as the only female in an otherwise all male environment, she couldn't risk hanging out pink knickers and pink bras. I was fairly convinced they existed as very occasionally I saw a pink gleam from Mrs P as she negotiated some cupboard or corner in the house. Very rarely I caught a glimpse of the interior of her bedroom – although I think boudoir might be a more appropriate word. The overwhelming sensation was one of pinkness.

As a student in digs I had a motorbike, giving me freedom; I used to drive to lectures and organise my life based on coming and going as I pleased. I remember one night I stayed really late at one of the halls with a few friends – I could have stayed the night but decided that it was better to return. I drove on the back roads very carefully – the road shimmered with crystals on the surface. I stopped to take a better look at the road surface in the moonlight. As I tested to see how slippery it was I heard a car coming. I didn't get a good look but I thought it was Mr P in his car but I'd a distinct impression of a pink haze in the driver's seat. I was fairly sure that Mrs P didn't drive. I came up the back stairs trying to make as little noise as possible, I was worried that Mr P would be in the process of going to bed. I need not have worried, as there was no sign of him.

The term continued and I flowed along gently with my student life. I decided that I would look for a new place next term.

The last day of term came and I'd a lecture in the morning that finished at 11am. With a light heart I made my way to the bike sheds where my somewhat scruffy bike stood amongst gleaming machines and also one or two that looked similar to mine. I sped away taking the back roads round the University. As I cranked the bike over on a big wide bend I saw tyre marks on the road and I slowed down to see that the tyre marks lead off the road through the hedge. I slowed to a stop and dismounted. I followed the clear marks down a bank and was amazed to see Mr P's car had driven right across a field; it seemed the car had crossed the field and stopped tucked out of the way but at the back of a service road to a new hospital that had opened recently. I contemplated trudging across the field or going to fetch my bike – from this distance I couldn't make out if Mr P was in the car. I decided I better walk over and see but before I got very far I saw a police car arrive. I kept still and watched from behind a tree. Two policemen investigated the car, it was obvious that they found nothing. I decided that I'd make a discreet exit.

Next term I came back to the lodgings early – I spoke to Mrs P on the phone. I came in the side stairs and found Mrs P where Mr P used to sit on the rare occasions I saw him.

The first thing I noticed about Mrs P is that she was much more radiant and colourful – not just pink. She was wearing tighter fitting clothes and her feminine curves seemed more pronounced – however she did seem to be moving cautiously when she bent and walked.

I explained I was thinking about finding another place –
a flat with some other students.

'Yes dear,' she said, 'I can see how that would suit you
better. But you need not worry about Mr P now – he won't
be bothering us any more.'

I'm not sure what made me ask but I blurted out.

'Have you been to hospital? I hope everything is ok. I
saw Mr P's car by the hospital on the last day of term.'

'Yes, Mr P took me; everything went very well thank you.
You're a nice lad but it might be easier if you don't explain
to the others why Mr P has disappeared.'

I looked into Mrs P's eyes and saw a mixture of relief and
jubilation in her. I still didn't understand her sexual
orientation but I'd a better idea of what it must feel like to
be released from being born in the wrong body.

Apr-14

Lovesnake

When Miranda arrived at the office, she was surprised to
find a snake on her desk.

'I think it is a love snake,' said Jean her colleague.

'I've never heard of such a thing,' replied Miranda.

'Oh yes, it was all over the Internet about six months
ago – they aren't real,' added Jean.

Miranda studied the snake carefully; from a safe
distance, she could see the creature moving slightly,
breathing but lying still over various things on her desk-
pens, post-it notes and so on. Occasionally the snake's
tongue flicked so fast that it was as if her eye twitched
and nothing was left to confirm the tongue's existence.

'What do you mean – they aren't real?' she asked Jean who'd returned to her tasks for the day.

'Oh – they are computer generated images of real snakes – after a while the power runs out. That's a very beautiful snake, deep colours – but it will fade away and leave a little cylinder. Do you know anyone who's been to China or Hong Kong recently and is lusting after you?' asked Jean smiling gently.

'I don't know anyone who's lusted after me in the last five years or so,' said Miranda. In truth probably longer, she thought. She'd got married quite late when she was in her early thirties. Her husband hadn't got much get up and go but it seemed he'd sufficient to get up and go off with one of her friends. She didn't have many close female friends so he'd picked the most promising and in an amazingly short time babies started arriving.

After that there was a very fit younger man – who used to call round whenever he could. It didn't take Miranda long to figure out he was only there for one thing but as she quite liked it she didn't put a speedy end to it. It did finally come to a bitter end with much screaming and gnashing of the other girlfriend's teeth. The other woman was pregnant.

Miranda lapsed into unfulfilled solitude keeping herself busy at work and with a few friends who stayed the course. She was keen to meet the right man to share her life with – maybe not live together all the time but for trust and companionship. The years passed.

The snake began to glow brighter and shimmer in the shape of a heart round it. Gradually it began to fade away. Miranda picked up a small cylinder that felt hard and cool to the touch and put it in her bag. The image of the snake was very much in her mind.

That evening she went with some friends into a local

wine bar. She looked down at the bare arm of the waiter and saw the snake on his arm. She looked at his face and saw a gentle smile and steely blue eyes. She had known him for years but only now was he coming home to settle down. She guessed he would still want to go on occasional trips.

Apr-14

Walrus Man

He was a walrus of a man. When he woke each morning a coin spun in the air – one way he was mild and well mannered, the other way a roaring moaning heap, a mountain of aggravated flesh.

He would limber out of bed and you would know how he was. Not to say he was easy just you knew from his happy sounds or his belches and groans what to expect from the day. He might mellow in the evening in his favourite reclining chair but that would be dependent on how his day developed.

Success would bring an atmosphere of contentment – failure would bring brooding determination or truculent bull-roaring bolshiness. Rarely or indeed never did he slide into despondency.

He rarely womanised, when he felt the need to woo he would choose a small slim, younger woman who on the face of it would be an impossible goal. Very occasionally he succeeded but was somewhat perplexed as to what to do next.

He was a creature of habit but liked to explore the exotic – a man of contradictions.

Boris might be a suitable name and he was most likely a successful scrap merchant which brought him into contact with a wide social scale.

Feb-14

Land of Minds

Imagine the land of minds. Your imaginations are the entities of this land, as are all the minds I will conjure in your mind, these minds are similar to yours. Without your mind of course, you would not imagine. To help describe the composition of the minds I will begin with a short journey in to the study of minds.

It was no ordinary door, it had taken a long time to develop, finally ensuring that it shut out all mind-waves. On the door was written:-

Department of Mindology – This door is to be kept closed during working hours.

Behind the door, years of dedicated work have led to instruments of detection and measurements being invented and refined. The door with the walls were vital in this pioneering work; only by excluding extraneous mind-waves could work really begin to map out the land of minds. For a long time it was understood that brains reside in heads. What was not clear until relatively recently is that brains cause minds. Or indeed what a mind really is. In the study of minds, their anatomy, their psyche - it is necessary to extend consciousness to meet the subconscious. To describe a mind needs in-depth analysis of mental, emotional, motivational and even the physical nature of the mind. At this point, I think it might be best to look at a few everyday examples. Not surprisingly, each mind has characteristics unique to that mind, analogous to shape, size, texture, colour and so on. In the Department of Mindology, techniques have been developed to detect and measure these characteristics. Finally instruments to observe native minds in the field have been developed. As yet these do not work as well as the more precise instruments behind the door of the Department of Mindology but they will suffice to explore today.

The first mind which I wish to describe is neither common nor rare, but sleek and superficial, staying mainly at the surface. Quite happy to be blissfully unaware of complexity. There are very few blemishes on this mind as it is rather unaware, not only of others but also of itself. This particular individual I wish to describe is a rather beautiful hue of purple gold. It can be quite difficult to work out gender from the mind alone but I feel that this one is fairly obviously a male and called Purvis. A keen golfer, which I have nothing against, but in Purvis' case limits conversation to holes.

The next mind to describe is a might ungainly one which may have sagged slightly through lack of use. Faded blues and pinks shimmer on the surface but give the idea of strong vibrant colours within. With the smell of roses. Self-conscious and of diminished ego through constant belittling over the years I have a feeling that she is a female, called Belinda, slightly past her best – which was probably when she worked in a bank about five years ago.

Purvis knows Belinda slightly and is rather taken with her,

not noticing the sagging. He sees her in the street and says.

'What a fantastic day – would you like a game of golf?'

'Well, er, I do not play golf,' replied Belinda taken aback by the question but flattered by the attention.

'Well, today is a terrific day to learn – I could show you how.'

I can see the two minds reacting – Belinda turns deeper pink and loses her blue with excitement and fear of making a fool of herself. Purvis' surface seems to become more rigid and gold – he has run out of golfing partners and Belinda would be ideal to beat.

At the golf course, Colin is working out the games and teaching rounds for the day – this mind is like a series of interlocking prisms, steely grey; his mind has little empathy and thinks there is only one worthy goal in life, to win. There is a faint whiff of leather and rubber together with a stronger smell of hot metal.

He catches a glimpse of Purvis and Belinda coming into the Club – he stops in his tracks and speaks with the brutal cruelty.

'For Christ's sake, can't you find a partner your own size?' he says to Purvis.

Belinda's mind flips into an inverted jellyfish, like some sort of whipped dog begging for sympathy. The pink excitement fades away and blue embarrassment sets in.

Purvis bursts into laughter and says, 'I'm sure she will be putting all the beginners into the shade in no time at all. Just you see.' His mind hardly changes at all, looking only slightly more slippery than before.

Colin nearly slips into the trap of offering to play Purvis himself but just in time his mind snaps shut, turns dark grey and spiky as if to repel borders.

Sally is in the office but is keeping an eye on what is

going on. Her mind is like a cornucopia, plenty of flowers and fruit combined. Vibrant colours, yellow, blue, red and deep purple. Smell of freshness and growth in the spring. Generous to a fault she goes out of her way to help everyone, not just the worthy, but also complete losers like Purvis.

'Hello,' she says to the incongruous couple, 'have you brought a new member to join us?' Sally's mind is idling, radiating good will; Belinda's mind responds accordingly, losing its deathly blue sickness and slowly being restored to hopeful pink'. Purvis' mind remains more or less unchanged but basks a bit more in the presence of the two women. Slowly and reassuringly, Sally completes Belinda's provisional membership. By the time the shiny new membership card shoots out of the machine, Belinda has found the confidence of a timid rabbit and her mind is glowing pink with a hint of blue here and there, amongst the sags. Purvis and Belinda head for the putting area. Purvis' grip on the vulnerable mind increases with each step.

Sally looks benignly after them, thinking thoughts of romance and true love ending happily ever after, rather than the more likely twilight of drudgery and self induced misery for Belinda. I see her active mind turn to more hopeful topics - her mind radiating with excitement and pleasure. I cannot tell what she is thinking but it is clear it is a lovely thought.

Mar-14

Most Experienced Lecturer in Mathematics

Iosef Borilin was the most experienced lecturer in the Mathematics Faculty. He was the senior Reader in Pure Mathematics. He had two places of work, his office and the lecture theatre. His office had one shelf of books and on his desk were usually three issues of different mathematical journals including the latest Fundamenta Mathematicae.

However, when he walked across campus to one of the lecture theatres, he took nothing with him. No briefcase, no file, not a scrap of paper. He would step on to the rostrum exactly on time, pick up a piece of chalk and start writing on a roller board they used in those days. He would pause from time to time to explain the greater context of what he was teaching. Occasionally he would pause to ask if there were any questions. When reviewing problems he would sometimes ask which we found easy, which ones hard. He knew which ones we could not do.

I went to a Faculty party, I forget for what now, and he was there smiling and nodding benignly. A junior lecturer prompted him with the story of why he never used notes. Early in his career he was lecturing in India and his students complained that with his notes he had access to information, which they did not. He promptly put his notes away and never used them again.

The other thing I should mention, he did not teach the same courses year after year, but different ones each year.

Mar-14

Birdman Comes in a Van

Birdman comes in a van. Like white van man but his van

is blue. The door is a sliding one, on the passenger side of the van. When it opens you can see how he lives and flies. On every space on the walls there are things to make life more livable and flying possible. Mostly they are held in place with small strips of elastic, knives, forks, spoons and an altimeter or two. There is a cooker and woodburner opposite the door. A bed towards the rear of the van. A shower made from a sprayer more usually found in a greenhouse.

Under the bed are the harnesses and para-gliders magnificent to see soaring out over the downs and across country. Few are skilled as he is, for he has clocked up thousands of hours flying time in the last thirty years. None have survived so long. Few have flown so high. Some have flown further, including his son, who holds the British pilots record of 376 kilometres and first went flying with his father in a hang glider when he was eight.

Birdman has two para-gliders to choose from depending on wind speed. Usually he is on top of the stack spiralling up, taking tips from the birds as to where the best lift is, watching the other para-gliders. Usually he lands back on top of the hill, but if he flies off across country with a paraglider, he hitches a lift or catches the train back.

Mar-14

Love at Last Light

Christopher dropped Georgina off at her parents' house and drove straight on to his mother's. The honeymoon was the first extended period he had spent with Georgina, or with any woman come to that. And if the strain resulted in a slight relief in being on his own, Christopher put this aside with the thought that this was only natural as he had got married so late. He was nearly forty and Georgina a couple of years older.

'Hello Mother,' he called out as he entered the spacious front hall. When his father died, his mother moved to a smaller house - this one was only five bedrooms. She came sweeping in to the hall like a sailing ship in full rig.

'Hello darling - how did it go? Did you manage to perform?' she asked, smiling benignly. Her question was a general one, but in this context was slightly more to the point than usual. Christopher took it in his stride and replied in kind.

'Well I don't think the earth moved off its orbit but I think we hit it off with a distinctive tremble. It is a bit tricky adjusting to being a couple and all that sort of thing but it seems to be going well.'

She tilted her head and looked searchingly at him. 'So we will see but it seems you might be ready to settle down to married life.'

He grinned sheepishly back at her.

Christopher would be going back to work soon; he was a successful merchant banker as his father had been. Next day he put off getting up as long as possible and drove slowly back to Georgina's parents' house. It was a huge imposing manor with a sweeping drive. He went directly to an upstairs drawing room. As he stepped into the room he saw Georgina by the window looking out at his car.

He started saying, 'Hello darling...' but then he stopped as she turned round. He felt a rush of emotion and embarrassment. He started stammering at his mistake but then he saw that she too looked struck silent as their eyes met. He walked slowly towards her and stood very close to her without her moving. Their proximity was intoxicating.

Christopher said, 'You must be Philippa - I'm sorry, I got confused but you're wearing clothes very like Georgina's.'

'Don't apologise - all my clothes are worn out or in the wash, so I borrowed some of Georgina's. I have always borrowed from my big sister but I think now the opportunity will decrease. I'm sorry I missed the wedding - I only got back the day before you did from your honeymoon.'

There was a silence and her fingers fluttered on his arm. With a single movement they embraced, a deep passionate hug that was natural and spontaneous.

Christopher had been back at work for a couple of weeks and he and Georgina had been adjusting to married life. Over supper one evening, Georgina lurched into conversation.

'I am going to take Philippa to the airport tomorrow.'

'Is she off on her travels again? I got the impression she wanted to do a bit of consolidation back here for a while.'

'I think you were right - but she has fallen in love with a married man and I think she wants to consolidate away from England.'

'Oh I say, that is bad luck - she is awfully noble, that sister of yours.'

Georgina looked at him, strain showing in her face, 'Yes - it was the way we were brought up, doing the right thing is not always obvious or so easy to do.'

'Quite.' His smile was as strained as hers.

Christopher knew she knew, and she knew he did.

Years went by with Philippa living in the States - Christopher saw her at her father's funeral but he missed her when her mother died as he was on a long business trip. His own mother died and he decided to keep her house as an investment. Georgina fell ill a few weeks after their twentieth wedding anniversary. She was in and out of hospital several times as they found more; chemotherapy and surgery. She fought hard for three years but then quietly started putting her affairs in order. Christopher took a long owed holiday and they sat in the garden. Fortunately it was a good summer, not too hot but warm and dry with beautiful sunsets.

Christopher went in to get a drink for her, lemonade and grapefruit, and when he came out she had died looking breathtaking.

On the last page in the file Georgina had prepared was a single sheet written in her neat handwriting giving Philippa's contact details. Nothing else.

Christopher telegraphed Philippa.

'Georgina died in the garden in the sunshine yesterday. Funeral Thursday week. I can meet you at Heathrow.'

The reply came back.

'Landing Tuesday week at 8am. See you there.'

He waited at the exit. So different to all those years ago in the drawing room. Full of people and noise. He caught sight of her as the number of people coming out was thinning away.

She stopped on the other side of the bar. They could not hear any of the noise nor see anything but each other.

'I will sell up here. If you will have me, I will come to America.'

She kissed him and clung to him.

Mar-14

Dead Ring

She chose her clothes carefully – from the less used end of her wardrobe. Nothing too colourful or garish; her aim was to blend into her surroundings and not stand out in the crowd. That was difficult as her figure usually attracted attention in most situations. She managed to find a suitable grey combination that went with a shapeless coat. It was a long journey the last leg of which was by rail through beautiful countryside. The line had been upgraded since she last travelled home, but the country was still just as beautiful. Running along the valley in that beauty would bring out the best in most people, but she was unmoved, fixed on her mission with obsessive intent. She glanced up when the ticket inspector came into the carriage. Outside the window, the hills had changed to be more jagged and hostile.

'Tickets please,' said the inspector despite the fact she was the single traveller in this carriage. She stood up and slipped her coat off making him stare even though she was wearing the dowdy outfit.

'I'm so sorry, you've caught me unprepared, I wasn't expecting a ticket inspection just now.' She bent over in front of him to pick up a large handbag and start rummaging through the content. Now and again she'd stop and fix him in a hypnotic stare.

'I expect you're constantly getting ditsy women like me who misplace their tickets?'

'I've seen my share – but few as comely as what I see now,' he said with a grin.

'I showed it at the station but I wasn't sure it would be valid as it is a while since I bought it.'

'I'm sure we can sort something out,' he said with another knowing grin. Finally she produced the rather tatty ticket.

'This is it but I've to get off here – is it ok?'

'Just this once - but only as it is you. Don't expect I'll let you off so lightly on your return journey.'

She got off the train hurriedly and started walking into the wind as quickly as she could. She knew she didn't have much time to spare. She covered the distance to the church in record time and managed to slip in with the last of the guests, before the bride arrived. She sat quietly at the back on the groom's side, there was more space there. No one challenged her.

The bride arrived in all her glory and the familiar ceremony started to wend its way towards the all-important vows.

She caught the words "....Lawful Impediment ..." and stood up, moving into the aisle at the eleventh hour.

'I do – she's already married.' Her voice carried all around the small church as she took a folded wedding certificate from her bag and held it high.

She walked down the aisle right between the unhappy couple and handed the certificate to the Minister, who looked bemused – they'd never covered this in his training.

A screeching banshee wail came from the bride, 'The bitch, the f-ing bitch, she's lying just to screw things up, she's made this up. She's a jealous cow that I went to school with, but she can't bear the thought of me being happy.'

The groom went a grey white, like a streaked sky. He didn't say anything as she smiled at him and fixed his eye. The bride catching the interchange started to spit and hiss like a malevolent kettle.

The best man was transfixed and let the groom's ring slip down while he just managed to catch the bride's ring. The church was deathly quiet, you could have heard an angel drop on a pin head. Instead the sound of a dead ring, as it slipped slowly and bounced away, carried through the arches of the church. Followed by an audible sigh as the collective breath was expelled from the guests.

She turned and walked away, back down the aisle, through the wooden door and out into the wind.

She hoped the same ticket inspector would be on the train. Fresh meat. She'd worked up an appetite.

Mar-14

Boris and Doris: Match Made in a Mangle

Lillian had a flat white face that constantly verged on the expressionless. When her husband had been alive there had been someone she could talk to, providing an audience for her endless jibes against others. Now he was dead these treacle covered barbs made their way out to anyone who hesitated by her side, in a shop, on the steps of a hall or museum - or in a café.

'I suppose he is salt of the earth – but from where I am sitting it looks like he should be doused in salt – like a slug.'

Lillian was sitting at the table next to Doris when Boris walked in. Doris was startled by the unexpected comment from a mere acquaintance in a café. Doris looked with disinterest at the man Lillian was talking about. Boris did not frequent this semi genteel establishment – he was here on a mission. He walked past the tables and went through some lifeless curtains to a staff only area. Doris looked dubiously at Lillian as raised voices came from deep in the bowels of the restaurant.'

'There – you should get hitched to that mendacious man, the two of you would be well matched.' Lillian almost spat the words out as if driven to be hurtful.'

'You vicious old trollop – if you are such a cupid you should prove you are not just a loud mouth bitch but get us together, rather than yack, yack on about it.' Meek and feeble Doris was enraged most uncharacteristically. Doris blushed a faint pink in her tired cheeks and looked so contrite that it was surprising the floor did not just open up and swallow her through pain of embarrassment.

Lillian also seemed to suffer discomfort but it was not clear if this was embarrassment or too tight a waistband. She spluttered and blustered.

'To match you with anything less than a hippo would be nothing short of miracle genius.'

'You are nothing more than a shrivelled up old hag intent on destroying all happiness in your path,' said Doris – again suffering embarrassment and derision at the hands of the other, who was more experienced and had a better-versed barbed tongue. Lillian stopped to consider, what perverse form of human nature caused this consideration is difficult to say. However, she resolved something, behind that flat expressionless face she came to a decision. She strode down to the end of the café and bawled at Boris.

'Boris when you have done your worst there I want a word with you.'

There was a respectful hush for a moment or two, then a bull-roaring stampede from Boris with much thunder and little lightening. He emerged outraged and disgruntled.

'That silly cow, that ungrateful slag,...' Boris seemed to be unclear what to say next as he lumbered out through the curtain.

'Never mind that,' said Lillian, 'I have got a far better

proposition – do you know Doris?'

'What, little sour puss Doris?'

'Yes – well do you know her?'

'Well not in the biblical sense but I have met her once or twice.'

'Well if you do get to know her - in the biblical sense – then we could make a killing as no one in the town thinks you are man enough for the job.'

'So - would you split the winnings with me?'

'Oh yes – if you bed that witch woman you can have half, if you marry her you can have the lot.'

'Will you shake on it, knowing if you go back on your word I will crush you?'

Lillian's face twitched, showing a rare glimmer of emotion.

'I will not go back on my word – I will show her.'

Feb-14

Remarkable Place

On the way from Mukalla to the Empty Quarter in Arabia, after you have been passed Shibam, you come to an unusual place. Well, I suppose Shibam is unusual, the New York of the ancient Middle East first mentioned in our third Century, seven stories high made entirely of mud. Only baking each floor in the midday sun ensures it stays standing at that many floors high above the ground. On the way you need to continue north east until you reach a high area where there are two rows of big stones set six feet apart.

For some reason the sand here is made from big, vicious

grains, that embed themselves in tender skin stretched out in the sun. The wind hurls the sharp particles nearly horizontally, stinging round the neck and over the cheekbones.

All around the two rows of stones lie flints, made into arrow tips, spear tips, scrapers and a few axe heads; a pre-historic site where flint tools were made by aspiring artisans. Well, maybe, but history seems like it started at different times. In Europe and ancient China, history started before it did in some other places, like North America and here in the Arabian peninsular not far from the Empty Quarter. When history started here is a bit unclear.

Looking at the two rows of big stones it looks like they may have been used to have been sat on – had there been a table or workbench in the middle? Alternatively, it may be more likely the large stones were work positions and the craftsmen sat beside them holding their work down, while chipping away at the flints. How many? Would it have been hot then? How long ago? Were there trees up here then? Shafts for spears, arrows, handles for scrapers and axes.

I looked around at the barren landscape screwing my eyes up as much as possible. Never had I envied camels before but now wished I could close my nostrils to slits, like the camels do in a sand storm. Not that this was a storm but rather a perpetual state of hissing wind, that wore stones round but let flints stay as sharp as the day they were chipped into shape. No trees as far as the edges of this place. Maybe they had taken the flints far away to the lower areas where the monsoon blossomed, most but not every year, and fitted wood to their flints there.

Chipping flints causes regular sparks – they would have

fallen on rock and sand up here. I picked up a flint and looked at the honey brown faces that met on ridges along a backbone. This was a scraper for preparing the skin of an animal, a goat for a large water carrier. The skin weeps a little water, which evaporates and keeps it cool. Some things have not changed; this method has not been improved on even now.

There are no signs of living here – just regular work. Most likely they slept and ate in another more hospitable place and came here to work. Something had changed and the time had come to move on, leaving the flints on the ground.

Feb-14

The Two Wolf-Cats

The two girls were like wolf-cats, not pretty but they were very striking. They had wide generous mouths, wide eyes and extraordinary eyebrows that started slightly above their nose and made a steep climb up their foreheads like a pair of wings, giving a feline wolf-like appearance. They were so similar that at a very early age their father had decided that one of them needed a private and distinguishing dot so he at least could tell them apart.

He set a precedent in that they had to pick a bead each from the jar to decide which got the mark. Serina was the one with the dot and Selena the one without. Only the girls and their father knew that the dot was just on the hairline on Serina's neck. While she was young he could just feel it raised on her skin, as she grew up then he sometimes would need to check her neck to make sure they did not play tricks on him.

Their father, Afanafisy, was a large criminal in every sense of the word. A big man who bore little resemblance to his two oldest daughters. A ruthless animal who loved his children fiercely. Successive women came in his life but he made them sign an agreement that meant that they could leave at any time. They could go but they had to leave any children behind and take 100,000 for each full year they had stayed. Of course, the agreement was not enforceable in law but the alternative was also clear, in a concrete pillar, the bottom of the river or from a tall building. No one could remember Serina and Selena's mother except perhaps Afanafisy, the memory of which he kept to himself.

Serina and Selena did not mix much with their half brothers and sisters – very occasionally one of the brothers would not take the hint to leave them alone and came out of it very badly, either through humiliation or sometimes tied up somewhere, stuck until another member of the household freed them. Before the girls left him they would circle round him, grinning at him, teeth gleaming whitely but seemingly dripping with blood.

The two young girls grew into two young women more similar than twins. As they grew up, from time to time the jar of beads came out and they got picked at random and one thing for one and another for the other. They took jobs in two different hotels that Afanafisy owned, of course chosen at random. Day managers to give them plenty of time for other activities.

Every now and again there would be a crackdown on crime and Afanafisy would bide his time to come through making more money then ever. Until a new Senator was elected who was incorruptible, and the self-declared enemy of crime and Afanafisy in particular. Very closely guarded he escaped assassination twice.

The two daughters were called by their father and the pot of beads produced. This time it was important that he did not know who got the bead with the dot. The one that matched took the small packet of crystals. One daughter went with the Senator the other with his wife. Soon they had coffee and a little while later the senator was writhing in agony and died. Serina and Selena met up in public, with the distraught widow, before the police arrived.

No one could say who killed the senator, indeed when they did tests on the two young women they found something very curious. Every other set of twins ever investigated by the police in modern times have a slight difference in their DNA – out of three billion DNA code sequences they differ by a few, a dozen or so, in some way. Not so with Serina and Selena - their DNA was identical down to every one of the three billion sequences. They did find a small tattoo on the neck of Serina but that did not help them. The women were not twins at all but clones made from the same cells of life in the first few moments. In a democracy, you need to know who to prosecute for a crime and who for a conspiracy. In their case, it was not even clear they knew that there was a conspiracy.

After the police had to release them, a young detective followed them to a nightclub. He observed them unnoticed as they were together in a private box watching others. As they moved round each other, the red and white lights played over their faces and bodies. It looked as if they had a prey between them and they were steadily tearing it to pieces.

Next day Afanafisy was found torn apart amongst the

garbage. A mystery that the police were happy not to solve.

Jan-14

The City is New to Me

The city is new to me, and the language is a jumble of discordant sounds that mean nothing to me as yet. The temperature and smells are also alien, but there right in the middle of the city is a huge shopping mall similar in appearance to those found back home.

One evening after work I walk through the glittering shops on a high walkway, some of the shops familiar household names others not. I find a food hall of cavernous proportions. Around the outside, fast food from around the world; of course the US is represented by burgers and fried chicken but there are also pizzas, nachos, noodles, sushi, paella, curry, local Arabic food and also fish & chips.

I pick spicy Arabic food and sit alone watching the unfamiliar world go by. Mostly I see expat workers and visitors crisscrossing the hall to sit in groups eating meals of babele. Co-workers from opposite sides of the globe working and eating together. It is the same in my work; there are fourteen people of eleven nationalities in my team. Communications take on a couple of extra dimensions. Even facial expressions differ considerably between the cultures that come together in this city.

I notice a family of Arabs making their way towards the food hall; four women lead by a lozenge of a cocooned woman. She has a headscarf but face showing and is well padded. Next to her is a smaller woman talking on her mobile phone. Behind her is another taller woman – maybe I read the signs wrong but I would say at a guess this lady is not happy. Maybe she has had a bad day at the spinning wheel but I would suggest things are not going her way. The final woman in the column is younger, more animated, prettier and talking faster on her phone. Last in the line bringing up the rear is a man aged before his time, pushing a pram – not an old fashioned one with big wheels but a cot on what will be a buggy. There are quite a few children ranging in age around the column of adults so I guess the pram has seen some service. The disgruntled woman answers her flip-phone and her manner brightens. The small woman at the front hangs up and starts talking to the woman at the helm. They make their way to the same outlet my meal came from, only they clear two shelves. The main man bringing up the rear, peels a wodge of Riyal to hand over – I wonder why he is using cash rather than a plastic card as most do. They take over two fair sized tables while the baby is parked still by his father. I wonder which of the four women is the baby's mother. Just possibly the mother is the fifth wife and is away visiting her sister. If that is the case I can see most of the time one or other wife would be away and he would be left holding one or other baby.

A new group of Arabs catch my eye – well in fact there are two groups, young men showing off to a group of young women. The same the world over but this reminds me of Russian Roulette. These women have full veils, their slits of eyes giving away the least with crinkles and gleams. They get their food and sit looking discreetly back and forth, a choreographed dance of eyes to ensure they never meet in full. One woman attracts my attention, she had been bold and strident wearing her veil. Now she has to eat her demeanour dissolves – her confidence flows away as she has to show her chin, mouth and lips. She crouches in her seat, her face coming as close as it can to the plate. She uses her hand cupped round her food to protect her mouth from chance eyes.

The big family is on the move – I don't think anyone, except maybe the baby, has taken an interest in the head or maybe more accurately tail of the family. It is time for me to leave too, as I walk towards a lift a small family of Qataris emerge – they have a child of about four, twins of two and a baby. One father, one mother. Each one of the four children has a Filipino nanny.

Outside the temperature gets to about 50 centigrade, inside the food hall it is less than half that. They do everything differently here, look below the surface and keep an open mind. The city is still new to me but it begins to mean more now.

Jan-14

Person Unknown

In a category of your own, a giant in the garden of your imagination, wit and humour abound and knowledge of World War Two second to hardly anyone.

You defy normal detection, having a very different exterior to the depths of the interior of your writing. By stealth you creep into our minds and spill out laughing.

A fair-weather roar heralds your arrival but no lion in sight.

If you know who you are don't expect anyone else to believe you.

Dec-13

Hopper Bar

The shiny new bar had just opened; it was a bit out of the way. It was very clearly a theme bar lifted directly from Hoppers' Nighthawk.

A man was sitting alone at the bar with a small drink into which he stared moodily – his face had a curious flattened appearance, his nose pointed and hooked.

A woman in very tight jeans, or pants as they'd say in the USA, walked into the bar not looking at him but came and sat close to him.

'What's an ugly bastard like you doing in a nice joint like this?' she asked, her voice smooth and urbane as a tilting train.

'Just trying to figure out how exactly you get into those jeans,' he said. He'd been admiring her figure-clinging jeans as she walked into the bar by looking in the mirrors, which gave him a good view of her, in front and behind, but without being obvious.

'Well,' she said with deliberation, 'you could start by buying me a drink.'

'Sure, but you seem mighty familiar, have I seen you around here before?'

'Often trash like you is familiar with me, but I don't get familiar – I don't recall you.'

'Will your drink be an Icebreaker – or I think they do a special here "The Ice Maiden Breaker" – with a cherry. Would that be your drink by any chance?'

'Well, well, maybe I have you wrong, maybe you've the

staying power to get in my good books – you might even manage to get in my jeans one day.'

'If you're willing to give it a second chance then they look as if they will just peel off you – they're so ripe.'

She laughed for the first time and looked at her watch nervously.

'Only half an hour before we open – do you think our marketing will have worked?'

'Oh yes, I'm sure it will have done – loads of time for me to get into those jeans. I know just the place, the broom cupboard will be perfect,' said her long-term man and business partner.

Nov-13

State of Jeopardy

I remember venturing out with the girl from next door, Jill. It was a warm spring day, arriving after a long and dreary winter. We must have been nine going on ten. Encouraged by the weather and being a year older than last spring we went further than ever before, under the bridge and into the woods. Just as we were on the point of turning back we saw a clearing and beyond it there was a crazy wooden house.

We crossed the clearing and looked at the path that led down to the house. There was no gate but a sign by the path showing the passage of time. On it was written,

"State of Jeopardy" then underneath in smaller letters "You enter at your own risk".

'What does jeopardy mean?' asked Jill with a slight quaver in her voice.

'I'm not sure – but I think it might be like danger.' I replied in all seriousness.

Jill giggled then pointed at a bench and said,

'That looks safe enough – shall we sit there and see what happens?'

'Fine.' I replied not feeling as brave as I sounded.

We sat in the sunshine tensing for a shock that never really came. But after a while we both noticed a man sitting under a tree. He was difficult to see as he blended in to the trees and plants around him like 'coordinated wall paper'.

Jeopardy, as we came to know him, was an extraordinary person. A timeless creature, scarcely human, so wise his eyes could swallow up evil, like whirlpools of forgiveness. His face was weather-beaten with creases that beckoned you in. His hair was long and wavy down to his shoulders. He was a formidable oracle of knowledge, knowing an inexhaustible supply of almost every aspect of human activity. He could astound and amaze for hours if he put his mind to it; but he very rarely did – rather letting interesting snippets out like inadvertent mishaps.

Like most knowledgeable people he didn't rush in to reply – instead he'd explore first, to understand what you were asking and if the answer was inside you. This could be quite frustrating – especially if you did have the answer but weren't sure.

When we saw him that first day we weren't sure if he'd seen us – of course he had. He spoke in a calm musical voice that sounded as if it was produced from his core.

'Well, what've we here? What've you come to learn?' he beckoned to us.

'Why do you think we've come to learn?' asked Jill.

'You've no choice – you'll have to wait until you're old to forget,' he said.

'Is forgetting the opposite to learning?' I asked.

'Not really, not learning is more like not being able to remember,' he said.

'Oh – I see how forgetting is bit like unlearning,' I said, getting interested.

'Yes – it seems that when we're young we learn things that stay with us for life but as we get older it gets more and more difficult to learn new things – eventually some people seem to go back into childhood.'

'My gran is like that,' said Jill.

I looked at him, narrowing my eyes in the strong sunlight and he seemed to merge into the background of trees and plants. I listened to the sound of the wind in the trees – it had a strength that seemed to flow all around him like the sea but he didn't drown or get wet. I could imagine him flying with a powerful strength beneath his wings. In a man sized kite.

I went to visit him many times over the years, sometimes with Jill, sometimes on my own. When we were young and we tried going too often, when we were bored, we'd find he wasn't there. Well I think he may well have been there but we couldn't see him – I think it was something he could do, blend into his surroundings so well that he could remain unobserved.

All through my schooling and studies I went to see him and he encouraged me with many questions – I'm sure he knew the answers but waited for me to answer them. Tenacious as a thrush with a snail he'd continue to extract enlightenment.

By the time I was twenty four he didn't seemed to have aged since I met him fifteen or so years before. I finally screwed up my courage – I suppose it was a risk that he might banish me from the State of Jeopardy.

I told him I was in love. With him.

'Do you think you've learnt enough to explain why some things can't be explained?' he said smiling; I think the smile was shining all the way through him.

Oct-13

Warrior Woman

Warrior woman wearied by time, once furious, often feisty.
Now prone, doing Saint Vitus' dance on her own.
Bruised with age, ring worn thin with passing years.
Her lover dead for half her life. His memory
the core of her grief.
Soon to pass.

Oct-13

Not Quite a Minute of Memory

Can art be locked into numbers,
rhyme or meaning?
For forgetting
art knows no bounds,
is crime indeed as well as words.
Memory crime,
not to commit
a clerihew,
is innocent of nothing new.
Just forgetting
this minute is
easy to do.

Oct-13

Trauma

Browley in Kent used to lie on the main London to Dover road but many years ago a new road was built and to the relief of the village the traffic declined to a trickle overnight.

At the bottom of the hill in a small house on the corner lived the Bulgers who were watching the quiz Family Frontiers. Despite the smallness of the house the Bulger family consisted of Ma and Pa Bulger, Granddad Bulger, Nana Biggins, the kids: Tom, Dick, Harriet and the twins Mable and Able.

The snow was falling silently outside. On TV the Smyth family had played the joker in an attempt to win a holiday to Iceland when there was a strange series of rumbling noises and the earth trembled as a lorry cab came in to the lounge and stopped just by Able's head, disturbing the domestic bliss.

No one was directly hurt – it is true that Nana and Harriet both went into hysterics and Ma had to slap them. Also Granddad's view of the TV was obscured and he missed the triumph of the Smyth family that he never really recovered from.

The cab of the lorry was partly in the bedroom above but eventually Joe, the driver, managed to climb out through the broken windscreen and fall on his back.

'God help me,' he said shaking, as he looked up afraid of all the faces peering down at him; he did not seem to know where he was.

Just then Able started yelling as the front wheel of the lorry was on his hood and he could not sit up. Pa went and got some scissors and cut the hood off to free Able and Ma managed to find space on the sofa for Joe to sit, so that she could go and make him a cup of strong sweet tea.

'It seems like a case of amnesia,' said Ma after she had given Joe his tea and asked him if he needed to phone anyone. Ma held his hand and patted him on his back and he regained a little colour. But all he could say was.

'God help me.'

They all watched the end of Family Frontiers, which was at the stage of seeing how the family from the last episode had enjoyed their holiday. As the theme tune was playing the emergency services broke in through the back door. In actual fact they could have just opened the door, as it was not locked. Fortunately the house withstood this final assault and everyone including Joe was evacuated safely.

The lorry was more or less ok but the house was a complete write off.

Oct-13

Origin

He'd finished a busy week early. On the way back through the park he stopped at a junction. He couldn't be bothered to change his plans and go home to England; instead he turned in the opposite direction and walked to the Musée d'Orsay.

He decided to go to the top floor but as he was thirsty

and in no rush he went to the Café and got a cup of tea first. He lingered watching a beautiful woman, about the same age as him, reading a French magazine at the next table. She was sitting against the radiator. Her hair, soft dark chestnut, was arresting, he'd no idea if it came out of a packet, but if it did he suspected the people from the adverts would be interested in her. Her face had a beauty of symmetry and friendliness but also with lovely lines and serenity.

He looked at her curves and her clothes and thought "French". Her handbag was small and the flap not secured. She moved to get up and he noticed her matching wallet slide from her handbag, down the side of her table. As she moved past him he felt he was going to lose this opportunity to speak to her - he was tongue-tied. At the last moment he stood up and broke in to scrambled French.

'Mademoiselle, excuse moi, mais votre sac à main a glissé vers le bas …'

'It's all right mate, I speak English,' she said deflating him with flawless English but with a French accent.

'Oh – I see, it is just your purse fell out of your handbag and behind the pipes.' He moved to her table and pointed to her purse. She came close to him, bending over the table; he could see her curves and the smooth skin on her face and arm at even closer range now. He shifted the table but she couldn't get her hand between the two pipes. She looked at him with dismay.

'Maybe I could try to hold the bars apart and you could slip your hand in?' he asked.

'Can we try please? I don't want to get the Museum people to do it unless there's no alternative.'

He got on the floor and grasped the pipes and pulled as hard as he could, his body went taut with strain, his muscles bulged all along his arms and torso. She bent over next to him and slipped her hand between the pipes and grabbed the purse. His strength gave out and her hand was trapped by the wrist between the bars.

'Give me a minute and I'll open them once more – my strength will come back,' he said feeling her soft body gently touching his.

'I don't know why I trust a complete stranger, an English one at that, but I do,' she said.

He grinned at her, their faces only centimetres apart.

'Here goes then – now or you're stuck here for life,' he put his feet against the wall and his whole body strained as if the last thing he wanted was to be stuck to a beautiful woman on a wet autumn afternoon.

She managed to pull her hand with the purse clear and he let go of the pipes trying to deny the pain in his hands. She took hold of the outside of his hands, holding them tenderly, looking at the palms.

'Ouch – they look sore. No one has ever saved me from the grips of an old French radiator – how can I thank you good sir?' she said with an impish grin.

He looked at her astounded even in jest. 'Well I thought you were French but now you sound English – in any case as an English gentleman I couldn't ask for more than the pleasure of being of service to you.'

Her face lit up and her smile was caring, 'Well I'm both French and English. You must at least allow me to show you round the galleries, unless you've already been round?'

'Oh no, I stopped to have tea and study the map, I came to this floor as I knew I wanted to see the Impressionists – but it would be great if you'd show me. Are you half French and half English then?'

'Non – absolutely not, I'm wholly French but English

through and through,' she laughed at his confusion.

She led him through the gallery pulling him along with joy and exuberance to each major section but stopping quietly while he looked, sometimes holding his hand demurely until he'd finished studying a painting. They sat at the end of the top gallery and spoke quietly about themselves.

She was strict and said no real names. They should remain anonymous, and invent names for each other. He went first, quite quickly getting the point of this.

'I think you suit the name "Ingle" – I found you curled up by a radiator, which is like a fire, but it also means an intimate friend or caress. Maybe your whole name could be "Ingle Nook", what do you think?' he asked.

'Well "Ingle" is fine but I drawn the line at "Ingle Nook", we only need forenames,' she smiled quietly while she still pondered.

'Am I so unmemorable that you're at a loss for either English or French names for me?' he said as straight-faced as he could.

'No, the reason I hesitate is that my name for you may seem a bit forward - but it is neither French nor English – I'd like to choose a Norse name Oskar spelt with a K, which means "spear from the gods",' Ingle said.

'Well I'm glad that's sorted,' he said.

'What other pictures would you like to see, Oskar?' she asked.

He laughed and said; 'I think there are some Van Goghs, and then the "Origin of the World" too please.'

'Good choice, but most gentlemen I know can't look at the Courbet without blushing, well when they're with me they do.'

'I think I may fail your test as a gentlemen,' he said seriously and she laughed.

They spoke about their lives hesitantly – they were both engaged. They both had brothers and sisters, mothers and fathers, and jobs.

The Courbet was in a quiet part; there were only a few people in the room. They held hands as an established couple might.

'The Origin - it is more convincing as you can't see her face, just her body,' said Oskar without blushing.

Sep-14

Scuba-diving

In our family the story goes that I could swim before I could walk. It is true that the only time when I do not feel clumsy is when I am in or under water; my true habitat must have been the sea. I have swum with seaweed, jellyfish, dolphins, sharks (not too close), crayfish, cuttlefish, turtles and even rays (not too close to these either). I swam for my school team in England and for my pleasure in the Red Sea.

So when I discovered I was going to swim in the Caribbean Sea I was very pleased, but when I discovered I was going to go scuba diving I was excited. So OK, I was going to have to learn to scuba, maybe lose a bit of naturalness of being in the sea but I was sure this was something I was going to remember until my grey matter finally decided to emigrate.

Some things fill you with fear; skydiving would be one for me, but not diving in lovely clear warm water in the

Caribbean sunshine. In fact if I was recovering from illness then I guess I would like to go to such a place. Gentle exercise in the calm – with a fantastic backdrop. I know that hurricanes can wreck the whole place but not in April.

The thing I learnt about scuba diving is that it is good not to rush – in fact for me a more apt description might be scuba sinking, slow steady calm movements letting your body adapt to slip quietly below the surface, not startling the local inhabitants. In this way you could avoid missing out on the most beautiful sights, the rich plant and animal life living close to the shore. Of course sometimes the fish or other sea creatures were disturbed by the slightest movement and shot away into the distance; but often it was possible to come across underwater terrain that revealed the most amazing sights.

Sights that do not have fitting terrestrial similes. You could say that some of the vegetation is like underwater forests but there are some fundamental differences in the way vegetation is supported by water and blown in the wind. Fish and other sea creatures can move about in three dimensions underwater in a completely different way to birds in the air. It is as if some are spring-loaded, leaving one place and reappearing in another as if they were being teleported across the distance separating the two points. Another curious feature of watching these creatures from a seemingly different world is that they emerge from shells, holes and cavities in the seabed at unexpected angles – with no regard to up and down.

Even relatively near the shore the colours are very vibrant, sending one of two signals – "hey look at me" or the other more sinister "eat me and you are dead meat". Being a mere human out of normal habitat I err on the side of safety and do not try to eat anything at all, just in case.

I instantly forgot what PADI stood for but I enjoyed a brief course in how not to die. What I did not get from the course was that I needed to take things very steadily. Including breathing. If I took a deep breath when underwater I was likely to rise about six or seven feet and this could result in me shooting to the surface like some sort of manic buoy – when this happened then the rest of the diving party had to surface too, which was pretty annoying to everyone, including me. After a few mishaps I gravitated to my natural role, the art of breathing shallowly and sticking to the bottom. We came across a chasm in the seabed – in truth only probably 20 feet or so, but it seemed to us that we had reached the end of the earth and we were stepping out into an adventure.

Sep-13

Flune

Flune was a curious looking boy, a little below average height, broad but not fat, his face slightly flat and with eyes that were arresting for several reasons – their colour, they glowed and his look was very penetrating. His skin and hair were almost translucent too.

He lived in Surburbiton some distance from the centre of Metropolis. All the roads were extremely neat and tidy and as Flune walked along he kept precisely the same distance from the row of angled bricks along the side of the gardens. This superficial order was very thin and didn't conceal frequent crime and corruption.

His mother, Eileen, was a very average person, typical in many respects except in that she only had one child and there was no sign of a father. Flune knew she was not his mother but had not the heart to tell her he knew. What he knew was she had found him in the park on her way back from a drunken party. He knew the story she told, she very rarely went to drunken parties, hardly ever slept with a man and absolutely never slept with several and could not remember who the father was. However that is the tale she told, just to a few people who asked about Flune. He arrived about twelve years ago and now fewer people asked anything about Flune. They were too scared.

Flune came in the back door to find his mother bound to a chair with one man holding a knife to her throat and three more standing about with guns. The man with a knife looked at Flune and was amazed to see purple eyes looking at him from a strange translucent face.

Flune spoke, 'put those weapons down'. The knife and guns clattered to the floor. The men all gripped their heads and fell to the floor too, writhing in pain. After a few moments Flune moved towards his mother and the men passed out; he freed his mother from her bonds and she rubbed herself where she had been bound and gave him a hug.

Eileen looked at the men lying on the floor and asked, 'What are we going to do with them? I don't suppose there is any point in asking how you did that to them.' On previous occasions when she asked him how he did things he found it impossible to explain.

'Well we don't want to call the police – all that happens is we get loads of questions and they take ages to go away.' He replied. 'I think it is better if they just wake up in the garden in a while. Shall we strip them to their underpants like usual? How did they get in?'

'Oh they rang the bell saying they were collecting for something – then they burst in.'

Flune and his mother began to drag the men out of the back door and left them in an unceremonious and more or less naked pile.

'What did they want?' asked Eileen.

'Oh – they seemed to think they could force me into stealing lots of money for them by holding a knife to your throat. Obviously not very bright.'

It was nearing the end of the summer holidays and Flune, who had taken his A-levels early, got his results. He could go to any University but had decided that it would be best to wait a couple of years.

It was quite a surprise to Eileen when Flune brought her a letter one morning with plane tickets to Syria.

'What an earth are you up to now?' she asked.

'Well now I am twelve and not going to University just yet, so I thought I should start trying to solve world peace. If I get that solved then maybe I could move on to all this crime and corruption and maybe even illness and other suffering.'

'Ok darling.' she said fondly, looking at him through misty eyes.

For some reason Flune did not handle aeroplanes very well. Shortly after take off be began to look even more odd than usual – the tips of his ears started to go faint purple, a bit like his eyes. He told Eileen he would meet her in the queue at the bottom of the steps of the aircraft once it had landed. He stood up and got his rucksack down and draped a blanket over it in his own seat. Eileen watched him walk down the aisle and slowly fade away. She had never seen him do that before but she had seen him once gradually sink into a rock by the sea. That had been pretty scary, as it seemed he had to leave his swimming trunks behind.'

She had quite early on realised that his physics were

different to other people.

When she got off the aeroplane she was a bit laden with her own hand luggage and his rucksack, but within a few steps on the tarmac he was taking his rucksack from her.

Once they were through Passport Control and Customs they got a very unwilling taxi driver to take them towards the war zone. Gradually the firing began to cease and a grenade landed in front of the taxi but failed to go off. By midday they took a walk down a pot-marked street; in one of the bars there was a CNN news broadcast all about a new unexplained cease-fire.

It seemed that Flune could stop guns firing and bombs exploding as well as sink into rocks.

Aug-13

Party Time

I have always had a soft spot for Harry, it has always been proper, he is a bit of a rogue and a bit of extra attention never goes amiss when you are slaving away to keep things nice and nobody notices. So when he first asked me to go to parties with him I was surprised, well actually gobsmacked, as he would say. He is a strange mixture of gentleman and lady-killer. I think he wanted me along, so he would not look so desperate – do you know what I mean?

He took me shopping the week before the first party to get me a lovely dress. It looked really good, not too showy, just tasteful and well made. Really expensive, it was in subdued colours, that's what Harry said - to suit my complexion. It was a fitted evening dress not too low but enough to make Harry twinkle as I came out of the changing room and turn this way and that to show him. Then, even though it felt fine, Harry wanted to check how well it fitted. He he didn't try anything this time and I went back in the changing room and we went to pay. I was very proud that he bought me that dress.

On the evening of the party he did me proud too, he was looking very smart and distinguished in a dark suit and neat trimmed hair. We came in a specially hired car. When we got inside the place there was this really beautiful looking maid ready to take our coats. I thought that Harry was struck dumb but no, he started talking as soon as he could.

'Wow, we are guests of honour to get such a lovely lady to take our coats,' he said beaming at her.

She smiled politely and gave him a ticket, 'Oh no sir, all are guests are special and we treat them just the same.'

Harry managed to catch her hand as she handed him his ticket, 'Look,' he said to me, 'she has given me a ticket – the last place I went she just took my coat so when I left I asked the girl how she knew it was mine. Do you know what she said? She said, "I don't – but it's the one you came in with."' Harry roared at his own joke and the maid looked relieved to get her hand back and laughed politely.

'Come along my dear,' he said to me, 'we better leave this gorgeous girl and find our table.' I smiled at the maid and shook my head and rolled my eyes to show I was used to Harry and his ways.

As we made our way up to the dining room in the lift, I said to Harry, 'This lift seems as old as the building – do you think it is going to break down?'

'Don't worry I would love to be stuck in a lift with you my darling – I can think of something to do that would pass the time – I am sure these good people could be prevailed on to look the other way.'

I could not help blushing – all those people in the lift, what must they be thinking. Fortunately the lift lurched into motion and we made our way to the dining room.

I was beginning to enjoy myself, the food was very tasty all in grand surroundings. I think Harry was in a sort of mini heaven too. He had two maids attending to his needs, every so often he would catch one of them by the arm and she would stop and lean forward to listen to him and off she would go to find him what he was after. He had very little to drink and was content to lay his eyes on their curves not his hands.

After dinner Harry led me out on to the dance floor and I think for a brief period we were the centre of attention with all the lights on us. I think the others looked at me and were impressed that I was holding my own as Harry danced his feet off.

Of course the evening did end and Harry was a total rogue but I did not mind. He dropped me off at home covered with kisses. My husband knows I was out dancing but I don't think he missed me – he just grunted and pointed at the TV. As Harry says, what he doesn't know can't harm him.

Harry said we could go again next month, I hope so.

Aug-13

The Bridge

It was the day after the monsoon had finished; the sun shone and drove away a few pools of rain in the hollows of the rocks. The old white rope and wood bridge creaked in the sun as it dried. It swayed in the breeze as it dried too. The termites were on their veracious march and came across the bridge. In a heavy column they ate their way over and left it so fragile the breeze alone was nearly strong enough to blow it away.

One Time

A goat came scrambling across the bridge. As it reached the far side, the bridge parted and swung into the ravine.
A jeep came roaring up to the bridge; standing on the brakes it skidded to a halt just inches from the edge. Just in time to avoid the drop.

Another Time

A goat came scrambling across the bridge. As it reached the far side the bridge still looked sound.
A jeep came roaring up to the bridge and hit it at full tilt. The bridge fell away. So did the jeep, as it spun in the air the engine cut out. There was a brief eerie silence before jeep and bridge hit the valley far below.

Aug-13

Woodlands in Shadow

In the evening the noises change,
it seems the sights coalesce into shapes not noticed
until now,
some unsettling, some familiar,
the imagination unleashed like a wolf with fear of the
unknown,
if we survive until the morning
everything is imagined and nothing is real in our
memories

Jul-13

Shadow

Not always attached but definitely belonging.
Has no direct use but useful in the heat.
Quite often disturbs as it flits and flickers
in the corner of your eye.
But try to live without one –
the only way is to die.
Ghosts do not have one.

Jul-13

Jurisprudence Hegemony Dies

Jurisprudence Hegemony (1962 to 2011) was a highly successful barrister and politician. It is true she did have one or two foibles, one of which led to her untimely death. But as a character she'd a significant impact on the law courts and on British politics. A truly eccentric person, a woman of all time.

As a young woman she was incorruptible. While she was studying for her law qualifications she was a model of decorum – there was never any hint that she'd achieved any of her very good results by using her physical attributes. But when she got to Chambers it did seem after a few years that her fortunes changed rather abruptly. None of her biographers have ever managed to establish a particular event but it was noted that at some point in the summer of '89 she did appear to dress in a far more eye-catching way. Previously she'd a good relationship with the barristers' clerk (Mr Chumly-Smyth) and her junior barristers' clerk (Bertie Fotherington) but it couldn't be said she got the best cases going. After that summer she'd many very good cases to work on and both Mr Chumly-Smyth and Bertie seemed to be most satisfied with the way Chambers were running. In fact her success lay in obtaining more work for Chambers; generally everyone had more interesting and more high profile cases as a result of her success. Both men were asked from time to time how Ms Hegemony's fortunes changed – they were both completely loyal in saying, with a quiet smile, "through hard work and aptitude". However it is true that rumours did persist.

The rumours didn't confine themselves to Chambers either. If she ever had any dealings with a powerful man socially or through work usually a rumour started circulating after a while. As you can imagine

Jurisprudence Hegemony came in to contact with many powerful men and there were many rumours.

Several times she stood for Parliament and finally secured a marginal seat for Labour, she was accepted directly into cabinet as a junior minister. Rumours of how she got there abound but the tabloids never dared to run an exposé. She made significant contributions to the campaign for equal pay for women as a very young minister.

She lost her seat at the next election and went back to Chambers – both Mr Chumly-Smyth and Bertie were exuberant and business rapidly picked up again. Her usual powers of persuasion and influence didn't seem to have been diminished at all. In fact both political parties seemed very keen to make her life even more influential and she appeared on many boards of important companies and quangos.

Her female critics were rare, as she worked tirelessly to improve equality for women. She took on female clients and won against all the odds. The uncharitable pointed out that these cases usually involved very powerful men.

By the end of the millennium Dame Hegemony had reached a level of respect that's unparalleled. The list of men who'd taken an interest in her seemed endless. If any powerful man in politics, media or other business was rumoured to be having an affair then his associates, and his wife, would breathe a sigh of relief if it was Jurisprudence Hegemony. They knew it would be conducted with the utmost discretion and minimum fuss. In fact it would never be proven. There were never any kiss and tell stories.

Jurisprudence Hegemony had one other weakness apart from powerful men. She loved all the latest gadgets and gismos. She even had a weakness for those handheld digital pets called Tamagotchi. About the size of a digital wristwatch with a similar screen they're generally carried on a keyring. The digital pet has a pseudo life cycle from egg through to adult pet that requires regular attention. Like feeding. If the owner doesn't feed the Tamagotchi then the pet will go through an electronic death, but it should be noted that no living creature suffers during this process.

The precise details of Dame Hegemony's death can't be given for legal reasons but it is understood that she was driving her car – a Jaguar given to her by an admiring client. It appears she'd neglected to check her Tamagotchi before starting out and as a result the little beast started to whinge about being fed or otherwise it would die. It isn't documented who her passenger was; there were a great number of rumours all involving high office or royalty. What's clear though is that there was a witness in the car. We know Jurisprudence Hegemony put her hands through the steering wheel and tried to press the correct buttons to feed the little critter. All while she was driving at about 60mph. Unfortunately there was a bend in the road and without full control of the car, she veered across the carriageway and hit a telegraph pole. Directly where the driver sits. Jurisprudence Hegemony died more or less instantly, the passenger and Tamagotchi survived unscathed.

Jurisprudence Hegemony never married but her knowledge of men wasn't in doubt.

Jul-13

BWV1001

BWV 1001 is more or less as difficult to listen to as this index reference implies. I remember the mosquito nets and heat with the slowly rotating ceiling fan, going to sleep hearing the first bars being played by my father. I was probably about five going on six. We were living in a palace in Mukulla in what is now southwest Yemen.

I was already accustomed to Johan Sebastian Bach so I listened to it with acceptance – it was not until later that I realised it caused in some people uneasy edginess and one girlfriend became quite agitated and had to stop it or go away.

As I grew up I did not get to see my father that much – we spent the summer holidays in Arabia and usually I would get to hear it a couple of times. There was a book published by a travel writer Thessinger in which he described my father as an eccentric political officer who used to fiddle as Arabia burned. This was a bit unfair as my father's playing, both the violin and the recorder, did help him establish a good rapport with many different Arabs from a cross-section of society. Also his musical ability undoubtedly helped him to learn to speak Arabic. This led him to learn to read and write Arabic – quite rare amongst the British at the time.

I also got to hear it in England, usually early in the morning. Every nine months in Arabia he would come home for three months; mostly playing and studying in the British Museum.

BWV 1001 is one of several of Bach's Sonatas for solo violin. It is in G Minor and launches right into a haunting monologue. If you do not like the violin you are not going to like this. If you do not like Bach there is not much hope of you liking it either. To me it is as if it is crafted out of sound into music. From large bending ribs to small ear bones. It is smooth running into rough. It provides questions and solutions simultaneously. It is hard work to listen to but given enough will power it is ultimately satisfying. Every time I hear it, it is familiarly new.

My father came back to England for good when I was about twelve. I got to know him a lot better and heard much more of his music. I was his youngest son and as all good sons do I rebelled – I chose maths, which was a foreign land to him, not England, not Arabia. More like a planet far away in the reaches of his awareness.

I was seventeen when I last heard my father play it – a few days before he died.

Jul-13

Bat Box

Professor Craig was a tall gangly man, old for his years, with a dusty, shabby appearance and he seemed to creak when he moved, if he either stooped or flexed his body.

Rose Wild was a plump woman, slightly gone to seed in her early thirties, cigarette hanging from her mouth. Twice as wide and half the height of the Professor.

They are standing in the staff room, just the two of them.

'Do you think that box moved?' asked Rose.

'I took my eyes off it to look at you,' said the Professor wheezing and creaking as he swayed from side to side. Slowly he started to move towards her, she began to look apprehensive. He came to a stop a few feet away from her as if coming out of a trance just in time before he ran into her.

She crossed her arms over her chest and said nervously,

'Are you alright mate?'

Then changing the subject she said, 'I could have sworn that box just wobbled a bit and I think there is a faint noise coming from it.'

He looked at the box in a puzzled way, 'What sort of noise?' he asked, 'we must not open it but I can prod it if you like.'

She looked very dubious, then compressed her mouth to give the overall impression of a citadel not allowing anything past her.

'Suppose there is something dangerous inside the box?'

'Well,' he replied, 'if there was, I think it would have to have a warning on the box. Don't you agree?'

'I don't know – be careful', she said as his long bony finger reached out and gently nudged the box. The box started to rock and when he retracted his investigating finger it continued to rock.

She panicked and squealed, 'It's making that noise again.'

'I can't hear anything,' he said. He leant over the box like some bent conductor or wizard. He listened intently.

'Yes – that is very strange I can hear a very faint noise – it is as if it is disappearing into a crevice.' He added in a bemused tone.

'You better open it,' she said.

He started to prise the lid open and for the first time she dropped her arms and her lips changed – she came close to him; all notion of her being a citadel and him a predator was gone.

Slowly he opened the lid and revealed the most unexpected sight. Inside was a small creature that most people fear and are repelled by, for inside the box, trembling, was a bat, all fangs and wings. Her hands rested on his arm and she let out a low sound of awe.

Even more extraordinary and for no apparent reason these two people both liked bats.

Jun-13

Purple Time

Sally was one of the most successful scientists of all time. Depending on which way you are travelling through time that is.

She got up that morning, it was a lovely bright morning, came downstairs and found her daughter Lucy on FaceTube making light pictures with her friend Tracy who lived a few miles away. She caught sight of Lucy's pale neck. Sally checked her own hair, she looked in the mirror to see her hair was neatly brushed and her complexion was pale with pink freshness.

Today she had to journey to her laboratory for the experiment – the first interventionist time travel ever. She had all the approvals from the Time Travel Ethics Board and she had volunteered her great great grandfather. He was terminally ill and had died before her great grandfather had been born.

The android, Arthur-ZA23, was going to travel back in time and administer a lethal dose of poison to her great great grandfather three months before her great grandfather was conceived. Arthur would go dressed in clothes of the time, "jeans and tee-shirt" Sally seemed to remember they were called. He would go as a locum doctor – in those days doctors were human so that is why they needed to send an android like Arthur back in time. The robot XZX373 was there to operate the time machine and ensure that Arthur was retrieved safely.

The experiment went perfectly, not a single hitch. As Arthur arrived safely back in the lab Sally, mentally and physically, checked to make sure she had survived.

When she got home Lucy welcomed her. Sally did not think it at all strange that Lucy had purple skin; neither did Sally think it odd when she saw the family photograph in the living room – the whole family were purple.

Jun-13

Fallen Giant

It was a dry summer's day with a hot sandy wind blowing. A long winding road ran along the side of the mountain range, down into the valley. The care worn Land-Rover rocked from side to side, juddering and lurching round the bends. There was no air-conditioning in the Land-Rover and as it descended the oppressive heat sapped the energy to do anything very much apart from maybe breathe.

There were two men in the front; a youngish Arab was driving with natural skill and impressive timing and anticipation. In the passenger seat sat a small Nepalese man, which was unusual in that part of Arabia at that time. He did look very much as you might imagine a Gurkha would look in casual clothes. Behind them both with the wide seat to himself sat a British man – you would have been forgiven for thinking he would look more comfortable in uniform.

They were still high up the side of the mountain but they could see in the middle of the valley there was a camel walking a grinding wheel round and round. There was a haze of dust and chaff drifting slowly away from the wheel down the valley.

The Land-Rover came to a hair-pin bend and just as they turned the corner the Nepalese shouted, "Stop" and the driver ground to a halt sickeningly suddenly.

The driver stayed with the Land-Rover while the other two men walked up the gully. Although the ground was uneven it was not far until they came to what they were looking for. What they feared to find. It was a huge bird lying on the ground, its last breath exhaled into the dust of this remote ditch.

The Bearded Vulture looks more like a massive eagle than a vulture. Unlike other vultures it does not have a bald head. It is one of the biggest birds in terms of wingspan, not quite as big as the Wandering Albatross, Great White Pelican, Marabou Stork or Andean Condor but stretched out it is longer than the Land-Rover at just three meters - that is just under ten feet. It can fly very high; at 24,000 feet most of us need help breathing. They grow to quite an age, maybe thirty to forty years old. Numbers are recovering now but at this time the numbers were low.

That morning, very early, hungry from the previous day, the bird took off for the last time from the ledges high up in the mountains. He was not young but he flew up high. In his youth he would have chased away any competition in the form of another male. Now he rarely saw another male. He was a solitary bird, who had been so for some time. Now he was flying east. Much of the time he did not need to beat his wings but endlessly trim them to catch the lift of the sea breeze. A beautiful curve with washed out wing tips and his regal head, craned, with curved beak, scanning far below for anything to eat.

Every so often he would spiral down in large graceful circles to take a closer look at something then straighten out and start to climb once more with nothing.

As the day wore on he began to lose height – now less likely to see food his chances of survival started to spiral down too. Tired and exhausted from lack of food he sees a suitable ledge on which to land and rest. As he comes in for his final approach he makes a fatal mistake, missing the ledge with one foot and crashing down the shear rock face, he ends up tumbling wing tip over wing tip like some ungainly smashed kite.

Stuck in the ditch close to the road unable to move – the rescue comes too late.

Jun-13

Warlords at the Dinner Party

Few people could remember what peace was like. It was twenty, maybe thirty years, since all semblance of civilisation had slipped away. All that was left now was war torn urban areas, mile after mile of wrecked and ruined houses, schools and factories. Wrecked railways and broken roads.

All hope of peace had gone when an unexpected invitation came from the chief of the salvage union – known not unkindly as Chief Scavenger Sebastian. An invitation to sit down, civilised, to eat, drink and talk about peace, went to all the warlords, an invitation to reintroduce peace. It took some time and a lot of patience to arrange this dinner party. All other hope had receded over the horizon.

Finally they all agreed to meet, hosted on neutral ground, at the Scavenger Hall. Either the warlords would come to some agreement or the fighting would continue to a final and irreversible destruction.

Not all the warlords were men but most were. Of the eleven that Sebastian let in, nine were men and two were women. Checking the women for weapons had not been as tricky as Sebastian had feared.

When each warlord arrived, at agreed 10 minute intervals, Sebastian would let them in through the outer door, but the inner door would remain locked until Sebastian was satisfied that the warlord had removed all weapons and placed them in a secure box, for safekeeping until after the meeting. The first woman warlord was slim, she took her cloak off and placed it in the box. She stood before Sebastian dressed in what appeared to be a suit that had been painted on her body, a mixture of blue and green, glittering as she moved. She passed through the scanner without a murmer. The other female warlord was a huge bodybuilder of a woman, small breasts perched on her muscly chest. She stripped off without demure and went through the scanner while Sebastian checked her cloak carefully.

The men came in all shapes and sizes, generally fit and not shy about stripping in front of Sebastian while he carefully checked the clothes passed to him. These were war torn people many with scars, one small warlord had a scar running from below one eye down across his body and on down to the opposite thigh.

When the final guest had arrived, Sebastian followed him into the main chamber to serve drinks. Unlike most dinner parties there was not much noise, no sound of chatter or laughter. Sebastian served drinks and offered round snacks. The table for twelve was set at one end and after a while he ushered them down to take their places. As they ate the starter of crispy locus Sebastian heard them grumbling about the difficulty of getting a good supply of weapons. Later as he led them to collect the main course, of jugged rat, the subject had moved on to the difficulty of getting new recruits.

Sebastian had arranged the seating; he looked round the table at the groups that had formed from the positions he had placed them in. At the top of the table were the three most powerful, these three held the most land and the biggest armies. You might have expected that the fiercest battles would be between these three but in fact they spent more time and energy fighting with the smaller factions, having come to a tacit agreement that it was best not to fight each other. It was this that Sebastian hoped could be built on. Two of the three were craggy, wary, battle scarred veterans, but the third was smooth, urbane slightly younger and a more persuasive man. As Sebastian looked round the he saw the odd groupings being formed. They all knew each other but over dinner the vestiges of civilisation showed faintly through. '

At the end of the meal Sebastian picked up a loudhailer. 'The people are fed up with this continual fighting. You have four hours to come to a solution. If you do not achieve a workable plan in this time then the food you have eaten will kill you – one by one. If however you produce a lasting agreement that ensures peace I will give you the antidote. Remember I have eaten the same food as you and I could be the first to die. Do not waste your time tearing me apart but rather react to the gun I am holding to your head and come with a solution. Let me start with the first assertion - does anyone disagree that we must find a lasting solution to this war?'

Not one of them did.

May-13

The Lake

A dark beach sloping sinister, anthracite grains ground to a standstill. The lake is completely undisturbed, mostly dark, an hour before dawn. Very little vegetation grows round the shores so nothing disturbs the surface. The low moon is mainly obscured by clouds, moving slowly across the sky. Patterns of light and dark play on the surface of the large expanse of the lake. Hard to discern, like shadows, the hills are reflected weakly in the water.

The lake is nearly a mile wide and twice as long. Towards the bank of the north side is an island cradled in the darkness of the hills. The island is formed from a single rock which has been eroded over time. It has a flat spire that rears up deceptively shapely to point at the sky, like a hand with circled thumb and index finger. In certain winds a curious eerie noise, a cross between sounds – a resonant note that plays up and down your spine, is created by the hand-spire.

As dawn breaks just such a wind starts. The lake which is generally silent starts to drone, chord like, gently from the island. The sun is starting to climb and the water begins to shimmer as sun and wind bring a mechanical life to the surface. Very little real life is visible. Should any make its way up here, it would die in the heat of the day or the cold of the night.

The wind shifts slightly and the intonation of the sound changes, part of a tone. There is a crack so loud the shock waves are visible above the water. The surface of the water erupts and there is a noise that numbs the mind and deranges the senses. The hum stops as the island is blown away in an ashen geyser. Bubbling lava shoots with liquid fire of the Earth's core.

The day has only just begun and the lake has boiled away.

May-13

The Lost Theorem

The stone cottage was on the edge of the North Yorkshire moors. It had been just a farm store when I bought it almost 20 years ago now. It had taken years to convert it to a dwelling, it was spartan, almost austere, but there was less to go wrong. I moved in the day after I had retired from my job, nearly five years ago.

The farmer I had bought it from used to drop by occasionally but last year he died of cancer and so now I get no social calls. Once a week, on a Thursday, the van from the village comes by with my week's supplies and any mail, which is hardly any. The rest of the time I have to myself.

A fair amount of each day is spent just dealing with household tasks, tending the fire, cooking, cleaning (house), washing (clothes and body), and drying but no ironing.

Mostly I spend time thinking and watching the moor. In some ways a sea on land, but really a thing like nothing else. It has moods; sad wind sighing through the heather, anger raging with wind and rain and heather lying flat under force, serene shimmering on a warm summer day. But always it has smell, beautiful and elevating.

I watch the moor from my small window, while walking and while sitting outside. I try to think mainly about mathematics; von Neumann's lost theorem, but sometimes my mind strays onto other things, memories. I have found that it is best not to try and block these thoughts but rather to limit the time that I spend on them, say five minutes.

von Neumann probably spent five minutes on his theorem and I have spent nearly five years on it, but I think I am getting closer to proving it. It did worry me a bit what I would think about if I did solve it – maybe this dulled my keenness to solve it. There was another theorem left by von Neumann called the von Neumann conjecture, which had been disproved in 1980, so there was also the worry that his lost theorem was false too.

I bought the cottage after Charlotte had divorced me. For me she was my one love, I suppose that I never dared, wanted to get close to another person after that went wrong. She had got pregnant and the joy was forgotten when she lost it. She could not try again and finally got over it by finding another man – a professor of mathematics. The only way I could deal with it was to think, "shit happens" and make sure it could never happen again.

So I bought the cottage for thinking about mathematics and proving von Neumann's lost theorem. Is it valid to say I also bought it to avoid meeting people too?

I do not enjoy the daily tasks much; I have even lost a bit of enthusiasm for cooking. Rather than thinking of different things to cook, I have a chart above the range cooker which dictates what I cook and eat each day. If all the food on a Thursday is good quality then there is no waste in the week – it also ensures that I do not eat too much.

I try to walk out on the moor every day and only miss that if it rains hard the whole day. I have decided that if I meet anybody it is best for me not to speak, so instead I raise my hand in greeting, and keep moving. It is now almost three months since I have spoken to anyone. My record is four months but I expect to exceed that sooner or later.

While I am walking, I keep thinking about the theorem and my mind does not wonder off to forbidden territory. Of course my mind is looking after my feet, keeping track of the way and taking note of things of interest and changes in the seasons. After a couple of hours I find myself back at the cottage ready for some writing up of how far I have got, both with the theorem and where I have been.

Mostly the big advances on the theorem come when I am in the bath. Most days some time after I have eaten my evening meal I have my bath. As I relax and empty my mind then quite often solutions to problems come floating in.

Last night in the bath a few things fell into place and I worked late into the night. This morning I woke late and all parts of the proof seemed valid. It was a complex proof but then it had remained unsolved for many years after von Neumann's death. It took all day to write the proof out neatly by hand and post it off to the Royal Statistical Society. Today is Wednesday so I will give it to the man in the van for posting.

I will go for longer walks and spend some time drawing – I was never much good at it but I always enjoyed doing pencil drawings. I have no paints.

It is weeks since I sent the proof off, the Royal Statistical Society had it reviewed by more referees than usual and they all agreed the proof is correct. I have been nominated for the von Neumann Theory award – I will wait and see.

This morning I received a letter from Charlotte. She picked up the news of my success with the theory. Her professor has died. She would like to come to see me. I have been for two walks today. And I have had a long bath. I will write back that she can visit. But she should expect nothing to come of her visit. I cannot see me changing my ways now – shit will not happen to me again. It will be okay for a social visit now and again. Maybe she will let me draw her. I never was much good with people though.

May-13

Ted and Fred

Ted added sponge-sanding block, grey paint and a paintbrush to his shopping list to pick up at the hardware shop. He was an odd-job bod who worked freelance on many of the surrounding farms. He often worked with Fred, his best and most long-term friend.

Fred had married his childhood sweetheart and they were still married with three children. Ted had had a few long-term relationships and been married once but he was living on his own now, feeling embittered and cantankerous.

They had just put a 30mph speed limit in the village. Ted could see no reason for this; the village school had long since closed down, the pub had closed down, the post office had closed down. There was still a small village store and a few grand houses but there were more houses out of the village beyond the new speed limit. Ted had a plan.

Ted picked up Fred as they were working on a farm, one of their main customers, a huge farm which had a lot of buildings and machinery. As they came from the side road to the junction in the middle of the village Fred said,

'You will need to be careful not to go through the village too fast now there is a speed limit'.

'Bloody waste of time and effort putting a speed limit here at all – someone in the village must be in with the powers that be to have got that one through,' replied Ted.

Ted asked to borrow one of the tractors with a post boring attachment. He quite frequently asked to borrow equipment from that farm and usually brought whatever he borrowed back the next day.

At 3am that night, Ted came quietly into the village and moved the two speeding signs on the east side about twenty feet towards the village. There were a few marks round the posts where he had lifted them out of the ground. He carefully sanded them down and painted the marks out with the grey paint. He disposed of the sanding block, paintbrush and remaining paint in someone's bin. He was also careful to fill in the old holes and cover them with turf from the new holes. Light was breaking as he finished and he drove the tractor back to the farm. Fred came to the farm in his own car and they worked happily together; Ted seemed more cheerful and relaxed than he had for some time.

Each morning Ted picked Fred up and they had to go through the village. Ted would stop at the junction and then speed away through the signs. If he had to go the other way he would scowl and stick to the speed limit.

One day there was a police car in the lay-by opposite the junction and Fred said,

'You better be careful now,' with a thumb gesture at the police car.

'Bah – if he thinks he can do me he better learn the law,' retorted Ted with venom.

Ted turned onto the main road and hit 56mph by the time he got to the speed limit. Sure enough, the police car was behind him and put his stoplights on. The policeman approached Ted and asked him to step out of the car. Ted grinned and stood by his car waiting for the policeman. The policeman asked,

'Were you aware what speed you were doing?'

Ted replied very politely, 'Yes officer I am aware what speed I was going at, but under the law I did not commit a speeding offence.'

'How do you arrive at that conclusion?' said the police officer, looking quizzical.

'Do you agree that I was stationary at the junction in the middle of the village?'

Ted took the policeman's silence as agreement and he carried on,

'As you were monitoring my speed from a moving vehicle, you need to observe my speed over a distance of two tenths of a mile, which is about 340 meters. The distance from the junction to the speed limit sign is 330 meters,' Ted paused before continuing,

'I have a theodolite in the boot of my car if you wish to check it – I will need collaborated evidence if you take this to court.'

'That will not be necessary – I will let you off with a caution this time.'

Ted grinned at the policeman but said nothing.

May-13

Confrontation

Peter had been away from home for just under three years and before that he had been away at University. He had grown up, matured and toughened up a lot. His mother responded to the change better than his father. With his job as a field archaeologist the demands in the Middle East were mental and physical. They showed in his face, his eyes and his skin.

In his second week home Peter had a major confrontation with his father. Many years before there had been a very similar argument between Stephen, his elder brother, and his father. It felt like his father had engineered this argument. Peter had grown in maturity but he could not defuse this explosive argument before it went off.

The whole argument was dear to both their hearts but rather than leaving it his father first poked it alive then fanned it on both sides in to a raging inferno. The central point of the argument was, were there absolutes in art, music and literature. The argument did not stay in the lofty reaches of the subject but tended to slide down int to the human condition with snide comments about each other and Anglo-Saxon descriptions.

'Your ideas of the arts are much like what your

generation has done all over the Internet – porn and bestiality, rather than the true absolute beauty of form, colour and sound,' said his father

'You have become stuck in your views and ways. You fail to see that language is living and developing just as sound, light and colour are changing so that a new form of beauty may emerge both via a conventional route but also via an unconventional route.'

'You are talking about the debasement of art – you should know in your job that the baser parts of every society come out and daub obscenity and deface art. If you are talking about a true new form of art these will not affect those already established.'

'Well there I think you are wrong. Your head is in the sand; your so-called absolutes are as vulnerable to changes in nature as the rest of the world. A case in point are those like you, stuck to outmoded ideals of absolute beauty but who will not survive the test of time against a developing and vibrant beauty', said Peter with clearly drawn lines of emotion.

'That is what every youth is hell-bent on, to make obsolete the previous generation. You will fail as you do not have the strength to perceive the absolutes like Bach, Shakespeare and Escher.'

'Neither would I - they are of enduring beauty but not some constant absolute doomed to isolation and neglect.' Peter could feel he had outgrown the constrictive confines imposed by his father. He could see his father bringing the argument to end by expelling him from the family home. He felt an understandable need to break free and thought of a neat way to turn the argument to help him escape. It would also help avoid his mother getting completely caught between his father and him. He turned deftly before his father could re-join the argument and said, 'Maybe I should go up to London and Oxford to look again at some of your examples of absolute beauty – it is some time since I have seen civilisation at close range, I can barely credit the fuss you have made of it'.

May-13

Calculation

Colin & Wendy were both on their second marriage. Colin wondered when his first miscalculation was. Suggesting they came on this holiday or further back.

On the second to last day of the holiday they stayed in and had a room service meal. Wendy had already had a few drinks in the bar – in fact Colin had not really taken much notice but she had had quite a few drinks before they went to their apartment.

They moved out on to the balcony of the apartment. As he followed her with his eyes he got the clear impression she was like a Rottweiler. The alcohol blurred his judgment.

'Look at you pacing about waiting to leap out like a demented Rottweiler bitch,' he said.

'Look at you like some wishy-washy impotent leech,' she thought it was just another row.

'Clearly the holiday has not helped this marriage, it is beyond repair – there is nothing left for either of us in it – only destructive stuff,' he said.

'You calculating bastard,' she screamed at him, 'you selfish unfeeling bastard you got me here...' Her hysterical uncontrollable tirade became incoherent as she started throwing random things at him. This included her glass that he managed to dodge and it shattered behind him. She moved rapidly towards the railings to pick up a pot plant, missed her footing and teetered for a moment. In this moment Colin was paralysed by anxiety as to what to do, his brain and muscles ceased to function during this crucial time. He struggled to his feet but he was too late, a lifetime too late. She fell over and down nine storeys. She must have hit her head on the balcony below as her scream was cut short. There was a horrendous noise as she hit the ground. Colin would not forget that noise for a long time.

It took Colin quite some time to recover and make his way down to the ground floor. The ambulance had already arrived and the Spanish crew were picking her up and talking to the hotel staff. The Police arrived; one policeman had relatively good English and came with Colin to the apartment to have a look round. Colin explained to him about Wendy's drinking and anger. The policeman said very little and made some notes. His radio crackled into life and after a short conversation the policeman looked at Colin.

'I am sorry to inform you that your wife has died,' said the policeman.

'I suppose there was not much chance of her surviving such a fall,' replied Colin.

'We have no further questions as this stage but you must not leave the country for the time being, I will collect your passport from the hotel,' concluded the policeman.

Colin spent a restless night going over in his mind time and time again how he had decided on a sequence of events that had led him to this. He also thought about what was likely to happen to him and if there was anything he could do to change this.

Next morning the police came and took him to the police station. This time an older more senior policeman conducted the interview; his English was good too. Colin thought about each answer but thought it best to answer as truthfully as possible.

'How long have you been married to Wendy?' started the policeman.

'About eight years,' replied Colin.

'After you ate supper last night there was quite an argument and yet you maintain that Wendy lost her balance and fell.'

Yes,' said Colin wondering why the policeman kept using her name.

'It is quite a small balcony – why were you not able to reach Wendy and catch her?' said the policeman fairly naturally.

'She had been throwing things at me and I was jammed in my chair. I did try to stand up but it was too late.' Colin was aware he was being defensive.

'From your own account and also from what the neighbours said it seems more likely you pushed her over the railings,' said the policeman aggressively.

'No,' said Colin and he froze. He noticed the policeman said 'her' now he had mentioned murder.

'Is it the case your wife was wealthy?' asked the policeman bluntly.

'It is true she had her own savings but I earn money,' said Colin sensing defeat.

'A neighbour says she shouted out you were a 'calculating bastard' just before she fell to her death. Also you do not seem to be so upset.'

Colin could see a long time stretching out ahead of him, time to consider how the trial for murder would go and even longer time serving life sentence in prison; a long time to consider when he made his miscalculations.

May-13

The Vicarage

Cathy, the vicar's wife, woke gently and remembered slowly that it was Thursday, and not just any Thursday but a special exciting one.

Her husband, Matthew, was already in his downstairs study near the front door as she leisurely got dressed. She went past the study and could just make out the fraught tones of a regular visitor – querulous Queenie. Matthew was quite a few years older than Cathy and they had not married until late. He had never seemed that interested in her physically and Cathy had formed the conviction quite early on that he had married her to fend off the likes of Queenie and others. Not a wholly successful venture, well not in this aspect.

Cathy made her way to the kitchen. The vicarage was a large rambling building left over from times when vicars had large families and a couple of servants thrown in. Cathy glanced furtively at the second stairs and thought about the lodger Peter with his easel. The diocese had agreed to a better use of the vicarage spare rooms for short-term lettings. Cathy was not hungry – she had a very small bowl of cereal and some sliced apple. She went into the garden to hang up some washing.

There was a broken wall between the back garden and the old churchyard – Cathy was fascinated by the plants and wildlife that thrived, entwined amongst the rocks. She had brought her digital camera, in the washing basket – her one stand, to be a woman in her own right, not just the wife of a vicar.

A fine delicate ivy ran over the rocks glued by white veins to the uneven surface of the broken stones of the wall. In some places other trailing weeds took advantage of the firmness of the ivy and wound round a branch or a leaf. Even though Cathy did not see any insects yet she waited with camera poised. She had won awards for capturing extraordinary events in the insect world. This morning she was impatient for time to pass but knew one of the most effective ways to do that, was to see what she could capture.

A very small creature, maybe a vole, appeared at the foot of the wall. Cathy was not sure what it was but she caught the movement of nose and beady eyes. Without thinking her camera caught an image of huge-scale wall, creeper and retreating eyes.

Cathy looked at her watch; the time had slid easily by. It was time to go and see Peter. She met Matthew in the kitchen requiring post Queenie sustenance – a cool drink and a biscuit.

'You look like you needed that,' she said kindly to him.

'Well I do not wish to be uncharitable – but yes frankly I do find her exhausting, well actually to be brutally honest knackering, ball breaking.'

Even after years of married life Cathy found Matthew a perplexing mixture of naivety and inappropriate language.'

He asked, 'What are you up to?'

'Oh I promised to go and see Peter in his studio and let him paint me,' she said without flinching.

'Oh yes I remember you told me – well don't let him wear you out, you know what these artists are like, very demanding. Why don't you take your camera with you so he can work from photographs too?'

'That's a good idea – I thought that I could take pictures of the painting in progress if he will let me.'

'If you take your kit off I am sure he will,' said the vicar looking at her with a twinkle in his eye, 'Nature at its best. See if the church magazine would be interested.'

Apr-13

The Heat Had Been Oppressive

The heat had been oppressive, the tension rising with the humidity, before the monsoon broke. It started slowly, huge droplets hitting the dry dusty ground with audible thuds. Soon however the rain picked up speed with long diagonal lines bombing into the ground and everywhere little rivulets of the precious stuff running away. Rahel had almost forgotten how the monsoon was. She'd been away for the last two years; her father had seen to that.

Rahel watched from the shelter of a shrine, she stood in an archway and saw the creatures, beetles, lizards, ants and chameleons thrown into disarray. Rushing madly from one place to another. The beetles could take a direct hit from an exploding raindrop scattering from their shiny exterior plates of beetle armour. However the ants didn't always survive, sometimes a whole column of them were wasted by one line of streaking rain.

Rahel's attention was suddenly caught by a car making its way erratically down the street – it was the sky-blue Plymouth and it lurched to a halt outside the empty house. Rahel could make out Baby Kochamma slumped over the wheel and she hurried to the car, braving the deluge to rush across the road furrowed by the escaping rain. Baby Kochamma was still alive but had fainted. Rahel opened the car door to find her sitting still in red liquid.

With the rain creating a continuous metallic drumming on the car roof, Rahel cleaned Baby Kochamma up. In fact the wound was superficial and only bled so much as Baby Kochamma kept the wound open by driving. It was an awkward position across her stomach and flank; Rahel tore the bottom of Baby Kochamma's dress off and used it as a makeshift bandage. As she did so Baby Kochamma began to regain consciousness. Rahel got in the passenger side, soaking wet.

'How are you feeling?' asked Rahel.

Baby Kochamma looked at her with slow recognition, 'Not quite as good as before that "scum" tried crude body modification on me.'

'What happened?'

'Oh – the usual, I was in the café, just cleaning up when this brawl broke out between these two savages.'

'Were they fighting about you?'

'Well if they were it was totally futile, I wouldn't have anything to do with either of them.'

'Have you seen them before?'

'Lowlifes like that hang around all the time – it's a job to tell one from another. I suppose I might have seen them before.'

Rachel paused and looked at Baby Kochamma speculatively, she was a bedraggled beauty designed to bring out the worst in men. Well, most men. Her thin clothes clung desperately to her vulnerable body.

'How come you got involved then – not just involved but nearly gutted?'

Baby Kochamma looked searchingly at Rachel and said,

'Well I'm sworn to secrecy – but I did get one of the lowlifes out of there. He was your brother.'

Apr-13

Runway Feelings

It was only just 9am but the heat was shimmering above the concrete runway.

For some reason the flight was a bit later than usual. We stood at ease with our rifles leaning slightly away. The flight was to take the Governor of Aden, representative of the Crown, together with the Commander in Chief of HM Forces on an internal flight.

The familiar crackle of radio came muffled to our ears.

'Perimeter checks complete'.

'Roger,' came a bit clearer at our end.

In recent years there was always tension, the regular terrorist attacks. Today was no different – the tension felt oily on the surface but with strong currents beneath.

Radio spoke once more, 'Governor's car approaching gate E.'

'Roger.'

The car made its way towards us; we were now standing to attention.

The Commander got out of the car first then came the Governor. The Commander stood to one side. They started to walk towards the aircraft, the Governor slightly ahead. A dark figure emerged quickly from the baggage cart.

A terrorist to us – a freedom fighter to them. He lobbed a grenade to the Governor's feet.

'Fire at will.' Sharp order from our sergeant - I'd never heard in action before.

An order for us not the Commander.

Protect the crown. His orders came from above and from within.

The Commander leapt forward knocking the Governor out of the way while he fell on the grenade.

We shot the terrorist – his freedom ended.

The Commander hadn't quite hit the ground when the grenade went off. A crack of death. He died and saved the Crown. The Crown walked away.

Of course my life changed today but not in the same way; mine goes on. A struggle of living, a struggle of thoughts.

The Commander already had medals for bravery so how can giving him a VC change anything? So he's a bigger hero now, is he? Just in smaller pieces. I don't think the VC is going to make things better for his wife, who's a widow now... of course the Governors wife isn't. Also his children will no longer have a father...

How could he make that decision? That his own life was more expendable than the governors? Of course he didn't; his mind was clear – so clear in fact there was no hesitation, the Crown, Britain, must be protected. Duty stepped in and eliminated hesitation - otherwise the consequence could be fatal - for the Crown. He lived and died to protect the Crown.

That's the reason why.

Was it a valid reason? If he's right then what happened was just. I can't agree. Which ever way I think about it 'injustice' screams in my head. The injustice came from the terrorist? The consequence from his sense of duty? I'm not sure.

He lived and died to protect the Crown – what a senseless waste. It makes no sense to me. Like fighting for peace. I'm afraid, afraid of dying, afraid that I signed up to the same thing that killed him.

Mar-13

Hero

Background

I thought long and intently about who to choose as a hero to write about. Finally I decided to write about a person in recent history who has had a big impact on my life. I did think about choosing a fictional hero as being of greater literary interest but decided finally that he has had a bigger impact on my writing.

In concession to choosing a real life character I will not confer with Wiki or other references but will rather write from memory. So please do not take me to task if some of the detail is a bit hazy.

I first heard about Turing when I was at university. I studied Maths not computing but Alan Turing's contribution spans both. A Turing Machine was defined by Alan Turing before digital computers where invented, based on a vision of how to tackle many problems.

A Turing Problem is one that can be solved by a modern computer; to give you an idea of what is and what isn't a Turing problem I'll give a couple of examples. A Turing Machine can go through a document like this and apply all common contractions to it without working up a sweat. Then read it out to me afterwards. However to take my original text with all the spelling mistakes I made and correct them without help is beyond a Turing Machine. Basically because I spell the same words wrongly in more than one way.

When Turing was at Bletchley he was key in the development of Colossus, the first electronic programmable computer built in this world. It was used to break the German encrypted messages sent by radio. This is a Turing problem as for a given code and encryption key there's only one answer; the problem is to find the key not knowing what the code says.

What's even more remarkable is that Turing developed a more generalised design for a computer that could not only crack codes but also execute many other tasks we see being done today on computers. From sums for flying the shuttle to searching the Internet. He did this around sixty years ago.

When I was at university what I didn't know was that after the war society rewarded his contribution by persecuting him for being gay. He was given the choice between prison and chemical castration. He chose chemical castration and was quite unwell.

It was thought for a while that he committed suicide but I think it was more likely he made a mistake while handling cyanide for an experiment. They think he transferred cyanide from his equipment on to his lunchtime apple. There's an urban myth that the bite out of the apple on the Apple Inc logo is a mark of respect for this man. However when the co-founder of Apple was asked about this he replied, 'I wish it was so'.

A few years ago as a result of pressure from the public the Government issued a statement apologising for the way Turing was treated. The original statement is at Bletchley Park not far from a working model of Colossus II and many other early computers.

Turing was liked by men and women, he had few of the normal traits of a genius, but he undoubtedly was. He was modest and thoughtful. He worked with other people and almost certainly achieved more that way than on his own. But for me he had all of the ingredients of a hero.

Eccentricity. Frailty. Humour.

I haven't found a worthy hero without these, and they always appear in my writing, even my computer heroes.

Mar-13

The Door Closes

You're the most extraordinary person – some days so perverse and difficult, impossible to guess what's going on inside you; other days loving and flowing lyrical.

You take no hostages when you surprise them with your insight, your wicked sense of right. Like when your friend came to you for help, her life was shattered in pieces. You took the time to look inside her life and gently show her that there were parts still in good shape and firm. Like her relationship with her father – strong bonds with freedom attached. The closeness to her father made her life feel different and you could see this clearly. You didn't try to wave a magic wand or tell her what to do. Instead you were there to show her little things that made the difference. Like how she's the one that others depend on. I don't know how you do it, to argue without heat or malice to show her; so she feels better about herself than she did before.

That day she came to see you a jangle of nerves, dressed so enchantingly but with no confidence. She'd met a man through her volunteering and now there was no doubt this was a real date. She'd been out with him in a group, but this time there would be silences in the conversation and she felt a total lack of confidence, first pancake out of the pan.

She came into the sitting room where you were plotting your latest fiendish scheme and immediately your brain changed gear. You'd most likely been lurking in a siding waiting for an unsuspecting prey but now, in an instant, your mind was working out the best route across a difficult terrain. You joked to start with.

'You look lovely – it isn't your man that will be the problem but rather stopping all the other men trying to muscle in.'

She smiled a thin misty smile not believing the flattery. So you go back for a more subtle approach.

'The dress is well thought out – it isn't too formal but it does tell him that you're very interested in him.'

'I'm not sure that I'm ready– it is so long since a man touched me, I'm not sure that I want to risk it again,' she said blushing against her words.

You're right there, guiding her over the uneven ground, 'Of course you're bound to feel like that after what's happened, and while he doesn't know exactly what happened, he'll know you've been hurt. He'll proceed with care and thoughtfulness; from what you've told me this is a new man of kindness and consideration.'

'I hope you're right.' She seemed to agree with you more than her words alone conveyed.

You're very good at knowing when not to talk. You wait with an accepting silence.

She says a tremolo, 'Will he expect to go to bed tonight?'

You give no opinion but rather see what she feels and thinks.

'Do you think it is as simple as that? Do you think he mightn't know either?' you say, serious and smiling.

'Oh – I see what you mean. I'm not sure when he last saw a woman.'

Friendly seconds tick by as you let her think it over.

Finally you say, 'Do you think he'll sense you might need more time? Or do you want his touch sooner rather than later?'

She said with not a blush in sight, 'I'm in no rush, I don't want to scare him off – I'm more worried he'll want to go faster than me.'

'Well,' you said, 'Often men feel they've got to prove something but that doesn't mean you can't reassure him and tell him you're not ready just yet.'

How did you think to put this so – it suits her to think like this; she looked surprised and pleased.

'Yes,' she said, 'I've never thought of it like that before.'

'Well how do you feel about going out now?' you said neutrally.

'Well I feel a bit more confident but not all together convinced it'll go well,' she said.

'Do you think that once you settle down you may be able to enjoy an evening out?'

'Well now you ask – I hope so.'

'And do you think he will?'

'I hope so – I'll try to put him at ease and have a bit of fun, he's good fun. I guess he'll be nervous too,' she said.

You said, 'I'd've thought so.'

You've guided her gently, her confidence growing and thinking how it must be for him. Now she's nearly ready to go but there's no rush, slowly you make your way to the door, as she's getting ready to take on the evening. She waves goodbye and neither of you say anything, she steps out. The door swings slowly shut.

Mar-13

Two Novices

Two novice nuns sitting naïvely outside Mother Superior's office soon to go in to have a final discussion to decide what to do. One by one.

The Mother Superior has great understanding, knowledge and wants the best for the women and for her nunnery. There are two doors in her office, one they are sitting outside waiting, this is off the entrance hall. The other leads in to the nunnery, it is an additional door to return to the nunnery.

Neither are youthful but rather women who have seen a bit of the world including suffering.

'Sister Kyle, come through please,' said Sister Anne.

'Take a seat,' said Mother Superior.

'Thank you Mother Superior,' said Sister Kyle. She is a well built woman with serious curves; while her face is rather plain she was always popular with the boys and enjoyed Friday and Saturday evenings to such an extent that she did not always remember what she had got up to or even who she had been with.

'How have you found being here, you've been here for just over a year – is it what you expected?' said Sister Anne.

'Yes Mother Superior, I have tried to behave as it was

expected of me and to learn to live as a Sister should,' replied Sister Kyle.

The Mother Superior looked at Sister Kyle and asked quietly, 'And has that been difficult?'

Sister Kyle felt like her soul was being examined, had she thought of not speaking the truth that now disappeared. She said with a vulnerability that surprised even herself.

'No - Mother Superior, it has not been easy, I will not deny that I have missed many things, a wayward freedom, having a good time, yes I must say it, men and pleasure. But it is what I have chosen. I know that this new life is for me I do not wish to return to a frivolous life.

Feb-13

Stream of Time

In the time it took me to wring out sleep from my body my mind had travelled an epic of mythological proportion. The phone was ringing but why at this time?

Plotless I stumble from slumber through the seaweed of time to see light above me and round circular images of the clocks of a brave world fighting against time, slowly or is that quickly backwards the great arches intersect with overlapping time so clearly depicted there is no one time, there is good time, there is bad time, time that stands still but never enough time and there is telescopic time, not time seen from a distance but rather telescoped together so that birth is close to death and all jammed in between.

Telescope time happens all the time but mostly in those few moments before you die, not just die at the end but also when you die from embarrassment or laughter or surprise or time of course.

Overlapping time only happens sometimes, good or bad, joyous and sad, birth and death but also unexpected like finding a flower on a bend or scarecrow down below, coming over a brow of hill and giving birth to twins, taking a wrong turning into a wheelbarrow as opposed to becoming a wheelbarrow which could be overlapping time too.

There is much that can be frustrating with time not least of which is inexorable time however elastic and plastic internal time is there is not much we can do about external time the time of ageing and the sound of hair turning grey.

Treacle time can be sweet but is more often frustrating, I come up towards the surface wondering if my breath will hold out that long and finally break through to gasp the air just in time to pick up the phone after it stops ringing.

Feb-13

The Right Thing to Do

Tom, Dick and Harry had a mother, Rose, of exceptional beauty and quality. Like all flowers time took its toll and gradually her body and mind crumbled. Many years ago while still of sound mind she wrote a Living Will full of fine words to die in dignity. Not so easy for her to achieve now, surrounded by thoughtful staff intent on caring for her and keeping her alive.

'She is still afraid of dying,' said Dick.

'But not wanting to carry on anymore,' said Tom.

'True,' said Dick.

'She is already gone – or mostly gone, she is not the Rose she once was,' said Harry.

'It's not kind to keep her here – they would only do that to a human, to be so inhumane,' said Tom.

It was her birthday and the boys had met in her room. But she was in another world, a silent world, a darkening world, of little taste, awful smells, tablets and no joy.

Each brother thought how best to help their mother. Each came to the same conclusion but did not confer, the upbringing of independence lasting long into adulthood.

Each saw her on their own and this time she took the tablet without protest.

They shoot horses don't they, thought Harry.

I hope my kids know what to do when the time comes, thought Dick.

Mercy, I hope the doctor signs the certificate, thought Tom.'

'I knew I could depend on you, son,' she said to each in turn not remembering their names.

Next day the doctor came and wondered which if not all the boys were involved. She signed the death certificate for her friend with relief.

Tom, Dick and Harry lived long, but not as long as Rose, and all died in their sleep none the wiser.

300 words

Tom, Dick and Harry have a mother, Rose, of exceptional beauty and quality. Like all flowers, time has taken its toll and gradually her body and her mind crumbled. She wants to die in dignity. Not so easy for her to achieve now, surrounded by thoughtful staff intent on caring for her and keeping her alive.

'She's still afraid of dying,' said Dick.

'She's already gone – not the Rose she once was,' said Harry.

'It's not kind to keep her here – they would only do that to a human, to be so inhumane,' said Tom.

It is her birthday and the boys meet in her room. But she is in another world, a silent world, a darkening world, of little taste, awful smells, tablets and no joy.

The Doctor comes next day. It looks like they all took it into their own hands but she signed the mercy death certificate.

150 words

Rose, mother of exceptional beauty. Dying to leave this world. Her three sons the only ones to help her. The doctor signs the death certificate.

25 words

Feb-15

Blur Learns

If you think that translating one human language to another is difficult you are correct. But this is relatively easy compared to translating between the languages of two different species. Even if I try to explain that the whole idea of the unit of communication is not really the same – there is no direct translation for the concept of a word. The equivalent of a dolphin word leaves our own word flat and one-dimensional. A dolphin word is more like a three dimensional object so it has a likeness to a musical chord but it also has a 'thought' component to it too. Mostly this thought component is embedded within the word and just reassures the listener that the speaker is calm and tranquil. However when there is an urgency, there is a need to communicate many pieces of information, then the thought component is like a thick hawser, which can convey speed, location, numbers and many other things simultaneously or quickly.

So my first difficulty is to translate the name of the young male dolphin on his way to meet the pod going hunting for the first time in this area. For a start dolphins have a given name and an acquired name, which within dolphin communication can be transmitted simultaneously. I am sorry but this is far too complex for me to translate, the name I have come up with is for his acquired name and it is Blur. If you can imagine associated with this name, a blend of notes and a streak of multi coloured blue-green light then you are getting closer.

Blur was around five years old, still with his mother but powerful and an extra fast dolphin – hence his name. The pod had found a new hunting area near where humans were swimming inside a wired off area. There was also an old disused wharf seen clearly through the water. As Blur and his mother approached the rest of the pod there was a stir and the dolphins were forming a ring; the usual response to a threat.

Blur noticed a female human swimming outside the wire and for one instant froze with fear as he saw a shark coming round the pod towards the human. Then Blur began to move at the same time as his communication to the rest of the pod went into overdrive. He told them his plan and the shark had no idea what was going to hit him. Blur accelerated as fast as he could hitting the shark between its eyes. Blur's nose connected with the shark and drove it into the uneven rocks below. The rest of the pod whirled round the stunned shark battering its sides until finally it split apart.

The female human saw the commotion and beat a hasty retreat to swim inside the wire.

The pod closed round Blur, the communication acting like a healing blanket as every aspect of the incident was discussed.

Feb-13

Resolutions

Tim Brown was a strong boy of a bit below average height. In the term before Christmas he had been miserable as one of the older boys had been picking on him at the bus stop to come home - every day for weeks. Over Christmas this had been forgotten, but on the morning of the New Year he and his mum were back to normal in their little house on their own and Tim got to thinking about the big bully.

At breakfast Tim looked out in to the little back garden.

'What is it called when people decide something at the start of a new year?' he asked his mum with quiet deliberation.

'Do you mean when someone makes a new years resolution?' she replied.

'Yes,' he said, looking determined.

'What is your resolution going to be?' she asked gently.

'That I'm not going to be pushed around by that Tommy Spanner.'

His mother looked at her young son with dangerous emotional stirrings.

'Well make sure he can still walk when you've finished with him,' she said seriously while trying to lighten the atmosphere.

Tim looked up at her with a flicker of a smile, 'So it is ok if I beat him to a pulp just so long as he can walk, well at least crawl away afterwards, is it?'

His mother looked doubtful, 'Well I should not like you to get into trouble.'

'Ok,' he said, 'that is my other resolution – not to get into trouble.'

The bus stop was crowded the first afternoon at going home time. Tommy Spanner kept taunting Tim about being a mummy's boy while Tim got redder and redder.

Tommy poked Tim once too many and suddenly there was a flailing of arms, legs and vicious head butting. Both boys were on the ground with the younger small Tim on top beating Tommy to submission. There was plenty of time for Tommy to beg for mercy before the bus came.

Finally, just before the bus did come, Tim stood up and shouted, 'You keep out of my way or next time you'll not walk away.'

As they were getting on the bus one of the big girls with lovely long legs said to Tim,

'He had it coming to him – if he makes any trouble tell me and I will say so.'

Tim thought of his mother and his second resolution – a bit late.

Jan-13

Lush at the Checkout

Stephen Cranford was not in the habit of going to supermarkets and waiting in a queue – but over the New Year he had given all his staff leave and was visiting his daughter. He was a very successful businessman in his early sixties, with no intention of retiring, a widower – his wife had died just before Christmas three years ago.

He was disturbed from his mournful reverie by the woman in front of him. Mutton very nearly dressed as lamb. She must have had a pretty heavy night out; she was emptying out the content of her bag – dogeared book, keys, stuff normally found in a Christmas cracker and a clear plastic bag with what appeared to contain a brief pair of knickers. The image did not really sink in on Stephen, but before she could reach in and haul out the kitchen sink, he uncharacteristically intervened and paid for her shopping which was not quite five pounds.

'Who says chivalry is dead?' she said looking him straight in the eye. 'Thanks mate, you are a natural gent or was it for some other reason?' she added quizzically. Stephen was struck by her earnestness; he also had a feeling she could see right into his soul. He did not feel any sympathy but rather felt a faint rise in his baser instincts. He had not had any interest in women since Helen had died; rather he had thrown himself in to making even more money.

He bit his tongue, stopping himself from saying cruel things and said as pleasantly as he could, 'This time of year's normal routine has gone by the board, I expect you've left your purse at home or somewhere. Do you want to get a bite to eat or a hot drink?'

This engagement was not like him. He looked at her in a new light – was she right? Did he see her as an easy touch? Amazing when he thought back to the women who would have loved to ensnare him before and after Helen died. In her last year any physical intimacy had become increasingly painful for her. On one occasion towards the end when he was cuddling her as tenderly as he could she had said if he needed to satisfy his natural instincts elsewhere then she would understand. Stephen had read about similar things but was taken aback. She had smiled and drifted off to sleep for a while in his arms.

'Ok then. It is definitely not chivalry now is it?' She made light of his schoolboy like confusion but shivered in the cold in her skimpy clothing. He led the way to his Jag.

'Lets get in the car out of the wind,' he said with genuine kindness. 'My name is Stephen.'

'Mine is Sheila. You don't need to feel sorry for me, err - but I'm not sure you do.' Again the lightness of the way she said it took out any bitterness that was there. It seemed to Stephen that she was a good observer and also accepting of the frailty of man's nature.

He called his daughter to say work had called him away. He took Sheila for lunch in a hotel and this turned to a room in the evening. Stephen was surprised to find how hesitant and shy she was but was convinced by her honesty that this was unfamiliar territory for her. They fell asleep in each other's arms waking in the early hours, embarrassed.

She asked to go home to be ready for her sister in the morning. He drove carefully but came to a hump back bridge on a bend as a gritting lorry came roaring round and ran into them.

Stephen was not sure how it happened but he was

standing on the side of the road. He sighed over the Jag, it was unlikely to be recoverable. He could see Sheila lying still with her clean knickers showing. He had known her such a short time but he felt a sharp pain of loss. There was much activity by paramedics beside another prone figure – was that the gritter lorry driver he thought?

The paramedics stood up disconsolate, giving up the struggle to save the man. Stephen saw that the man was not the lorry driver but himself; lying still, close to Sheila, he drifted away.

Jan-13

Wilhelm Tkoscz is

'Wilhelm Tkoscz?' asked the man at the door.

Only a trained eye would have spotted the slight hesitation before the answer, 'No. No one of that name lives around here.'

There was a pause as the man at the door, dressed in a smart suit, just the hint of grey about him to add to the air of experience, looked questioningly. The other man who had opened the door looked well worn but as if no trick would get past him, not that he had the air of a razor about him but rather he kept it under wraps.

'You are not from the authorities: tax, health, social welfare or insurance are you?'

'Oh no,' said the smart suit, 'From commercial TV.'

There was another pause as razor under wraps considered the risks involved.

'Well "Whiz Smelt-Lock" lives here,' he looked searchingly at smart suit and finally came to the conclusion that this remark may need some explanation,

'That is an anagram of "Wilhelm Tkoscz" do you see,' said razor under wraps as if explaining to a thick TV executive.

In fact the TV executive, who was nearly as smart as his suit, nodded patiently and said,

'You have quite a lot of people living here with strange names, like "Elisa Slalom" haven't you?'

'Oh yes, I am not sure if she knows if her own name is "Elisa Slalom", "Lola Melissa", "Salle Somali" or none of the above.'

'Then there is "Serene Condescension" which could be any number of obscure anagrams but just sounds like a joke name. Is she very grand by the way?'

'In a sort of tongue in cheek sort of way – yes she is.'

'How come you never get any obscene names like "Bigus Dickus" from Monty Python or the Carry On films?'

'Well we used to, but the residents formed a house committee which has to approve all names that a resident wishes to use. To avoid getting a bad name if you see what I mean. Just recently we have seen a few post-anagram ironic names like "John Smith" and "ffredric ffarquart". We even had a "Tony Flair" recently but I think that was a little too obscure and dated for most of the residents. All residents have to change their names by deed poll of course. I do apologise for keeping you standing on the door step, would you like to come in and have a cup of tea?'

'Well that is kind – this sort of research can be very disappointing but it really looks like this time I have struck lucky. So yes, I would love to come in.'

Razor under wraps took smart suit downstairs in to a basement kitchen with a homely fire in the grate and people walking past on the pavement above, visible through bars and windows that were below ground level.

They sat at ease and carried on their conversation.

'So what is your interest in a bunch of misnamed misfits?' asked razor.

'Well we have got two possible interests, one is a "reality TV" show where all the contestants have to use assumed names – maybe having a few "professional" name changers on the show would add an extra dimension. The other is possibly for the BBC, and looks at a series of British eccentricities – one of which would be people with amazing assumed names.'

'Some of them would have a field day – especially the ones that take anonymity to extremes, they would want to have assumed names for any programme. I suspect some would only appear in profile or chequered out with those blocks, with disguised voices too.'

'Do you think many of them would want to take part?' asked the smart suit looking cautious at the enthusiasm of the other.

'Oh yes, I expect that you will need some way of selecting the best for each type of show.'

'Where do they all come from?'

'Well there are a few ex-convicts but by no means a significant proportion. I suppose that there might be one or two with identity crises of their very own, with or without paranoia. A few who have won the lottery and want to avoid attention. One or two forgers and fakes plus a few fantasists I suppose,' he paused for a moment then added, 'It might be a bit difficult sorting one group from another.'

'Yes – I suppose it would.' Smart suit finished his tea and asked, 'What is the next step? How should we ask if any one is interested?'

'Well you are unlikely to get any names if you ask individually, or put a notice up. I think that the best way would be to let me go to the residents house committee and see what names come out that way.'

Nov-12

The Last Autumn

You might be forgiven for mistaking the first part of autumn as a final throw, a final extravaganza of summer, if you had never seen autumn before. But you have seen autumn many times before, in its decaying beauty. Like some monster lizard moving through the undergrowth, a torpid creature colourful in its final journey towards winter. Down its dry back gentle colours changing to reflect the death throws of the plants all around. Deep yellows and browns but also blood red.

It seeps into your mind that this autumn, in its spectacular glory, might be the last autumn. Slowly as the end of autumn is reached and it turns to winter you think that this time there will be no rebirth in spring. It worries you what we have done to the world, is it too much this time and that come the springtime there will be silence. No songs from the birds; not even the quiet of new growth bursting forth.

You feel a shadow fall across you and out over the landscape in front of you, a shadow of darkness and fear that grips your heart. So with the passing of the last autumn, as the last leaf falls your hope will begin to die.

At first you think to yourself, 'After the winter the spring will surely come.'

But as winter progresses and stretches out to when spring should arrive, you will say to anyone left to listen,

'I had a feeling that was the last autumn.'

Nov-12

Speechless

In life there have been a number of strange and amusing incidents, as you would expect. I could tell of rescuing a young woman from a scorpion, or when a camel ate my hair, or when our lion had to be sent to England, a few pranks and one or two tragedies.

But none of these are so strange as the story about Gillian Leigh.

We lived in a huge palace in Mukalla, in Arabia. It was way before internal telephone systems were common, in fact there was not even a public telephone system in Mukalla. The reason I explain this is so you know why I was often sent with messages to the other side of the palace. Our family lived on the west side, west wing I suppose, as you had to go down to the first floor to get to the east wing. On the ground floor there were the offices where my father worked. As all my three older brothers were at school in England there was only me to take messages.

John Leigh was a political officer working for my father. He was married to Gillian and they were a deeply loving couple. They had been married about three years and had a little boy when Gillian held forth one day, how wrong it was to have more than two children. She was a lovely lady but as the fourth child I felt a bit unwanted. I think she may have realised this as she changed the subject. Next day we heard Gillian had found she was pregnant. It turned out she had twins.

So it was that John and Gillian moved into the east wing

after the twins arrived until their new accommodation was ready. They were there for a couple of months. Quite regularly I made my way to the other side of the palace with a message, sometimes I was asked over to help with this or that. Gillian took it very well when I asked her if she liked having three children. She made quite a thing of asking if she should have another, it was like she was asking my advice whether she should have a fourth like me. The twins were boys. So I said.

'If you want a girl then you should have another one, but like me you might have another boy, so be prepared.'

She went all slushy and said, 'Oh well I think it would be worth the risk.'

Looking back I was in an unusual position, not like a male Arab helper as I was allowed anywhere in the apartment, not like a visitor either really. Not like a female helper either as I had more freedom to go to the market. I do not think I was aware of this at the time but I just looked forward to being more like my older brothers.

It was a really hot and humid evening near the break of the monsoon. I was asked to take another message. I am not sure what the message was. I suppose I was a bit traumatised by what happened. I went in to see Gillian and she was feeding one of the twins, a fascinating process but I was used to this and often brought her things or a drink as she fed them. She put the baby down and clutched her chest.

'It is so hot today the twins do not seem hungry. They have not emptied me. Would you mind finishing me off?'

I am usually quick to take up new opportunities when they occur but it was so unexpected. I am not quite sure why, such a surprise but I did not say "yes" quickly enough, unusually I was lost for words.

'Well if you are not sure I guess it would be a mistake. I

can do it by hand,' she said disappointedly.

Nov-12

Pocket Stuff

Alfie had a bounce in his step as he left Mandy's flat. He took his phone from his pocket and called two of the lads but got no reply. Very unusual and worrying. He could feel his long comb and wallet as he put his phone back in his pocket. He only carried the three items.

His peripheral vision caught sight of three menacing men – they looked like some guys from a rival gang. He quickly turned down a side alley to a closed back yard. He guessed one would have a gun. He was now like a taut spring but it did not really cross his mind that he would not win.

He took his metal comb from his pocket with its long sharp handle. There was a dog with them. It ran forward, teeth bared. Alfie ran straight towards them and kicked the dog with a steel capped toe hard in the mouth – it lifted up in the air with a horrendous yelp and landed on its back dying painfully. Alfie cannoned into the first man and sank the comb into him just below his lowest rib. One of the other men struggled to aim and fire at Alfie. Alfie lifted the stabbed man up and threw him towards the gunner. The bullets thudded into the dead man's body and both man and corpse fell in a heap. Alfie carried straight on and rose into the air and kicked the third man in the throat. He bent down, picked up this man's knife and also body to use as a shield. The man with a gun cried out for mercy as Alfie and shield closed in on him struggling up from the ground. Alfie showed no mercy slicing through his neck.

Alfie decided to leave his comb in the first man's chest but he did rub the second man's dead hand over the part sticking out.

Alfie walked away. There was only one person who could account for this attack; he walked back to Mandy's flat. She was still in her housecoat, hesitantly opening the door; she knew if she did not he would just kick it down. He did not speak but dragged her into the kitchen, took a knife from the draw bent her wrist back and drew the knife across her wrist. There were faint lines on her wrist where she used to self-harm. The new cut beaded with blood and she pleaded with him.

'Please, please don't kill me Alfie.'

'I won't kill you,' he lied, 'but you must do exactly what I tell you.'

He tipped her handbag out and found her phone. He looked at the calls she had made and saw a number she had called that was not in her address book. He grabbed her other wrist and said savagely, 'How much did he pay you? – Go and get me the money.' He stood by the door of the small flat while she went and got another handbag. She gave him a roll of notes. He looked and said '£5,000 before and you believed him £5,000 after?'

She nodded dumbly. He took her, a chair and a thin washing line out in to the stair well. She stood on the chair with the line round her neck attached to the steel handrail. He dialled the number in her phone. He heard a man answer and passed her the phone and she cried down it.

'Harry he is going to.....'

Alfie kicked away the chair. She did not die quickly of a broken neck but slowly from strangulation. Alfie watched as the phone dropped from her hand and he could hear obscenities coming from it as it smashed on the concrete. Her coat gaped open, good for a suicide.

Alfie's own phone rang; it was Nick his main man. They had been attacked too and a couple of the lads were badly hurt and one was dead.

Alfie said, 'take the two lads to hospital, then get the stun explosive we used in the last job and meet up at the shed.' They never used the shed normally but Alfie had decided to get Harry. Taking the lads to hospital would look like they were giving up. Harry was gone and all would know it.

Oct-12

Scarlet To Dark Red

She applied her scarlet lipstick carefully and smiled slightly at herself in the mirror, testing. The colour clashed with the red of her hair. She met the men in bars and the women in coffee shops – always choosing different meeting places. Tonight it was the third time she was to meet Erick; he was big and blond as a Viking. As on the previous occasions she took aspirin with her, already dissolved in water, it was totally clear.

He was very keen and had wanted to see her as frequently as she would agree, which suited her very well. As usual he talked about himself and she nodded encouragingly as if she was listening. As early as possible in the evening she poured the clear liquid into his beer. She lent forward and kissed him on the cheek, he was such a gentleman he could not tear his eyes away from her face to look down at her cleavage. Her pulse increased, she thought in either case he would not see her other hand by his beer glass. And he did not.

Men were much easier than women really, that is why she found women more of a challenge, more exciting. Still never mind, this man was by far the largest man to date. He was well over six feet and built broad to match. She held his arm and looked adoringly up at him, her small smile playing over her bright lips.

After three drinks she gently led him out of the bar to the bench by the river. She had taken him to different places each time so he said nothing as they sat down at the top of the bank. She nuzzled up to his neck kissing him repeatedly ensuring a large area of his neck was wet from the kisses. She encouraged him to lean down and kiss her so far neglected breasts. As he did so she bent her head and her sharp teeth sank into his neck. He did not feel her teeth cutting through skin and artery; her earlier kisses had a very special effect of deadening pain. Slowly his blood flowed from his neck into her. He gradually seemed to deflate and sink further down her lap. Finally he slipped from her and from the bench on to the ground, his head facing down the bank. She got up and lay next to him her mouth clamped to his neck draining every possible drop of blood from his body. The aspirin worked well keeping his blood flowing through the incisions in his neck. She thought it was cheating really. There are so few of us left nowadays we need all the help we can get. I will need to find a mate to keep the bloodline going, she grinned wickedly. It was far too risky to live together but meeting up now and again would be good. Just so difficult to meet a suitable mate these days.

Never had it taken so long, over an hour, to drain a person's blood before. She had a really lovely feeling of warmth and satisfaction, difficult to describe in human terms, the closest would be a huge helping of porridge laced with the best brandy. She unclamped her jaw from his neck and let go of him. Like a crumpled, deflated straw man he rolled down the bank. He gathered momentum and hit the river with a quiet splash.

She waddled home in a euphoric daze. She looked in the mirror at her flushed face as she slipped her wig off. Her lipstick all gone now but her lips were engorged and a deeper shade of red. She expected it would take a little longer than usual for her craving to return, maybe next time she would go for a large succulent woman.

Oct-12

The Web

The web creeps everywhere; all pervasive it saps our individuality and rules our lives. We have forgotten how it was before the web. However they have now made good use of the web at last, I can ignore eBooks and turn to Soft-books. Maybe in these days of forever changing jargon I should explain Soft-books.

For a start Soft-books are more or less hard, since they are like a physical book. They have a hard cover and a spine. You can turn the pages and it feels like paper that you can read in the sun. When you buy your first Soft-book (on the web of course) it will arrive totally blank. It does have a special sort of pen in the spine. You open the cover and search for your favourite book, which will only be free if you are lucky or you are an old fuddy-duddy like me who likes dead authors.

So when your favourite book is downloaded (from the

web) into a chip in the spine, then you can start to read. Just like a real book. You can write in the margins with the special pen. My goodness, your comments can be stored until you download the same book again and even shared with your friends (if you have any left after spending all your time on the web) on Facebook (which is not a book at all).

If you want you can make all the letters bigger. If your favourite book is longer than the number of pages in your Soft-book then you can just continue to read by turning to the start of the Soft-book again. It just knows. Unfortunately when you want to start from the beginning again you either have to turn all the way back to the start of the book or reset the Soft-book with a tiny little button on the spine with a paper clip. Why did life get to be so complicated? Maybe because we are. …

Oct-12

Lakeness

The lake was completely still in the darkest hour before dawn. Very little vegetation grew around the shores so nothing disturbed the surface. The low moon was mainly obscured by clouds moving slowly across the sky. Patterns of light and dark played on the surface of the large expanse of the lake.

Joe looked out over the lake. It was at least a mile wide and several miles long. The surface of the water erupted and there was a horrendous noise. A huge beast lifted up out of the water – it was as if Joe was watching in slow motion with the volume turned right up. Great sheets of water seethed and bubbled where there had been complete peace and tranquillity before.

The noise was of screeching and tearing and the beating of huge wings in air and on the water. The huge beast made its way to the shore with two enormous necks coming from a barrel of a body. Each head was weaving about each with one eye, it seemed that the heads were more in conflict than harmony. They each seemed to be struggling to make the most noise and gain the best advantage.

Joe lifted up his hand and stilled the writhing heads and heaving body. He tried to fix the beast with his eyes and willed it to lay its heads down. He shouted loudly:-

'Be still, beast, so that I may ride on you.'

Joe tried to approach the beast but the foul stench drove him back. The heads moved restlessly each eye looking defiantly at Joe from different directions. Joe tried once more to concentrate and focus his mind within the beast. This time he decided not to yell but to throw his will at the beast.

The creature lowered its body, bending its six powerful haunches and laying its two necks and heads stretched out towards Joe. The ugly creature seemed to be under control, both mouths closed and the smell more bearable. Joe wondered for how long and if it would be a good idea to test the beast. Joe decided against it as time was ticking on; instead he walked closer to the two heads and walked slowly up the necks, his boots unsteady on the creature's thick hide.

Joe got to the creature's shoulders and fastened a harness round its two necks and first pair of legs. In the harness were two loops for Joe's feet and reins to hang on to, as he stood on the shoulders of the now compliant beast.

With a cacophonous roar of rocks and wings they were

airborne, climbing up out of the lake's valley as the sun was rising. Fast they flew until Joe could see the city in the distance, tower blocks rising in the morning mist.

They landed on top of the tallest of them all, the Global bank building. The beast settled down for its long wait, chewing on a couple of seagulls.

Joe brushed his jacket and straightened his tie. What a way to get to work thought Joe as he entered the building using his security card, still it beats all that messing about with helicopters.

Oct-12

Sightless Words

Joe had been hacking away at a searing exposé - it had taken a few days and he was pleased when it was done. As always he'd see what the readers made of it. His savage way of attacking what he saw as wrong earned him the nickname of "The Beast", and he relished the image. He didn't care what the consequences of writing a story were. Sometimes it got him into more trouble than he expected.

It was fairly early evening and he turned to one of his favourite haunts to go and relax, a bar where journalists tended to go. Sometimes he headed away from his own kind but tonight he was still humming from his latest break.

He walked into the bar catching sight of his own ugly pitted face in a mirror and hastily turned to see a really beautiful woman sitting at the bar, half facing away. She had beautiful elegant lines and curves, a contrast of colouring, light and dark lines, a fantastic feline quality to her movements as she turned and smiled at him, then turned away again not wanting to appear too obvious.

A shy woman would not sit just there in that spot, in the brightly lit part of the bar. This was a woman as least as experienced as he was. She was probably much the same age as him, no longer young but not forty yet.

'Hello,' he said, 'I'm The Beast, I don't think we've met before – are you a journalist too?'

'Hello,' she replied, 'you must be Joe Gruychk, we've never met but of course I read and write about your articles. Yes, I'm a journalist but for specialist magazines which I don't think would be of interest. I'm Olivia Swannson.'

'How come I immediately feel like contradicting you? I suppose that you get guys like me coming on to you all the time.'

'Not guys like you,' she replied with a smile which made his heart and stomach tumble over each other, 'only men like Paxman and Morgan.'

He burst out loud at the way her pick-up line made his own pale away. He waited to see what she'd say next.

'You're the first man today to shake my hand that didn't make me want to wash directly afterwards.'

He looked down at his hands and realised he was still holding hers from introducing himself. Just as he was going to a little self-consciously remove his hands from hers there was a crash behind her at the bar.

She was startled and asked him, 'What's that?' She didn't turn round and he watched her carefully.

He replied, 'The bar man has dropped a full bottle I think.'

'That will be Jim, he can be a bit clumsy sometimes when he's been out running,' she replied.

'Have you got a good memory?' he asked, 'but not for

faces.'

'Yes, I need to have a good memory.' She paused, 'you've sussed me out haven't you?'

'You've such beautiful curves, would you mind if I touched you discreetly?'

She freed his hand and said, 'As long as every journalist in the bar doesn't think he can come and "cop a feel" too, then that would be acceptable.'

She smiled again. He rested his hand on her face so gently it felt like light, she didn't seem too demure as his hand travelled down her neck and ever so gently over her breast.

'What gave me away?' she asked, 'Was it when I didn't look round at the crash, or was it before that?'

'Yes before that, it was when you held my hands and I felt my entire life history draining out through my palms.'

He lay on the floor of his cell for three days, his beaten flesh recovering slowly. Never had his writing got him in to trouble as badly as this. He thought of Olivia as he lay there; it was a new relationship so he couldn't help wondering what she'd do, but he hoped she was making a bit of a campaign. He'd formulated a plan of his own, he must have been captured about 15 weeks ago and his little show of an attempt to escape had got him the beating. His plan was to try and escape on the fourth day – when they'd least expect him to. If he didn't try then he thought they'd move him and he would have to start all over again.

He could feel her under his hand – 'Everyone is focused on the smash at the bar so no one noticed,' he said quietly and moved his hand away.

She looked at him and said wistfully, 'You may have felt I learnt all about you through your palms but now I feel my innermost secrets have been revealed to you. They said you were sharp but I thought it might take you longer than five seconds to realise.

'Have you ever had close dealings with a blind person before?' she asked nervously after a pause.

'No not really – I knew someone at University and sometimes she forgot to put tea in the tea pot and we got hot water with milk.'

She laughed lightly with relief.

'Have you eaten?' he asked neutrally.

She grinned broadly, 'It can be a pretty messy business eating with a blind person.'

'Oh – so you've heard about the eating habits of The Beast then have you?'

She laughed genuinely. 'Well, if you're prepared to risk it then we could give it a go – it need not be a competition'

She chose a salmon salad, already cut in neat pieces, no dressing, but asked him to butter and cut her bread, he guessed to make him feel useful. They ate without saying much, companionable after such a short time. Afterwards they sat drinking coffee and liqueurs. He thought that their talking seemed to be like reminding each other what they already knew. She'd an amazing memory and knew lots about all the journalists that he knew, what they wrote, what they were interested in. He didn't feel uncomfortable that she seemed to know so much about him. At one point he was relating some of his journeys and she said that she thought he went to Africa after South America. He laughed and said, 'I think you're right – history was never my strong point.'

The guard brought food for the first time since his beating and left him to eat it. While he lay on the floor they didn't chain him but he expected that he'd be chained again that night. He waited as long as he dared then he climbed up above the door, his body aching with the exertion of wedging himself in the corner.

It wasn't late when they left and he naturally took her hand and led her out into the street, to a nearby square where he sat with her on a bench. This evening had been nothing like he'd expected. When he asked her, blushing she agreed but would not say much.

He sat holding her hand even though there was no need now. He started to speak slowly.

'I live to write and when I saw you I thought I'd love to paint you with words, then when we talked together I was wondering all the time, would you let me – I suppose that at least you'd be able to hear my picture.' He trailed off into silence.

After a pause he asked her naively, 'How did you get so experienced?'

'Living in cotton wool was not for me – so I suppose I needed to learn, thoroughly – being blind means filling the gaps as best as you can, but also taking advantage of what it gives you.'

She seemed genuinely touched by him holding her hand and the way he talked. She continued light heartedly, 'so long as you don't expect me to jump into bed with you before the painting sessions,' she could feel him tense and smoothly continued, 'but that you promise you will after.'

He smiled and wondered if she could tell he was smiling, 'I was thinking of doing the painting the other way round to artists – starting with a clothed sitting and then gradually working towards a nude sketch.'

'That might work,' she replied. 'Would you be insulted if I painted you with words too? Of course it doesn't make any difference to me if you're clothed or not,' she added helpfully.

He smiled directly at her and asked, 'Can you tell when

I'm smiling?'

'Only if you speak at the same time,' she said seriously. 'How are we going to do this portrait? Are you too tired to start tonight?'

'I think I might be able to make a start but how are you feeling?'

'Oh I'm not too tired, but then I haven't just finished a major story.'

He could feel the hairs stand up on his neck, warning of a trap; he hadn't mentioned any story. 'How do you know about that -'

'Just relax, I'm not after your story,' she laughed lightly, 'even if my feminine intuition was switched off I could have worked that out.'

He relaxed and returned to the previous subject, 'I could offer to take you to my flat not far away, but I suspect that might attract attention.'

'Yes, I agree,' she spoke thoughtfully, 'Would you feel it too risky for me to invite you to my flat? There's a spare bedroom – but can you be trusted?'

He put on a pseudo serious voice, 'I want to preserve your mystique, your allure until after you've posed nude but will I be able to resist you until then?' For the first time he felt at a loss that she couldn't see him.

He thought back to when they had been beating him - he'd thought of her; he'd chanted out the words of the word paintings like the Knight Templars chanting religious verses.

At last the guard came and he heard the keys turn in the lock. The guard hadn't even checked first to see where he was in the cell he just came blundering in and looked down at the blood stained floor. Joe kicked the steel door with all his might against the corner wall and it bounced back knocking the guard off his feet and he came crashing down. Joe dragged him to where he had lain for three days. He left the cell and locked the door behind him. He climbed up into the wooden arches to where the fuses were. He turned the master switch and unscrewed each fuse then turned the master switch back on. There were often power interruptions and he hoped that the guards would think there was a longer power cut. In the darkness he crept past the guards and down over the mass of roofs. Blind amongst pungent smells and nerve racking crackles.

'Just remember that a pepper spray would render you more blind than me,' she said. He thought about her kind gentle curves and the contrast with feline ferocity and claws. He stood up and held her hand and waited for her to instruct him how to find her flat.

He said, 'The Beast is tamed, I promise to be a gentleman until instructed otherwise.'

She sat for him for the first time in her small kitchen sitting on a stool. She was slightly turned towards him with her arm down and the curves of her hips and breast in a strong but not harsh light. Her long hair flowed over her shoulders leaving dark and light colours playing between hair, clothes and skin.

'If you were on your own would you turn the light on?'

'No – I have only learnt where the switches are so I can turn them out if an intruder turns them on.'

He began writing some short sentences but some long. He only spoke to ask her if she was ok if he touched her. She was cautious, saying within reason. He thought "A Sketch by Joe".

Several times he moved her almost like a mannequin, moving her to look the other way, swap which way she turned. Once she held his hand to her body as she steadied herself on the stool. He felt her body once more and tried to describe the vitality he felt pulsing beneath his hand. Not once did he describe her eyes as sightless. He described only what he saw, not what he knew to be so. Such a dangerous line for a journalist anyway, since so often what you thought you knew, were wrong assumptions.

He made his way to the railway sidings and found a goods train. His tired body dragged him down but he found what he was looking for, old rope that he used to make a hammock, out of sight and under one of the trucks. He couldn't be sure but he hoped that this goods train would leave before dawn. He'd no idea what time it was when the trucks started moving. He closed his eyes and focused his mind on Olivia, going over what he wrote about her that first time. He was stiff and cold when they finally came to a halt. He found his way to a road and a car stopped and took him to the British Embassy.

He told her he was nearly finished, but asked if it would be ok if he came close to her. He gave no explanation and she asked for none. He wondered if she realised it was in preparation for when she was nude. If so it seemed she'd thrown all caution away and had decided to be his study.

That night he slept in her spare room, later to become so familiar to him, yet that night still different from his usual surroundings. He rose early and made her coffee. He left her to drink it in peace while he revised what he'd written. After she was up they went for a walk in the park and she told him about the people who came in to help her, some paid professionals, some friends, and some relatives.

He learnt that Olivia had visited the British Embassy two days before he arrived there and they contacted her at her hotel. She'd made a regular nuisance of herself to push them to find him. They arranged for a passport and a flight home the next day. He was troubled that he'd chanted the word paintings to the kidnappers feeling he'd broken her trust. He went back to her flat – to her spare room. His body healed faster than his mind. One day she told him a friend was coming to have a chat. He didn't reply much to anything but he did start talking to Toby. A short man with short grey hair, but not old. Joe did not ask, but he knew Toby was there to help him.

'You will need to come and see me at 9am in the morning, every morning for a while'

'Why is that?' asked Joe.

'I need a controlled environment where I can get you to talk about what has happened to you, but in such a way as to help you heal.'

When Joe went to Toby's office he saw his business plate – Psychologist: Trauma Specialist Counsellor. Toby did not ask many questions but listened a lot to the answers. He encouraged Joe to talk about what had happened and also suggested many different explanations as to why Joe felt the way he did. He was skilled at getting Joe to see things differently, especially what Joe had thought of as weakness.

One morning Joe said, 'You've told me so many theories about trauma you must be wanting to jack it in and turn your business over to me.'

Toby smiled back, 'Another possible explanation could be that you are ready to try writing for a living. And to talk to Olivia about chanting the word paintings to your kidnappers.'

He took her home then went back to his flat to collect some things and have a shower. She'd lent him her spare key and he let himself in. She knew immediately that someone had come in and called out to him – he replied and she came towards him and put her arms around him spontaneously. They sat next to each other and he read to her what he'd written so far. She was completely absorbed listening to him.

Only at the end did she make a couple of comments. 'I think I won't be able to conceal anything of myself. That brings me to another thing which I should have asked before, what do you intend doing with this writing?'

'When I started on it I thought I might try and publish it but since I've worked on it and been with you I've realised that it is far too intimate and personal to us both. If you wish you can have the only copy for safe keeping.'

It was the next weekend that he came for the nude sitting. As she expected he placed her in the same position and studied and wrote, moved her, studied and wrote. She could feel how close he came and then he brought her dressing gown and they sat and talked into the night.

He held her in his arms once more. She could feel his healing wounds on his body and scars on his face had almost gone.'

'I'm sorry,' he said, 'I gave you the only physical copy of the word paintings but I have another copy in my mind. I used the words to fight them - the only thing that I could tell them and survive. To shout out the words of the paintings, over and over, it was all I'd say, word for word, including the nude one. They wanted to break me so I couldn't write about them again. I chanted the words out, to deflect them and give me strength. But I feel I let you down, especially afterwards, when I had escaped.'

At last he'd told her what was bothering him so. She put her hands gently over his eyes and felt the tears and said,

'It seems a small price to pay to have you back here with your limbs and sight still intact.'

'Yes,' he replied, 'I couldn't let them stop me writing.'

Aug-12

Desolation

When he came back from the hospital of course the house was quiet, untouched since he left it. He went upstairs to the bedroom. Delayed reaction to the shock set in and the sheer pain of the grief and anguish made it difficult to think straight, or even move. To try to get through the pain he started to pack his stuff into a couple of suitcases, tears streaming unchecked. The rest he would burn in the back garden. He knew now that he had to leave. He looked out of the back window to where the small greenhouse stood; he could see a couple of pots were laying over where Susie had fallen.

They had talked about it often enough, maybe too often; mainly about Susie taking her life – she hated the expression 'committing suicide' – too much like a crime, which it was. He had gone that morning to get milk and a few small things they needed on a Sunday. When he came back he saw her lying amongst the flowerpots. It was a beautiful morning, the sort that makes you pleased to be alive. But Susie had been struggling for some time. He had tried to help with support and encouragement as much as he could but Susie felt her life was unfulfilled.

In their discussions he had said how crushed he would feel if she tried to take her life. He had never threatened to leave if she did; that seemed wrong, partly as he did not know for sure but also he did not want an undue threat to be hanging over her. They had both attempted suicide before they met – his further in the past than hers.

Since they had been together, they seemed to have built a healthy relationship but Susie wanted children and so far that had not happened.

His stomach had turned and he rushed to her as soon as he had seen her. She could not have been lying there long; cold and clammy to the touch and looking glassy. He found a small, unmarked bottle in her hand and wasted no time in going to the phone. Dialling the emergency number and telling the operator seemed to take forever, but nothing like the wait until the ambulance arrived. In fact it was probably only about 20 minutes but in that time his life unravelled. He sat on a garden chair and stared at her – this was the person he loved and this was the person who had attempted to destroy the person he loved. He gazed in the sunshine and thought about all they had – they should have a full life together helping and supporting each other. They should be able to be happy with what life had handed them. They could adopt or foster, fat chance of that now. All those coulds and shoulds. His mind was going around and around when he heard the front doorbell go.

More waiting around in the hospital; hours until at last a nurse came to see him. 'We think she will pull through – do you want to come and see her?'

'No thank you, not now,' he said. Not ever, he thought.

He finished packing and made a mound of everything he did not want to keep. And set fire to it. The summer evening was closing in – it had taken a whole day to change this life.

Susie had not left him a note but he decided as part of the catharsis from old to new, he would leave her one. He often left her notes and signed them with a single descriptive word. Today would be no exception and he chose a red pen.

Dear Susie,

You tried to murder the person I love, and I cannot risk that one day you will try again and succeed. I am gone.

Desolation.

Jun-12

Austin the Author

I first met Austin the Author by pure chance. We were crossing a busy road in London. I stopped on the central reservation in the middle of the road while Austin carried on. He saw his mistake and stepped back to the central reservation. He missed his footing and fell into the road we had just crossed. I grabbed his coat lapels and dragged him to safety before he was knocked down. He was profusely grateful. He did not stop thanking me for the next ten minutes. He insisted on buying me a coffee and as I was in no hurry I agreed.

Over coffee it came out he was an author. He explained to me that he had been a writer for years but now he was an author. He had written books all of his working life but no one had read them. When he retired he had set about trying to get his best book published and establish a readership. He got 78 rejection slips from publishers. I did not know that there were that many publishers. Maybe he had more than one rejection from the same publisher for different drafts. He had looked at vanity publishing and ePublishing but decided that did not qualify in terms of true authorship.

Finally he saw a workshop for new authors where several publishers were present. He signed up for it and took along his latest draft. He listened all day to the spiel from successful authors and dull publishers. He could find no one to take an interest in his book.

At the end of the day, defeated Austin decided to give up writing. As he walked past a bus stop he dumped his manuscript in the bin and walked on. He decided to take up painting.

About a week later having started with watercolours there was a ring at the door. Austin answered the door and found a small wizened man looking up at him.

'Are you Austin the author?' asked his visitor.

'Retired and not really an author as no one has read my books.' replied Austin.

'Well I have. I really enjoyed your book. I found it in the bin. Have you any more?'

I had been worrying that Austin's story would not have a happy ending. However now Austin has a readership of one he is happy. He has decided to take up writing once more and sees that he is as entitled to call himself an author.

After all he does not want to disappoint his readership.

May-12

The City was Hot and Sweaty

The city was hot and sweaty, restless with thunder rumbling round the rim, the backstreets a mishmash of oriental buildings, the streets themselves ingrained paths from long ago. The planning and construction of buildings was a haphazard process in this place leading to a mottled effect of no two buildings looking the same. No buses ran to time. No shops opened promptly. No clocks chimed on the hour.

The very nature of the place was likely to irritate someone who came from a cooler climate and well ordered city. I could see a young German man in his far from suitable khaki suit sweating and getting in a worse temper as he tried to negotiate his way through the animals, plants, people and parked cars. It seemed he was on his way to our apartments – we get quite a lot of Germans these days. I guess that applies to a lot of tourist places like ours. I also suspected he was going to be an even more unhappy German when he found our lift was not working and he was on the thirteenth floor. Of course there was a free apartment on the second floor but it just looked like too good an opportunity to miss so I allocated him one on the thirteenth floor to see if the pent up temper would blow his head off.

He came to reception and stood fuming as I explained to him in Chinese, English, French and finally, very bad, German that I would be with him in a minute. He acknowledged he understood the German by wincing. So I was right, he was German and, as his details confirmed, from Bonn, a very well organised city.

He went to his apartment disgruntled that the lift was out of action – I saw him taking two steps at a time, his heavy suitcase knocking against the wall.

He got his own back though, we did not see him for two, maybe three days and finally I had to investigate as the cleaners said his door had "do not disturb" on it. I climbed the thirteen floors and opened the door to his apartment.

There he was lying dead, nearly naked with a towel neatly round his waist. He died in a most extraordinary way for a frustrated German. I am no detective but he must have come out of the shower, slipped and fallen on a low coffee table. In his neck there was a large multi coloured plastic angel that he must have placed on the table himself. The angel had been driven into his carotid artery from the force of his fall.

When a foreign national dies there is always more paperwork to do and things to arrange so I guess he is up in heaven with his angel thinking it serves me right for not putting him in a second floor apartment.

May-12

Deception

Sally drove slowly to his house. Even though they had been lovers for three years she had never visited him as he was married. She had come to accept that he would not leave his wife and now she felt it could not continue. She did not know if she was going out of malice or rather to make it easier for her to finish with him. His wife, Kate, was wealthy but the address turned out to be a ground floor flat in a small close.

She rang the bell without really working out what she was going to say and rather than anyone coming to the door the intercom crackled into life and a woman spoke,

'Who is it please?'

'I wondered if I could come in and speak to you – I know your husband Colin...' Sally's voice trailed off not knowing how to deal with this unexpected situation.

'Well I do not have many visitors and tire very quickly but if it is just for a while, you will find me in the living room just off the porch,' said Kate over the intercom. A buzzer went and the front door opened.

Sally stepped in to living room and saw a frail woman lying on a bed with an artificial lung helping her to breathe. The room was very warm, an invalid's room. Seeing Colin's wife lying helpless in bed Sally felt an effect like a physical blow. She said without thinking, 'Colin never mentioned about you being bedridden.'

'No I guess he would not – he would not want you to feel sorry for him. He had quite a hard childhood with no father and I think when this happened on our honeymoon the last thing he wanted was for people to know he had a cripple for a wife – what did he tell you about me?'

Sally was at a bit of a loss but decided to stick as closely to the truth as was comfortable, 'When I first met him it was to do with work and I thought I had heard he had a rich wife – so I just came out with it and he replied that yes you were rich. Since then I think he has just left me to imagine.' There was a degree of chagrin in Sally's tone.

'You are the first friend of Colin's to visit me – I guess you are quite close to him. How long have you known him?' asked Kate showing signs of tiredness.

It was Sally who felt vulnerable and embarrassed, 'We met about three years ago – he was doing a piece on "Fair Trade" and I was one of the businesses trying to promote it. I run a business supplying body products.'

'He sometimes brings me lovely creams – I wonder if they come from you?' Kate did not sound at all malicious and went on, 'We have not had a physical relationship for years – we did try after I got polio on honeymoon but Colin could see it distressed my breathing too much. He is so loving and kind. It bothered me a lot what I was expecting of Colin – I had a talk once with my doctor about him. I have never been directly aware of his other "friendships" but I am bound to fear the worst aren't I? I am not going to ask you to tell me anything you do not wish to, but of course Colin's happiness is important to me,' Kate paused after this long speech. After a while she continued, 'I know it is asking a lot of you but I wondered now you see the situation if you could bring yourself to deceive Colin – not letting on you have been here? Also carrying on just as we were. For me it is better than not knowing.'

Sally let the silence stretch out, all that she had felt that morning had been turned upside down. What did she feel now, about herself, about Colin and now Kate? She took Kate's frail hand in hers, 'Would it be too painful for me to come and see you on the quiet?'

Kate smiled, 'So long as you do not come out of a sense of pity.'

Sally smiled too, 'Do you think we will be able to keep up the deception?'

Feb-12

VE100 a Room Built

A room was built which opened to the public on 8-May-2045. On this one hundred year anniversary, this anti-shrine was completed. To help humanity to remember, so it would not forget the awful savagery of war made by man.

The room is large and grand. Superficial and sinister. Around the walls are flags of domination hanging limply not stirred in the wind, as there is no life in this room. No one goes in, they just shuffle past looking at the horrors laid out for all to see. Each artefact meticulously documented, evidenced past any denial known to man.

There is a huge glass wall down one side of the room, if you look at something in the room and touch the wall details of the atrocity will scroll up and down as your finger moves over the glass to provide the details. Of course written by the victors, but history of the events, the inhumanity done to man by man.

Visitors have a choice, they can watch and read in silence, or they can have earphones to listen to commentary and audio from the time. There is guidance by each item to warn how distressing it is. A scale of one to ten swastikas. Advice is given to limit the number of items above five swastikas that are watched at one time to no more than three or four at the most. There are trained counsellors available if they should be needed.

There is a huge desk at one end with papers waiting for the Führer's signature. These are orders that will changes lives and destroy lives.

I have been influenced to write something which is anti war, in particular anti Holocaust. When I saw this brief I thought of Hitler's office. I am not sure where I have got it from but I believe he did not get up early so often his office must have stood empty. I think it was in the same building as his bedroom but I have not really followed the domestic brief.

The room is large and grand. Superficial and sinister. Around the walls are flags of domination hanging limply, not stirred in the wind, as there is no life in this room. No one goes in, they just shuffle past looking at the horrors laid out for all to see.

Material for the history of the events, left lying around, the inhumanity done to man by man. Columns of figures showing the financial side of the extermination of five or more million Jews. Evidenced past any denial known to man. How profit increased as the process was refined. But no record of screams, or suffering so extreme, are kept here. Just the quiet of pure Nazi dust landing on the polished floor.

At one end there is a grand chair like a throne with a statue on either side, based on the ideal Roman male.

There is a huge desk at the other end with papers waiting for the Führer's signature. These are orders that will change lives, orders to destroy lives. These are orders that were nearly always obeyed; until finally when the Führer faced defeat a few of the most futile orders were ignored by his staff.

Unlucky for Some

Punishment: Write Thirteen Lines for not Writing a Poem

I saw a cat
with a can.
In the can
I saw a poem.
Can the cat
see a poem.
If the cat can
I will say damn.
That cat is
sure sore

that I saw

the cat

with a can.

Certain Images

Certain images, without any reason, even though they may apparently have no significance for us, stick obstinately in our memory, even if we are hardly conscious of having registered them, and they seem to mean nothing important at the time.

Such was the yin-yang symbol when I first saw it in some far-flung shop.

Much later I began to learn what it meant – the balance in nature or rather the complementary opposites that are so necessary in nature. That you need a back of a hand in order to go with the front of your hand. Yes, it does seem to be bound up with Eastern philosophy too – the sound of one hand clapping and that sort of thing.

Yin is the black side with the white dot on it and yang is the white side with the black dot on it.

The relationship between yin and yang is sometimes described in terms of sunlight playing over a mountain and in the valley. As the sun moves across the sky, yin and yang gradually trade places with each other, revealing what was obscured and obscuring what was revealed.

Yin is characterised as slow, soft, yielding, diffuse, cool, wet, and passive; and is associated with water, earth, the moon, and night time.

Yang, by contrast, is fast, hard, solid, focused, hot, dry, and aggressive; and is associated with fire, sky, the sun and daytime.

So not surprisingly the yin relates to femininity and yang to masculinity. However there are several ways to interpret this; to some, things are not so simple as a straight diagram seems to suggest, but rather the masculinity and femininity in us all whether we are male or female. To others it is as simple as yin is female and yang is male; they fit together as two parts of a whole.

Sometimes I have heard that the yin and yang symbol refers to the balance of good and evil; however I do not think that this can be literally that one of yin or yang is evil and the other is good. It may be that at some level yin and yang symbolise the balance in nature of good and evil but as a product, not a single realisation or outcome.

There is a beauty of symmetry in the image and also the feeling of life and balance. Sometimes I have seen variations on the image, with colour or with three or more lobes – all or these do not have the power and simplicity of the original. Whatever it means to you it is worth thinking about more than that first discarded glance.

May-12

To the Rescue

With one mighty bound the dragon leapt up on to the ledge, scattering the goblins in all directions. Colin watched as a few goblins were brushed like dolls over the edge of the ledge and down in to the ravine with cries and screams. Colin was petrified as the dragon came towards him, the ledge crumbled behind the dragon with a few more goblins slipping into the abyss. Colin's fear turned to surprise as the dragon spoke to him.

'Quick, climb on to my back, we need to get away from here before the ledge crumbles.'

Colin shook himself into action, he gritted his teeth as he climbed past the dragon's grisly head, the foul stench of sulphurous breath making his eyes water. It seemed a little unkind to think ill of his saviour but he nearly passed out as the dragon turned its head to see if Colin needed any help. Colin grabbed the scaly wing and was surprised to find that it felt smooth and flexible like soft kidskin gloves. The Dragon shifted its body almost shrugging Colin into the gap between his wings.

'Hold tight,' exclaimed the dragon as he more or less dived into the ravine as the ledge broke around them. Colin felt the strength of the dragon gather beneath him, the wings beating powerfully as they avoided the rocks and crags around them.

Seemingly effortlessly the dragon turned the dive in to a soar. On the way up they passed a goblin clinging on to the rock face. The dragon turned its head and breathed fire on the goblin who shrieked in pain, curled up and fell from the rock face with a tortured cry.

Steadily the dragon flew on. Colin never found out how the dragon knew where his home was.

Poetry For Mortals

Poetry is to me the most complex art
A poet must be a writer of brevity
With adherence to rhythms
A dancer of characters
A philosopher
A worthy wordsmith
A sequence choreographer
A master of timing and piquancy
A selector of syllables and sibilance

Oh dear I nearly forgot to mention the rhyming too

Mum's the Word

I was back home after the third autumn term at

university – so my final year. A small pile of post was in my room. One letter from a solicitor in town.

"Dear Sir, We regret to inform you that Silas Fortescue has died. He has bequeathed £500 and a small gift to you in his will. Please find enclosed cheque. We would be grateful if you could collect the gift from us during normal office hours."

I went downstairs to find my mum.

'Do you know who Silas Fortescue was?' I asked her as she was bending low over a drawer in the kitchen. She stood up hastily, slightly pink and flustered.

'Yes, that's Pentecost, he has died hasn't he?' She carried on not waiting for an answer, 'I got a small bequest from him too; I was surprised when I saw your letter. What did he leave you?'

'Five hundred pounds and a gift to be collected.'

She looked surprised and pleased.

I thought back and remembered many happy occasions stopping in to see Pentecost, drinking ginger beer and sitting on the bank of the river at the end of his garden. Sometimes building tree houses or falling in the river, we spent hours together. As I had grown older we spent time talking homespun philosophy and playing chess. I had seen him last holiday looking frail and only up for playing draughts but pleased to see me.

When I picked up the gift it was a painting in a lovely carved frame. I could see he had spent many loving hours on it. The picture was of my mother in a low cut dress – smiling and radiant. I remembered her blushes and that she never said what he had left her.

Human Situation

If you hear a lament does it make you sad?
Do you feel a pain of human missing and loss?
Would you do without this pain if you could?

If you sit too close to a barbecue, on a lonely evening,
when the heat gets uncomfortable you turn or shift
away.
But that is not so easy when the pain comes from
within.

There are some kinds of pain which do not discourage
you
from probing – like the socket of first tooth gone on a
thread
what is not so easy to flee is the chance encounter that
is the end

before the beginning is underway, do they feel the way
you do
how difficult it is to tell, how hard to make way for
feelings
that you hardly know yourself. Listen to your inner

self and be true to the human condition or
else venture, so little nothing gained
in the end only pain

A Visit to A&E

Roy struggled awake at 2:15am as his work phone nagged him out of his sleep. He worked for Global Oil and was "on call" as medical advisor for the night.

They were calling him from offshore to tell him that one of the men had gone berserk and also fallen. They had him in a straightjacket, sedated, and the chopper was ready to leave if he and his colleague could be at the airport to meet him.

Roy was on his way with his colleague within 20 minutes. Roy had been working for Global Oil for a couple of years and had done this a few times now. They picked up the offshore guy and took him to A&E.

Roy saw a woman at A&E he had never see there before. He felt the hairs on his neck rise. He could only see her face. He said his name, of course he gave his adoptive name, and for some reason he said his date of birth. The woman looked longingly at him – she could remember that day so clearly over twenty years ago. She was Roy's birth mother. That day their life changed forever.

"Hello son" she said.

Oct-11

List of Pieces

32425363R00171

Printed in Poland
by Amazon Fulfillment
Poland Sp. z o.o., Wrocław